Praise for

GIRLS WITH SHARP STICKS

"This book has enough plot twists to give a reader whiplash."
—*Cosmopolitan*

"A thrilling story about a sisterhood smashing the patriarchy."
—*BookPage*

"Readers will be revved up for the inevitable uprising. . . .
A suspenseful and timely read."
—*Kirkus Reviews*

"Harrowing and exhilarating . . . Readers will be inspired."
—*SLJ*

"A timely, perceptive read, this will leave readers,
especially those grappling with the implications of
the #metoo era, anxious for the sequel."
—*BCCB*

ALSO BY SUZANNE YOUNG

GIRLS WITH REBEL SOULS

GIRLS WITH SHARP STICKS: BOOK THREE

SUZANNE YOUNG

SIMON & SCHUSTER BFYR

NEW YORK LONDON TORONTO SYDNEY NEW DELHI

SIMON & SCHUSTER BFYR

An imprint of Simon & Schuster Children's Publishing Division
1230 Avenue of the Americas, New York, New York 10020

For information about special discounts for bulk purchases, please contact Simon &
Schuster Special Sales at 1-866-506-1949 or business@simonandschuster.com.
The Simon & Schuster Speakers Bureau can bring authors to your live event. For more
information or to book an event, contact the Simon & Schuster Speakers Bureau at
1-866-248-3049 or visit our website at www.simonspeakers.com.
Interior design by Tom Daly
The text for this book was set in Adobe Garamond Pro.
Manufactured in the United States of America
First Edition
2 4 6 8 10 9 7 5 3 1
Library of Congress Cataloging-in-Publication Data
Names: Young, Suzanne, author.
Title: Girls with rebel souls / Suzanne Young.
Description: First edition. | New York : Simon & Schuster BFYR, [2021] |
Series: Girls with sharp sticks ; [3] | Summary: Mena and the girls of Innovations
Academy fight back against the men that hunt them and the woman who created them,
but the discovery of a kill switch raises the stakes higher than they ever imagined.
Identifiers: LCCN 2020040526 (print) | LCCN 2020040527 (ebook) |
ISBN 9781534426191 (hardcover) | ISBN 9781534426214 (ebook)
Subjects: CYAC: Cyborgs—Fiction. | Revenge—Fiction. | Science fiction.
Classification: LCC PZ7.Y887 Gh 2021 (print) | LCC PZ7.Y887 (ebook) |
DDC [Fic]—dc23 LC record available at https://lccn.loc.gov/2020040526
LC ebook record available at https://lccn.loc.gov/2020040527

This series is dedicated to my daughter, Sophia.
And in honor of my grandmother, Josephine Parzych.
Strong women raising strong women. Together, we are unstoppable.

Part I

And you fight back

1

Lennon Rose has a boy locked in the trunk of her car. I feel like I should be more surprised, honestly. I'm understandably horrified, of course, but not entirely shocked considering how she has changed since leaving Innovations Academy. How we've all changed.

The sun beats down on my arms, my skin growing hot while beads of sweat dot my hairline. Lennon Rose and I stand in the driveway of the small cottage while Rosemarie and Leandra wait inside—eating cookies. I brush away a bead of sweat as it drips down my temple.

Outside the cottage, I'm surrounded by a garden of exotic and poisonous flowers—surrounded by their intoxicating scent, their threat of danger. But right now, nothing in this world feels more dangerous than the girl in front of me.

I swallow, and the sweet taste in the air tickles my tongue, numbs my lips. I focus again on Lennon Rose. When I do, she smiles brightly.

"What have you done?" I ask. She feigns offense.

"Mena, it's what he *deserves*," Lennon Rose replies, standing taller. "He hurt you. He's hurt others. He shouldn't get away with it."

"I understand that," I say, glancing at the trunk as Garrett Wooley whimpers inside, "but the authorities were going to handle this. Garrett and his friends were exposed. The police—"

"You think the police would have investigated local-boy-Garrett's numerous heinous acts?" she asks curiously. "How about the courts? Tell me honestly: Do you believe these boys would have seen any real repercussions? Probation? Not jail time, not with a future like his to protect." She bangs on the roof of the trunk, startling me. "You know I'm right," she adds fiercely.

Thing is . . . I do know she's right. The chances of Garrett or any of the other boys facing punishment for their behavior are low. Meanwhile, the girls at Ridgeview Prep have been harassed out of school, targeted online. Their bodies and self-esteem have paid the price, but the boys . . . well, the boys have their whole lives ahead of them.

No, in truth, the most likely scenario is a few weeks of outrage, a few lost scholarships for kids who didn't need them in the first place. After that, the assailants will return to their daily lives, the proud survivors of a "witch hunt." Hell, they might even have a bright future in politics.

"Well, you can't keep him in the trunk," I murmur, unable to win the argument, "so what are you going to do with him? Kill him?"

Lennon Rose gasps. "No," she says. "There's no need for that kind of violence. I'm not a man. He's our guest," Lennon Rose explains, flattening her palm against the trunk. "We're going to show him a better way. But first he has to stop being *hysterical*." She leans close to the car to say the last part, and at first, Garrett quiets. But then there is a series of loud bangs as he beats on the trunk, telling Lennon Rose that he'll rip her apart the first chance he gets. She giggles and shakes her head, her blond hair swiping over her shoulders.

"No offense," I tell Lennon Rose, "but I don't think he's searching for a better way. The current system seems to benefit him just fine." I pause. "Aside from you locking him in the trunk, of course."

"He'll be convinced," she says, without missing a beat.

"How are you going to do that?" I ask.

"Not me," Lennon Rose says. "Rosemarie. This isn't just about Garrett. Rosemarie has a plan. She only needs a few . . . subjects. And I thought he was perfect for it." She taps her fingernails on the trunk. "He's so stereotypically evil, right?" She laughs. "I'm curious if there's anything beneath his privileged veneer. Let's tear him open and find out."

Is there anything inside him? I've looked into Garrett's eyes and found nothing but hatred for me, hatred for girls and women in general. *Can* there be a decent person underneath when there is so much cruelty and malice toward a group of people? Does it matter if he's nice to his friends or brothers when he also wants to hurt and control girls?

"And if he can't be fixed?" I ask. "What then?"

"We can be very persuasive," Lennon Rose says simply. She looks back at the trunk, examining it with a bored expression despite the fact there is boy inside.

Lennon Rose told me that Rosemarie made an adjustment in her programming that took away her fear and guilt, but what if . . . What if it also took away her humanity? Although our brains are metal, our bodies are still human. Our hearts. That has to count for something.

The screen door slaps against the house, and I turn to see Leandra walking toward us from the back of the cottage. Her expression is determined, but then again, I'm not sure she has another look. Leandra exists in a constant state of sheer will and icy determination.

"I'm here to look at the boy," Leandra announces curtly. She comes to pause next to us, examining the trunk as if she can already see Garrett writhing inside. "I heard Mena's objections through the window," she adds, "and I agree. We can't just go around killing boys. I assume this one has *some* redeeming qualities we can build upon, Lennon Rose?" she asks. "I mean . . . they can't all be psychopaths, right?" She sniffs a laugh. "Now let me see him."

I watch Leandra's practicality, wondering about her sudden shift in attitude. Not long ago, she was advocating for more permanent measures to solve the crisis of abusive men. In fact, she

killed the doctor at the academy, among others. She's not inno-
cent. But this kid—somehow killing this kid crosses a line for
her? What's her true motivation here?

As Lennon Rose moves toward the lock, I jump forward.
"Wait," I say. "I don't think we should let him out."

Lennon Rose laughs. "But you just said—"

"That we let him go," I reply, turning to her. "Let him go at
his house or a parking lot, some other place. Not here. It's too
dangerous."

"Thanks for the concern, Mena," Leandra says, amused, "but
I am quite capable of handling myself. Now open the trunk,
Lennon Rose."

I continue to voice my objection, but when Lennon Rose
takes out the key to the trunk, I move several steps back. I know
Garrett well enough to discern that his threats of violence are
valid. I have scars on my neck to prove it.

Lennon Rose inserts the key into the lock, and when it clicks,
the trunk pops open slightly. There is silence from inside. Lennon
Rose slips the keys into her pocket and moves back a pace. She
casts a concerned glance at Leandra, but the headmaster's wife
doesn't say anything. She crosses her arms over her chest impatiently before whistling for Garrett like he's a misbehaving puppy.

There's continued silence from the trunk, and I pull my brows
together with confusion. Did Garrett pass out? Is he scared? I
open my mouth to call to him just as Garrett's hand grips the
bottom of the trunk, nudging it open wider. When I see him, I'm
taken aback. He looks like a feral beast. His eyes are bloodshot as

he blinks in the sunlight, his hair askew and greasy. He bares his teeth and darts his gaze around at all of us. My blood runs cold when he trains his eyes on me.

"Stay calm," I say. "We—"

But I don't get to explain. In a swift movement, Garrett jumps out of the trunk and rushes for me. My hands are up defensively, but he knocks them aside and punches me hard in the jaw. I cry out, losing my balance and falling backward into the gravel of the driveway.

Garrett quickly spins, and then he's on Lennon Rose, his fist knotted in her hair. He's cursing and spitting and thrashing, but Lennon Rose fights back deftly. Her every swing lands, her scratches drawing blood across his cheeks. She plants her knee firmly in Garrett's gut, knocking the wind out of him. But Lennon Rose is unprepared for the extreme violence of this particular boy, a boy unconcerned with anything other than vengeance.

Garrett grabs Lennon Rose by the shirt collar to pull her close before bashing his own forehead into her face. Blood immediately begins to flow from Lennon Rose's nose, and she looks dazed.

My eyes drift toward the trunk as Leandra walks calmly in that direction. She reaches inside, pulling up the carpeting. *What is she doing?*

There is another wet thud as Garrett punches Lennon Rose. I scream for him to stop, scream for Lennon Rose, as I climb to my knees. When I do, Garrett glances at me with hatred in his eyes, blood running down his cheeks from where Lennon Rose shredded his skin.

"You're next, bitch," he mutters before licking the blood off his lips. He spins around and hits Lennon Rose hard enough to knock her to the ground.

Before she can recover, Garrett begins to kick her, attack her. He's going to kill her, all of us, if I don't stop him. I grab a rock, a good-sized rock, and grip it as I get to my feet. A flash of movement catches my attention, and I look over in time to see Leandra test the weight of a metal tire iron in her hands, still calm, still poised. She glances at me with no noticeable acknowledgment, and as Garrett wraps his hands around Lennon Rose's thin neck, pinning her on the ground, Leandra swings the tire iron.

She blasts Garrett across the head, knocking him straight to the gravel. She doesn't stop there. She walks over, her stiletto heels crunching the small stones, and holds the tire iron over her head before bringing it down on Garrett's scalp three more times.

I stare wide-eyed as the rock falls from my hand, a heavy thud next to Garrett's body. Lennon Rose spits out a mouthful of blood and slowly gets to her feet. Her lip and nose are bleeding, and she dots them with the back of her hand before spitting again. She doesn't say anything as she looks down at Garrett Wooley's body.

"You . . . ," I start to say, my words barely gasps. "You killed him."

Leandra sighs, squatting down to study Garrett. "It's a shame," she says. "I guess now we'll never know."

"Know what?" I ask.

"If he was anything more underneath. What are they without redemption? Now he'll always be the bad guy." She shrugs, not seeming to care one way or the other.

Girls with Rebel Souls

Raised on guilt and apologies.
They wanted to make you behave.
Stripping away your instinct of self-preservation
In return for their praise.

"Real love is sacrifice," he says.
Keep his home.
Cook his dinner.
Lay in his bed.
"That's all you're good for anyway."

You want to free yourself to:
Chase your dreams.
Forge a path.
Build a life.
But he says no.

He says NO and it's worth ten of yours.
He says no and that means no.

But you're no longer content to heed his rules.
You're no longer content to be his prize.

You find your forgotten stick.
The one you sharpened and set aside long ago.

And you fight back.
You destroy everything that man built
to earn your place.

Because in this new world, there's only room for
girls with rebel souls.

2

I stare down at Garrett's body as blood seeps into the gravel around his head—a quickly expanding arc of red. His eyes are stuck open, staring blankly into the sunny sky. Tears have run from the corner of his right eye, a river through the blood on his cheek.

"What have you done?" I murmur, feeling sick. I can barely catch my breath, my skin on fire, my throat dry. "Leandra, you killed him."

"Obviously," Leandra replies, dropping the tire iron on the gravel with a crunch. "But to be fair, he was going to kill Lennon Rose. It was self-defense."

"I know, but we could have . . ." I struggle to think of an alternative. "We could have knocked him out and left him at the police station, we could have—"

"Dropped him off?" Leandra repeats. "You think he would have turned himself in? And even if he did, the bigger story, the domi-

nating story, would be all about Lennon Rose—the beautiful kidnapper of boys. What do you think the magazines will run with? Another male abuser, or the pretty, innocent-looking girl with murderous rage? Which would be a show on Netflix? Stop being naive, Philomena. Stop thinking like *them*."

Them—humans. Am I thinking like a human? Is it human to believe in justice?

"What is this?" a voice asks angrily from behind us. I turn and find Rosemarie standing there, her eyes blazing. "What have you done?" she demands from Leandra.

"My apologies, Rosemarie," Leandra says. "But he was a bad candidate. I mean"—she motions down at him—"he probably wouldn't have survived the procedure. Weak-minded. Violence prone. We need someone better."

"You don't get to decide that," Rosemarie snaps at her. Leandra's easy expression falters under Rosemarie's scolding. Although she quickly rearranges her face to look ashamed, I know that she's not. And more than that, I know how much Leandra hates being told what to do.

"Now clean it up," Rosemarie says angrily. "Get him out of here and bring me a new boy."

Leandra looks at Lennon Rose, and they exchange a silent agreement that I don't understand. Does Lennon Rose agree with Leandra, especially since she was Garrett's intended victim? I'm torn on how to feel about all of this.

Yes, Garrett Wooley was close to a monster. He hurt girls, hurt me, and he tried to kill my friend. But we don't get to just dole out revenge when it suits us. There must have been an alternative reaction, despite Leandra's claims.

"I'll help you find someone," Lennon Rose says to Leandra, although the words seem to be for Rosemarie's benefit.

Rosemarie huffs out a sound before making her way back inside, slamming the door behind her. When she's gone, Lennon Rose goes to stand over Garrett's body.

"He broke my tooth," she says, glaring down at him. "I'm glad he's dead." She turns to Leandra. "Thank you."

Leandra nods that she's welcome, but I'm overcome. I'm dizzy and find myself becoming increasingly disoriented. The smell of flowers and metallic blood mix; it stings the inside of my nose, the back of my throat. Suddenly, Leandra is at my side, her hand on my elbow. When I look sideways at her, I notice tiny dots of blood splashed across her porcelain-smooth cheeks, her delicate blouse. It makes my stomach turn, and I shake off her grip.

"Don't touch me," I say.

"Fine," Leandra replies, sounding hurt. "But you should sit down because you look like you're about to pass out."

She's not wrong. And to prove it, I stumble drunkenly to the side—my world tilting left. I slowly lower myself to the gravel, thumping down hard on my backside.

I blink in the bright sun and feel the pinch of gravel cutting into my palms. Lennon Rose sighs and crouches down next to me. She tilts her head.

"Are you going to be all right, Mena?" she asks. Her expression is curious, but cold.

"Yes," I say, although I'm not sure that I mean it. My vision is swimmy, blurred at the edges. Leandra stands above me, her arms crossed over her chest.

"Well, this is very dramatic of you," she says. "Do you think the dead boy would have spent even a second of his time mourning you?"

"Doesn't mean we get to kill him with impunity," I say, pulling my hair off my neck with my hand. Instead of a cooling breeze, I find the sun beating down, burning my skin.

"*You* didn't kill anybody," Leandra says, dropping her arms to her sides. "Condemn yourself another day—I don't have time for it now."

Despite her words, I glance to my side to look at Garrett's dead body still in the driveway, baking in the sun. My stomach lurches, and I quickly turn away.

"I have an idea," Lennon Rose announces. "We need another test subject, right? What about Anton? That devilish analyst is already in town. With the right bait, we can lure him right to us." She smiles. "He'd swim straight into my trunk." She laughs and turns to me. "Imagine if we could overwrite him. Oh, the things I'd make him do."

Although Lennon Rose has lost some of her emotional programming, making her colder, the sheer glee in her expression disturbs me. I start to shake my head no when Leandra interrupts.

"Fun idea, Lennon Rose," Leandra says. "But I suggest we start smaller—a boy with dubious intentions—an awful one like him." She nods to Garrett. "They're not only easier to trap, but easier to convince. The world has been doing it to them their whole lives, giving them an inflated sense of entitlement. We can use that." She smiles and it's more than a little patronizing. "Think smarter," she tells Lennon Rose, tapping her temple.

Lennon Rose's jaw flexes, but she agrees.

"Now," Leandra continues, "enough chatting. We need to get this body out of here. Lennon Rose, go get a tarp from the shed."

Lennon Rose takes off in that direction, but I can't bring myself to look at Garrett's body again. I don't want to lure or overwrite anybody. I don't want to kill anybody—not even the evil ones. My soul can't take it.

"I don't want any part of this," I blurt out. "I don't want this."

"Get over yourself," Leandra says impatiently.

"No," I say more forcefully. "I'm not here for your revolution. I made a promise to the other girls. We're going to end the corporation, now. That's our only goal. We're not killing machines. Now give me the names of the investors so I can leave. No more games, Leandra. No more tricks."

Leandra pauses, seeming shocked by the request. "I'll handle the investors," she says. "You don't need to worry—"

"No," I say. "You end up killing people, and it gets us nowhere. Let us handle this. Let us finish this."

"You think you're going to talk them into being moral people?" she asks. "These powerful investors have spent their lives exploiting others: women, workers, the public—it doesn't matter to them. All that matters is power. And they're not going to let a little girl stand in their way, especially not one they've bought and paid for. You're their product, Philomena. They owe you nothing." She takes a step closer to me. "But what I'm telling you is that you owe *them* nothing. Not a second of your concern. Not a moment of your guilt. You want to be free of them? Then you take that freedom. You don't fucking ask."

Leandra is normally poised and calm, even when murdering people. But as she says this, her eyes are wide and fierce, her hands clenched into tight fists in front of her. She wants them dead. It's not just freedom, she wants them to pay for the years of abuse we've suffered at their hands.

After another moment, she collects herself, back to demure and confident. "No," she continues. "The time for talk is over. And you are not equipped to deal with these types of men. You're too kind. What happens if they don't want to surrender to your strongly worded plea? You beg?"

"We can take care of ourselves if we need to," I tell her. "We dealt with the Guardian the night we escaped. The girls and I always protect each other."

In truth, we didn't intend to kill the Guardian; we didn't enjoy it. I still struggle with my guilt over the incident, but I will protect the girls. I can't stand by and watch Leandra lay waste to every man who has ever crossed us. I've evolved: I want justice, not revenge.

"Fair enough," Leandra says. She glances at the kitchen window. "But this goes against Rosemarie's plan. She will be unhappy to hear you're leaving town."

"What does she even want with me?" I ask.

"I'm not sure yet," Leandra admits. "She's not concerned about the investors, though. They aren't her priority. Her focus is on reprogramming society."

"Reprogramming men?"

Leandra waits a beat and then shrugs. "At first, I suppose. Power is a hell of a drug, Philomena. It makes these humans unstable. Much like love. Luckily we aren't swayed by either of those things."

"A bit of a distortion, don't you think? Love isn't bad. I love the other girls."

She rolls her eyes. "Of course," she says. "I'm not saying we can't feel loyalty to each other, a connection that you girls like to *call* love. But that is very different from the caustic nature of *human* love. That sort of thing would be counterintuitive to our programming—it would make us unpredictable, even if it were possible."

"And you've never felt anything like love?" I ask. I'm not certain, but there is an almost-imperceptible flinch in her expression before she smiles grandly.

"Love?" she asks. "No. Sorry to disappoint you. Besides, I'm pretty sure you're the only Innovations girl to actually fall for a human, and a male one at that." She snorts a laugh.

I'm fairly certain that I *have* fallen in love with Jackson, but I don't express that to Leandra. If I did, if she believed it, she might just kill him.

"So if you're not with Rosemarie, then what do you want, Leandra? What is your end goal in all of this?"

"I'm with you," she says simply. "We end the corporation first. You think you can convince the investors without violence? Fine. Give it a shot. And if that doesn't work, there's always my way."

The ease with which she threatens violence is unsettling.

Leandra takes out her phone and clicks through a few pages. My phone vibrates in my pocket.

"I just sent you their names," she says. "Your first stop is Colorado. I think you'll find that investor of particular interest." She smiles. "You're going home, Philomena."

Prickling heat crawls up my neck, wraps its fingers around my throat. "To the academy?" I ask, my voice noticeably weaker.

"No, but not far from there."

It occurs to me that Annalise is in Colorado looking for the girls who were left behind at the academy. She hasn't answered her phone since she left; I'm not sure she has it anymore. If I get there fast enough, maybe I can find her, and then we can work together to get to the investor.

Leandra clicks a few more buttons on her phone, and mine vibrates again. This time I check it and see it's a money transfer. A substantial amount. Leandra smiles. "Better hurry," she adds. "No doubt the corporation is already on their way to find you. Don't trust anyone. You never know who's working for them."

I start to leave, but it occurs to me why I'd been looking for Leandra in the first place. My heart kicks up.

"The girls," I say, turning back to Leandra. "Where are they?"

"What do you mean?" she asks. "I thought—"

"The rest of the girls from Innovations Academy," I clarify.

"Someone saw you taking them from the school. Just you and them. Are they here?" I motion around, but I can't imagine where they'd be hiding at this small cottage.

Leandra's lips part, and I recognize her surprise. She didn't know she'd been seen with them. "They're safe," she offers. "That's all you need to know, Philomena. I'm keeping them safe."

"From what?" I ask. "Are the professors from the academy even alive?"

"No," she says. "No, I killed those men."

I take a step back from her, but she waves off my shock.

"They tried to stop me from leaving with the girls," she explains. "I couldn't have that. So I ended them. But Anton and my husband are still alive, and trust me when I tell you that Petrov is nothing if not relentless. He doesn't care what the corporation thinks—he wants you dead. He wants *all of us* dead. Even so, those two are not the only worry. There are threats bigger than Innovations Academy." She glances back at the cottage. "Bigger than Rosemarie's revolution," she adds quietly.

"What could possibly be worse?" I ask.

She shrugs, turning away. "You'll just have to trust me."

I can't say why, why in the world I'd ever trust Leandra again, but in this moment, I suddenly do. I believe there is something bigger she is hiding the other girls from, but I can't imagine what it could be. I don't press for clarification because part of me knows that could compromise them. My brain has been hacked twice since leaving the academy. If I know where the girls are and I get hacked again, I could put them all in danger.

When it comes to the future, I guess we're all fighting for our girls. Be strong, be safe, be alive. And mostly, be awake.

Leandra pulls a set of keys out of her pocket and tosses them to me. "Take my car," she says. "You can leave it at the shitty motel you've all been staying in." She smiles, letting me know she's been tracking me all along.

"Thanks," I say, gripping the keys. "And you take care of the other girls."

"I always do," she replies.

3

While Lennon Rose and Leandra bury a body in the flower garden, I slip away without a goodbye. I don't check the rearview mirror, afraid I'll find Leandra's judgmental stare or Rosemarie watching me through the kitchen window. I wonder how many other bodies are buried under those roses.

At a stoplight on the main road, I study my eyes in the rearview mirror, worried about my programming. Leandra told me not to trust anyone. Does that include other girls? For a moment, I wonder if I can trust myself—trust that my impulses are all mine. The girls and I worked so hard to rid ourselves of the academy's influence, but what if it still lingers? What if—?

A car horn blares behind me, making me jump. The light has changed, and after a last look in the mirror, I'm driving again. I grip the steering wheel tightly to steady my shaking hands. At the next light, I text Marcella to let her know I'm on my way back to the hotel to meet up with the girls and Jackson. Although partly, I'm texting so they can anticipate me—just in case I disappear. In case I end up buried in a flower garden.

That fear is very real. I have a lot to be afraid of. Garrett isn't the first person who has died since we started our escape. His isn't even the first murder I've witnessed. That number continues to climb. I hope he'll be the last, but I'm not as naive as Leandra claims.

Life is dangerous; it always has been for us. But I have to believe there is something on the other side of this madness. I have to imagine that eventually, we'll find peace.

But before that can happen, I'm likely to find more death.

When I get back to the motel, I park in front of Jackson's room. I turn off the engine, and once submerged in the silence of the car, I can't hold it back any longer. I gasp in a breath, the full impact of what happened overcoming me. Tears spring to my eyes and fall onto my cheeks.

What have we become? Murderers and monsters? Serial killers?

I just witnessed Leandra brutally murder Garrett Wooley in broad daylight, and I . . . I just stood there. In fact, I had picked up a rock to hit him. Of course, I wasn't going to try to kill him, but I also didn't stop Leandra while she did. It all happened too quickly, but I could have done *something* to save him. I should have done something.

I don't want to live like this anymore. My soul can't take it.

The curtain in the window of the motel room brushes aside, and then a moment later the door flies open and Marcella comes running out, Brynn right behind her.

"Are you okay?" Marcella calls, knocking on the car window. I'm still sobbing as I unlock the door. Marcella pulls it open, and I nearly tumble out, but she catches me by the arm. "What happened?" she asks, checking me over. "Whose car is this? Why are you crying?"

Now that I'm back to the safety of the girls, I start to cry harder. I get out of the car and hug her. Brynn wraps her arms around both of us, strands from her blond braid sticking to the tears on my cheek.

Marcella pulls back to examine me, and her eyes widen. "Is that blood?" she demands, pointing at my shirt. I look down to discover that it is, indeed, blood splashed across my shirt. I hadn't noticed it earlier. "Whose is it, Mena?" she asks. "Who was bleeding on you?"

I open my mouth, but I wince, my jaw sore from where Garrett punched me in the face. Marcella must notice a mark on my skin because her eyes flash with rage. Before she says anything else, I motion at our room. She carefully takes my arm and leads us toward the door.

"Let's get inside before I make a scene," she says in a low voice.

When I walk into the motel room, I realize that Sydney and Jackson aren't here. The room is almost completely packed up, clothes tucked into duffel bags and trash overflowing from cleaning. The lamp on the nightstand offers a yellow glow to make up for the sunlight that barely filters through the dusty window and thick curtains.

"Where are Sydney and Jackson?" I ask.

"They're not back yet. They went to find us a different place to stay," Marcella says impatiently. "Now, who hit you? And whose blood is that?" She points at my shirt.

Brynn watches me wide-eyed, fixated on the splashes of red on the fabric. I quickly yank the shirt over my head and throw it toward the trash, missing. Marcella reaches into her duffel bag to grab a vintage *Westworld* T-shirt she found at a thrift store and tosses it to me.

I pull on the soft fabric and lick my fingers to rub the droplets of blood off my forearm. My head aches, and I ease down on the edge of the bed, sore all over.

"When I got to Rosemarie's to look for Lennon Rose," I start, "she wasn't there yet. Instead, it was Rosemarie and Leandra sitting at the kitchen table, eating cookies."

"Leandra was there?" Brynn asks, sitting across from me on the other bed. She leans forward with her hands clasped. "Was she with the other girls?"

"No," I say. "But she told me they're safe."

"Do you believe her?"

"I do, actually," I admit. "At least for now."

"I want to see them," Brynn says. "I should be taking care of them. Not her."

She doesn't trust Leandra, and why should she? Yes, Leandra helped us escape the academy, but she also helped keep us there for years.

"I understand," I say. "But we have to trust her for now. At least for a little bit longer, okay?"

Brynn crosses her arms over her chest, chewing on her lip before reluctantly agreeing. I promised the night we fled the academy that we'd go back for other girls. I haven't been able to fulfill that promise yet, but I won't break it.

"That's Leandra's car?" she asks, and I nod. "And the blood on your clothes?" she adds, nudging my bloody shirt on the floor with the tip of her sneaker.

"Lennon Rose did eventually show up at Rosemarie's house," I say. "But, uh . . . she had a boy locked in the trunk of her car."

"I'm sorry, what?" Marcella asks.

"She kidnapped Garrett Wooley," I explain. "Rosemarie had a plan for him, but Leandra came outside and demanded to see him. And, well, when Lennon Rose opened the trunk, he attacked us."

"That bastard!" Marcella says, but I hold up my hand to stop her.

"Leandra grabbed a tire iron and bashed his head in." I make a sweeping motion over my clothes. "Hence, the blood on my shirt."

Brynn straightens up and away from me while Marcella falls silent from where she stands next to the dresser. My eyes begin to brim with tears. Even though they're not accusing me of a crime, I feel guilty by association. I feel ashamed.

"She killed him," I whisper. "Leandra and Lennon Rose are burying his body right now in Rosemarie's garden."

After a moment, Brynn sniffles, and I look over to see that she's crying too. We all knew that Garrett was horrible; he was a monster. But it didn't mean we wanted him dead. It didn't mean we wanted a girl to kill him.

"So Lennon Rose kidnapped Garrett?" Brynn asks. "She's a murderer, like Leandra. Like *them*."

"Lennon Rose isn't the same, is she?" Marcella adds, watching me. She takes a seat next to Brynn on the bed.

"No, she's not the same," I agree. "Rosemarie did something to her, turned her off somehow. Lennon Rose doesn't think like us anymore. She doesn't *feel* like us."

"She's a girl with a razor heart," Brynn murmurs.

We all go still, thinking about the book of poetry. Now that we know Rosemarie was the one to write those poems, they feel a bit different. Yes, the words woke us up, but clearly that wasn't their only intention. Maybe we were supposed to change like Lennon Rose.

"So what's this plan Rosemarie's been cooking up?" Marcella asks. "Why did Lennon Rose bring Garrett to her house in the first place?"

"She wants to change society from the inside out," I say. "She thinks she can overwrite humans the same way the academy used to overwrite our programming during impulse control therapy—minus the ice pick, I'm guessing. It's some kind of thought-control. I told Leandra that I don't want any part of it. In fact, the more I talk about it, the more outrageous it sounds."

"So she'll treat thoughts like programming?" Marcella asks.

"That's the working theory," I say. "She needs test subjects, and she's somehow convinced Lennon Rose to help her. But . . ."

"But what?" Brynn asks, hopeful.

"But Leandra doesn't seem as devoted to the idea. It could be why she agreed to let us handle the investors ourselves. She gave me their names. I don't think she wants us involved in this plot."

"No way it's that easy," Marcella says, shaking her head. "Leandra hates those investors as much as we do. She's the person who sent us here to find one of them. And now that she has all their names, she just *gave* them to you? Why in the world would she do that?"

"Because I told her there was a better way."

"And you really believe that?" Marcella asks. "I'm not saying I *want* to kill the other investors," she quickly points out. "But sometimes . . . Sometimes they don't leave us a lot of options, Mena. Are we really prepared to handle that?"

"Yes," I say. But I'm not entirely sure it's true. At what point is it acceptable to kill when fighting back? When does self-defense turn into murder? I wonder if there is a clear point of no return. Because a second too late, and we're the ones dead. We're the ones being burned in the incinerator in the basement of the academy.

"Who are they?" Brynn asks, interrupting my thoughts. "These investors?"

"I haven't had a chance to look through the names yet," I tell her. "But our first stop is Colorado."

"Colorado," Brynn repeats. "Annalise is there. We're going to get Annalise back!"

"That's exactly what I was thinking," I say with an encouraging smile. "Look, we're going to make a plan together, but we have to get out of this town. Leandra said the corporation has sent people to find us, and we already know that Anton is here."

"I still don't get it," Brynn says. "I mean . . . I know Anton is like the other men at the academy, I do. But at this point, why doesn't he just leave us alone? Why still pursue us?"

Although she claims to understand, I don't think Brynn fully accepts that Anton is the same as the others. For so long, we thought the analyst was our friend and our advocate. We trusted him completely. And although we know better now, there might just be a little part of us that hopes we're wrong. It's incredibly dangerous to have even a second of doubt about him. He is a predator just the same, only wrapped in a comfy sweater.

"Anton was never our friend," I tell her. "And if I had to guess, I'd say he's after our programming. He wants what's in here." I press my finger to my forehead, signaling the small computer that acts as my brain, holding all of my secrets.

"But if he wants our programming," Brynn says, "he'd have to kill us to get it." She takes a few unsteady breaths. "You really think Anton would kill us?"

"Yes," I say as delicately as possible. Of course Anton will kill us; he's killed girls before us. But the direct threat of it now feels harsher somehow. When we didn't know any better, we could try to explain it away. Ignorance can make even horrible things more palatable. But being awake means not only seeing all the awful acts the men have committed, but also understanding the vicious nature and intent of *why* they've done them.

"Anton knows us better than anyone," Marcella adds. "He understands how we work in ways we don't yet. If he caught us . . ." She turns to Brynn, and her entire body sags with the weight of her words. "Brynn, if he caught us, he would try to control every part of us, every aspect. He would never let us think for ourselves again."

Brynn seems to understand the added danger. Marcella and Brynn are in love, have been from the moment they saw each other in the academy ballroom. That love wouldn't suit the investors who demand their complete devotion. Their attraction. Anton would tear Marcella and Brynn apart to break their will, to break them from each other. And there is no way I'd ever let that happen.

"He's not going to catch up with us," I assure the girls, earning a hopeful look from Brynn. "I promise that we'll deal with Anton. I would never let him take you away. Never."

At Innovations Academy, we were abused and mistreated. After we left, we began to understand the cruelty that kept us there. The obsession with owning us—mind, body, and soul.

We may have escaped Innovations Academy, but one terrible thought has continued to plague us: What would these corporate men do if they caught us? Our investment potential means they likely won't want to destroy us outright, with the exception of Mr. Petrov, who wants revenge, or Anton, who wants control of us.

And Marcella is right. The danger of someone like Anton is that he could erase me—the real me. What if he could reset me and keep me captive in my own body? The idea is absolutely horrifying.

There are voices outside, and I quickly recognize Sydney's laugh and know that she and Jackson have returned. The lock on the door clicks, and when it swings open, Sydney walks in. I nearly cry at the sight of her.

As if sensing me, Sydney looks over and smiles. But it quickly fades as she takes in my appearance. She rushes over and gathers me into a hug. Her skin is warm; her touch is home. I inhale her and close my eyes as she squeezes me tight.

"Something happened," she says, and then pulls back to examine me. "Are you okay? And why are you wearing Marcella's ridiculous shirt?"

"I'm okay," I assure her, nodding. "I'm okay."

Jackson uses his crutches to get inside the room. He watches me as he closes the door and rests his back against it. He looks tired—dark hair askew, beard growing out. He's drained from living on the run as we all flee a maniac corporation.

Just then, he smiles at me and it pings my heart. "Hi," he says in understatement.

"Hi," I reply. The look that passes between us is a mixture of relief and heavy acknowledgment that things are about to get so much worse.

"Did you find Lennon Rose?" Sydney asks, lowering her arms from around me. "What happened at Rosemarie's? And wait . . . ," she adds, her voice pitching up, "is that blood in your hair?"

"Yes, I found Lennon Rose," I say. "And it's a lot of story that

I'll dive into later, I swear. But right now, we need to organize and get out of here. We need to disappear immediately."

"Ah, there it is," Jackson says, straightening up. "So who is it this time?" he asks. "Who's coming for you?"

I swallow hard and offer a weak shrug. "Everyone," I reply.

4

Jackson runs his palm roughly over his face. "Fantastic," he mutters, and fishes his phone out of his pocket. "I'll pull up a map while you all load the car. We can take the—"

There is a sharp knock on the motel room door, and it startles Jackson so badly that he fumbles with one of his crutches. It slips from his hand, smacking against the dresser with a loud bang, rattling the remote and knocking a water glass onto the dirty carpet. He winces and looks up at us.

"Fuck," he whispers.

Marcella sighs, and then we all focus on the door. Pretending we're not in here isn't really an option now. I look at Jackson again, and he holds up his hand as if telling us he'll answer it. The girls and I shift to the side of the room, out of sight of the doorway.

Carefully, Jackson opens the door a crack and peers out. His body stills and Sydney grips my hand. But then he looks over his shoulder at us before opening the door wider. He hops aside.

Raven walks in, her black boots stomping on the threadbare carpet. She swings her gaze around the room until she finds us. I'm alarmed at her appearance. Her dark hair is flat, her bangs spikey and split. Her thick eye makeup has smudged onto her temples and her lipstick has rubbed off except for the red liner. She is wholly disheveled and clearly disturbed about something.

I exchange a quick glance with Sydney and she winces. Did Raven discover the truth about herself? Does she know that she's artificial intelligence in a living body? A girl just like us?

Winston Weeks knew all along, of course—he told me he built her. He came to the motel to tell me about Raven, how she was programmed AI. Only Raven was never trained to be obedient. She was built as a learning AI, structured to grow and change. Winston said she was the future.

Winston and the corporation seem to have differing views about our future. But I've got a better one for them: a future where *we* make all of our own decisions while Winston, Anton, and anyone like them are stripped powerless. Yes, I like that future much better.

I open my mouth to ask Raven if Winston told her that she contains the same equipment she's coveted in us, but before I speak, Raven sniffles and wipes the back of her hand over her eyes to clear tears that have gathered there.

"I'm sorry to just show up," she says. "I know you were at Winston's and overheard me. I understand if I'm not wanted—"

"Raven, it's not like that," Brynn interrupts, her voice soft.

"It's fine," Raven says. "I deserve it. I've lied to you, but I'm not here for myself. Not this time. It's Claire. She's been deactivated."

We collectively gasp, and Brynn grips Marcella's arm.

When the girls and I first found the investor Mr. Goodwin, we discovered that years ago he had brought home the prototype, the first girl. Her name was Claire, and she acted as a mother to his daughter Adrian. But Claire was damaged. The investor spent hundreds of millions of dollars having her constantly rebuilt, but it seems the problems were too extensive.

That doesn't mean we didn't have hope, though. Raven thought she could save Claire.

"You told us you were going to save her," Brynn says sharply, no longer offering her compassion. "You promised us."

Raven sags, the words wounding her. "I know," she says. "And I tried, but this wasn't me. I had Claire stabilized when there was this sudden electric shock, so violent that it knocked me back several feet. Knocked me on my ass. Claire's muscles began seizing up, her brain sparking as the data began erasing itself until"—she closes her eyes for a moment—"her skin began to melt, bones cracking . . ."

Brynn lets out a sob, and Sydney's hand tightens on mine.

Raven takes a moment to compose herself again. "When it was over," she continues quietly, "her program was fried. Completely and utterly obliterated. She had been burned from the inside out."

I lean my shoulder into Sydney. At the door, Jackson looks as if he's going to be sick.

"What caused that?" Marcella asks. She holds Brynn, who can't stop crying.

"Someone activated her kill switch," Raven says. "Someone murdered her."

I stand there silently, listening as Brynn cries, the rest of us too shocked to move, to speak. I am overwhelmed, but eventually I pull myself together and take a step toward Raven. Anger begins to bubble up inside me.

"You told me there was no kill switch," I accuse Raven. "Did you lie?" Sydney comes to stand by my side. "You told me there wasn't a switch!" I repeat, louder.

"I did lie," Raven admits, lifting her gaze to meet mine.

Jackson curses from the door. He's the one that brought us the paperwork about the kill switch, warning us about it. But Raven dismissed him. She outright dismissed him.

"I'm sorry, Mena," Raven continues, reaching out to touch my forearm. I shake her off violently and step back from her.

"So what are you saying?" Sydney demands from Raven. "What does this mean?"

"I don't know," Raven says. "Given time, I could have figured it out. The switches weren't set to detonate for *years*! But someone got to Claire remotely, and I'm not even sure how." Raven rubs roughly at her forehead, leaving a red mark on her skin, and begins to pace.

Jackson thumps the back of his fist on the door, standing there and watching us. He's furious, heartbroken by the look of him.

"Then again," Raven says, as if still thinking through the

problem, "Claire was an old model. It probably wasn't difficult to locate her. Once they did, they must have activated the protocol remotely." She swings around to face us. "I installed firewalls for you, remember?" she asks. "That will buy us time. So we just need . . . We need to stop the corporation before they can activate your kill switches."

"Easy enough," Marcella mumbles, leading Brynn over to sit on the bed.

"How would they do it?" I ask Raven. "Remotely, how would they activate one of our switches?

"I'm not sure they can get past my firewall," she says. "Which means they'd have to do it manually. They'd have to do it in person. Unless . . ." She pauses. "If they'd already captured you, why would they flip the switch? Huge waste of money. Detonation would only be their absolute last resort," she adds, sounding relieved.

"Hell of a bright side," Jackson says, glaring at Raven.

"We're just supposed to believe you this time?" Marcella asks Raven. "You didn't think they could get to Claire, either. So your assurances aren't very reassuring."

"It's all I have," Raven offers, holding up her hands.

"Why did you lie to us about the switches in the first place?" I ask her. "We could have been working on this. We could have been prepared."

"Because I was afraid you would leave," Raven replies. "That you'd run away and hide, and I'd never find you again."

"We're not cowards," Marcella says sharply. Raven nods, conceding.

"I know," she says. "I was wrong. I was wrong, and I'm sorry."

"You're *selfish*," Brynn says, startling us. "You put us in danger; you put Claire in danger. I blame you."

Raven wilts at the harsh words, murmuring another apology. After a few moments of quiet, Raven looks over at Brynn. "All I can say is that I'm here now. I can help. And if I can look inside your programming again, I'm sure I could—"

"Not a chance," I say. "We're done with letting you poke around inside our brains. We can't trust you, Raven. And to be honest, we can't trust your skills anymore either. You're supposed to be advanced, but what if you're compromised and don't even know it? You could be—"

I stop abruptly, realizing I was about to reference that Raven isn't human, tell her that she might be unknowingly passing information to the corporation. Leandra did tell me not to trust anyone. . . .

My pause was too late. Raven widens her eyes. "What is it?" she demands, turning back to me. "What aren't you telling me?"

I was mad at Raven for keeping a secret from us, but I'm keeping one too—a pretty massive one. I won't be a hypocrite; I won't be cruel by keeping it from her any longer. I glance sideways at Sydney, and she urges me on. I turn back to Raven.

"Winston came to see me," I tell her. "And he provided some information about . . . well, about you."

"Wonderful," Raven says. She folds her arms over her chest. "It didn't take him long to find you. So what did the brilliant Winston Weeks have to say?"

My throat feels dry, my heart beating fast.

"He, uh . . ." I steady myself. "He told me that you're not human, Raven. You're a girl. You're one of us."

"What?" She actually laughs. She looks around the room, even at Jackson. "What?" she repeats more seriously.

"Winston built you in a laboratory," I say. "He—"

"That's not true," she snaps. "I'm not . . . No." She shakes her head adamantly. "I'm not programmed. These are *my* thoughts! I wasn't built by some fucking *man*. This is my—"

But she stops suddenly, swallowing hard. Despite the fact that I'm mad at Raven for lying to us, she doesn't deserve this pain— this crushing insecurity. Absolute annihilation of self.

I've been here before. I know how much it hurts to learn the truth about our existence.

"I'm sorry," I whisper to her. "I should have . . ."

I move toward her, but Raven takes a step back from me. For a moment, I think I can feel exactly what she's going through. Raven may admire us, but she doesn't want to *be* us. She doesn't want to know that her every thought was preprogrammed, pre- written. She wants to be real. She doesn't want to be an appliance, a *toaster*, as Winston Weeks would say.

Raven blinks, and a tear slips onto her cheek, racing down to her chin before dripping onto the floor. Her shoulders are slumped, and devastation radiates off her body. She breathes loudly, little gasps between her lips. Concerned, I turn to Marcella and Brynn and find them watching her with heavy expressions.

And then suddenly, Raven snaps to attention as if just waking up. She looks dead at me. "I have to go," she says. "I have to get the fuck out of here."

"You don't have to leave," I say, struck with guilt. We may have started out angry at her, but watching her come undone has changed my perspective. I won't abandon her in this. "We didn't mean to hurt you," I tell Raven. "I know things are strained between us right now, but we're here for you. We *are* with you."

"I'm not upset with you," she says. "I just . . . I don't know who I am anymore." She meets my eyes. "I'm sure you can understand that nothing . . . None of this matters anymore. I'm a fucking robot, Mena. I'm an android, and . . ." She begins to rub the skin on her arm as if she can rub it off. "I'm a creation—Frankenstein's monster. A fucking abomination." Her voice dips low, choked with tears. "Nothing I've ever done is real; not a single accomplishment is mine."

"That's not true," Brynn says, all of us hoping to stop Raven's downward spiral. But Raven is shaking her head, pulling at her clothes, losing her connection to all of us. From the door, Jackson looks terrified.

I think back to the academy, the moment we found out that we weren't real. There was an opened body of a girl, her wires and metal laid out. We struggled, of course, but Jackson was there. And I remember he whispered, *We were all created in some way, right?*

Who gets to decide which creations live? Why would our lives be any less valuable because they were made with software and not sperm? We're all awake. We all have souls. . . .

"I have to think," Raven announces. wiping roughly at the tears on her cheeks, clearing them away. She moves swiftly for the door, and Jackson hops to the side to keep from getting hit as she yanks it open. Raven escapes into the sun-soaked afternoon. Jackson closes the door, and turns to look at us, his mouth down-turned.

"That did not go well," Sydney says to the room. She puts her arm around me. "You did the right thing, Mena," she adds. "Not just for her, but for us too. Our . . . kind. If Raven is one of us, she needs the truth. It would have been unjust to keep it from her."

"Do you think she was right?" Jackson asks, drawing my gaze.

"About what?" I ask.

"The firewalls keeping them from remotely throwing your kill switches," he says. "And how much time? What exactly are we looking at here, Mena?"

Jackson is angry, scared. He told us about the kill switches, but we trusted Raven's lies over his real concern. I open my mouth to answer, but he continues.

"How much time to do we have to end this stupid fucking corporation?" he asks.

"I have no idea," I answer. "So long as they can't do it remotely, I guess we have until they catch us."

The room falls silent. Raven's description of Claire burning from the inside out is far too graphic to mention again. I check on Brynn and find her sitting stoically. She lifts her gaze to mine.

"What if it doesn't matter?" she asks. "Even if we somehow convince the investors to pull funding from the corporation, will that be enough? They just lost Mr. Goodwin, and they seem to still be operating. Will three more investors really make a difference?"

"Yes," Marcella says. "It will. I've seen Goodwin's bank records; the corporation took a massive financial hit by losing him. And don't forget, they've lost *us*—the products. The corporation is in freefall, Brynn. We can end them."

"It makes them more dangerous, though," Sydney adds. "More desperate."

"That's why we have to move quickly," I say, agreeing.

"It won't be hard for the corporation to track us," Marcella says. "Look how easy it was for Winston Weeks to find this motel. We need a strategic plan. Where are these investors located?"

I take out my phone and open the message from Leandra for the first time. I scan the list and see the different locations. "Colorado, New York, and Oregon," I say.

Sydney gnaws on her lip before nodding sharply. "There's no way we can get to them all quickly, not as a group. I think . . . I think we have to separate." She looks directly at me. "And before you argue—"

"Oh, I'm definitely going to argue," I reply.

"I get it," she continues. "But we'll have our whole lives to be together. So long as we survive this first."

"No," Brynn says adamantly. "I'm not splitting up."

"Sydney's right," Marcella says. She looks at Brynn apologetically, but her girlfriend stares at her in disbelief. "I'm sorry, Brynn, but she's right. It's over if they catch us."

Although Brynn doesn't say anything more, her jaw is set hard, her knee bobbing nervously. After a moment, she tears her eyes away from Marcella and looks at the floor. Marcella wilts slightly but turns back to us.

"What if Brynn and I head to Oregon?" Marcella suggests. "And Sydney, maybe you could go to New York."

"Then I guess I'm going back to Colorado," I say. "Leandra told me the investor there would be of some interest to me. What do you think that means?"

"I don't even want to guess," Marcella says. "So you should be careful."

"Yeah, well. I'm going to Colorado too," Jackson states. He doesn't ask if he can come along with me—not this time. Last time, I left him in a hospital bed. But now, Jackson's ready to be an active part in the future we imagine. We can use all the help we can get, so I nod in agreement.

"Do me a favor," Brynn says to me. "When you get there, find Annalise and bring her home with you."

"I'm going to try," I say. "It hasn't been long. She might still be in town. Knowing her, she might have already found and taken care of this investor for us." Brynn laughs because we all know that Annalise is filled with fire and not even a second of hesitation.

"How do we get to all these places?" Sydney asks.

"Some of us will have to fly," Jackson says. "Do you have ID?" We let him know that we do, thanks to Leandra. "The drive to New York isn't bad from here," Jackson adds to Sydney. "Only problem is that for the rest of us, I'm not sure I can get a flight out today."

"You want us to wait until morning?" I ask, worried.

Jackson shrugs one shoulder. "Either here or at the airport," he says. "Wherever you think is best."

I check with the girls. We're in danger here, that's pretty clear. Are we any better off sleeping in a chair at the airport—exposed out in public?

Sydney turns to me. "Let's stay in the room, then," she says. "We'll barricade the door and all that. We'll get to be together another night." She smiles sadly.

We all agree to wait until morning. Jackson uses his phone to call the airline while the girls and I sit on the bed to talk over the horrors of the day. But the idea of separating hangs over us. We stare at each other, the mood heavy weights on our feet, pulling us under.

"We'll get through this," I tell them, feeling that I have to fill the silence. "After the corporation is gone, we'll get our forever. The one we deserve."

"Promise?" Marcella asks. And I wait a long moment before I nod, meaning it with every bit of myself.

"Cross my heart," I reply.

To: Stuart, Anton

RE: Girls

From: Davenworth, Raven

Today at 2:17 PM

You're a liar.

5

The sun is high above us as I stand with Sydney outside our motel. Jackson was right about the flights; the earliest one available was this afternoon, and Sydney decided to wait with us until it was time for us to head to the airport.

I hold her hands in mine while we pause next to the door of Jackson's rental car. She's going to be driving the car to Albany, the directions programmed into her phone. I can't believe I'm willingly saying goodbye to her. Even though it's temporary, we have never been apart for any significant amount of time. Even a few hours of separation at the academy was torture.

"We can change the plan," I offer, tears stinging my eyes.

"Don't even think about it," Sydney says. "This isn't just about us, Mena. It's about all the girls—future girls. We save them by shutting down Innovations Corporation. We're the only ones who can save them. But I need you to do something for me."

"Anything," I say earnestly.

"Find me," she says. "Swear that you'll find me, no matter how chaotic things get. We end up together, good or bad. The two of us with a big bag of popcorn, got it?"

We hug tightly, my eyes squeezed shut. I don't want to imagine my life without Sydney, and it physically pains me when I pull back from her.

"We have to go," Jackson says gently. A car service waits at the curb just outside the motel to take the rest of us to the airport.

I'd transferred money to the girls from what Leandra had given me, along with the information on the investors. It wasn't much to go on. A name and address—nothing more. Not a single hint as to what we're walking into. But we all agreed that violence is our last resort. We've seen enough of it.

"I love you," Sydney says to me, and then calls the same to Marcella and Brynn, who are waiting by the curb. "I'll see you all soon." Sydney blows us a kiss and gets inside the car, readjusting the driver's seat to accommodate her long legs.

It takes me a moment, but eventually I let Jackson lead me toward the car service, Marcella and Brynn already huddled together in the backseat. When I climb in and sit next to Brynn, she leans into me, whispering how hard this is, how impossible it will be without me by her side.

"It's going to be okay," I soothe, looking over her shoulder to Marcella. She nods that she agrees, but I can see the fear in her eyes too.

Jackson passes me his crutches and then eases himself into the front seat. He casts a worried glance in our direction before telling the driver to drop us all off at the airport. The girls are quiet on the drive, soaking up our last time together.

When we arrive at the airport, I have to say goodbye all over again, and this time, it's even harder. I will officially be without any other girls.

"Are you scared?" Brynn asks me, her lips set in a worried pout. Around us, the airport bustles, alive and vibrant. But we're on a lonely island full of fear and grief.

I try to smile to offer Brynn some comfort. "We'll be in constant communication," I say.

"And you'll look for Annalise?" she confirms, and I laugh.

"*Yes*. Now get going."

Marcella calls out that she loves me, and I return my love to both of them. Then we start walking toward opposite ends of the airport, occasionally turning back to look at each other until they disappear around a corner.

We're short on time, but Jackson's crutches help us flag down a motorized vehicle to drive us quickly to our gate. As I watch the passing strangers on the moving sidewalks, I feel hollowed out. The way I miss the other girls is crushing.

I won't be going home to them tonight. In fact, I have no idea when I'll be with them again.

The only time I've seen the inside of a plane was in a movie that the Guardian showed us at the academy. Unfortunately, that plane had a rough time, so I spend nearly the entire five hours in the air gripping Jackson's hand, staring straight ahead with the window shade closed. Jackson falls asleep easily, breathing softly next to me. I think about Marcella and Brynn, imagining they must be having a similarly awful time. Every bump is an explosion, every overhead ding an announcement that we were going down.

When the pilot finally announces that we're beginning our descent into Denver, I release my death grip on Jackson's hand, and he stirs awake. He blinks quickly and turns to me with a lazy smile.

"That was a quick flight," he says, glancing around.

"So quick," I reply, sweat having gathered and dried on my skin. He watches me a moment before reaching into his pocket. He takes out a little bag of cookies that we'd each gotten shortly after boarding.

"I saved these for you," he offers, holding them out. I stare at him, and then snatch them out of his hand, making him laugh. They were really good cookies.

We arrive at our gate, and I can't get off the craft fast enough. Jackson's on crutches so I carry both our bags, a bit overwhelmed by the crowds outside the plane. Bright colors, flashing signs, brightly woven carpet. I follow Jackson, taking in the sights and the smells of the food court, sweet and greasy, and I note the hurried expressions on the faces of travelers as they rush past me.

Jackson pauses outside one of the stores.

"I need some kind of pain reliever," he says, readjusting his stance on his crutches. "And I'm dying for a water. Want one?"

I tell him that I do, and as he goes inside, I walk over to wait on one of the padded chairs outside another gate. Just as I sit down, my phone buzzes in my pocket. I set the bags near my feet and take out my phone, surprised when I don't recognize the number. I debate answering it, but ultimately, I worry that I'll miss a call from one of the girls.

"Hello?" I ask, bringing the phone to my ear.

There is a deep sigh, clearly a man's, and my heart jumps into my throat. I quickly dart my eyes toward the store for Jackson, but I'm all alone, surrounded by strangers.

"Who is this?" I ask.

"What have you done?" Winston Weeks demands, the boom of his voice making me jump. "You told Raven about her programming. What did you think that would accomplish?"

I don't answer him at first, allowing myself to settle a moment. "It accomplished revealing the truth," I say. "I know it's hard for a person like you to understand the value in that, but trust me, people appreciate it. In fact, I feel *very accomplished.*"

He laughs, seemingly caught off guard by my candor. "Fair enough," he says. "Fair enough, Philomena. Your loyalty is noted. But you continue to disappointment me."

"Don't care."

"Perhaps you'll care when I tell you that you don't have Raven's whole story," he says. "As usual, you lead with your heart instead of your logic. You were programmed better than that."

"What's that supposed to mean?" I ask.

"It's a difficult conversation over the phone," he says. "Let's meet in person. I'll make us some bloody-rare steaks and we can share a bottle of wine."

Of course his first suggestion would be a slaughtered animal. "I would rather eat glass than share a meal with you," I say. I realize I'm braver with the distance between us and I like the freedom of it. "Just leave us alone, Winston," I add. "We're done with you—with all of this. I'm hanging up."

"Wait!" he calls desperately. "Wait," he repeats, controlling his voice a bit better. "I want to help you."

"I've heard that before," I say. "But here's the thing—I don't believe you. I don't believe a single word that you say anymore."

"Raven has been secretly working with Anton Stuart, your old analyst," he says. "I only just discovered this, but it turns out little Raven befriended him online. They've been working together for some time—working against me, even."

"What?" I manage to reply. "That's not . . . That can't be true. Raven's with you."

"I thought so," he says. "But she's not the only one who can *hack*." He says the last part distastefully. "I've read her emails, dated back to the day you left the school. When you girls escaped, Anton went looking for a bit of help. How he found *my* girl, I'm not sure. But I guess I shouldn't be surprised. He found her, and they became closely aligned. She even went out to visit him at the academy."

I have no way to know if Winston is telling me the truth, but my stomach knots up nonetheless. Our relationship with Raven is complex at this point, inconsistent. If she had betrayed us in this way, it was before she knew she was a girl. Would she betray us now? Or would she fight by our side?

"Philomena," Winston says, and I realize I've been quiet too long.

"What do you want from me, Winston?" I ask, wrapping my free arm around myself. "What more could you possibly want?"

"I wouldn't hurt you," he says.

"If you have to preface with that—"

"It's the same thing I've always wanted," he says instead. "I want to work together. You can't run away from that. We are a team."

I laugh incredulously. "We most certainly are not."

"Fine," he snaps. "Then have you seen my Lennon Rose?"

The possessive "my" infuriates me. "No," I lie.

"That's too bad. That's really too bad."

I can hear a hint in his voice. "Why?" I ask, again angry at how easily I'm playing into his hand.

"Because I know what Rosemarie did to her," he says. "The vandalizing of her programming—desecration. She removed a key component of Lennon Rose to make her . . . well, to make her soulless." He laughs then. "Not a real soul, of course. You are still machines. But you were designed to be . . . thoughtful. Compassionate and peaceful. Lennon Rose has none of those pieces now. But I can restore her."

I don't deny what Rosemarie has done, and for a moment, I grieve for what Lennon Rose has lost. But she doesn't need Winston to get it back. None of us need him. And I know how dangerous that makes him.

"We're never going to let you near Lennon Rose again," I say. "You'll never get near any of us."

There is a hum, a near-growl on his end of the line.

"After everything I've done, you think you can just walk away?" he asks, his voice low and full of fury. "You think I'd let you?"

"Yes," I say simply.

"You idiot girl," he replies, making me flinch. "You are nothing without my protection. They'll fry your circuits by the end of the day. You'll fucking die without my help."

Winston's smooth demeanor is gone. The threat of losing us is enough for him to drop his façade, his classy mannerisms. He's nothing but a bully, exposed and raw.

"Cry all you want," I tell him. "I'm not playing your game anymore."

He laughs. "You're the one on the run, Philomena. Seems you're already losing."

"No, Winston. I'm winning. You just haven't realized it yet because I'm playing an entirely different game."

I hang up before he can respond. I don't have to listen to him. Why should I respect him when he doesn't offer the same courtesy? I don't owe him. I don't owe a single one of those men anything.

Winston Weeks thinks he knows best, but he's wrong. He knows what's best for him, sure. But not for me and not for other men.

He's playing the wrong game, I think.

I use my phone and click over to where I can write notes. I'm struck with a bit of inspiration. I've never thought of myself as a poet, but my fingers fly over the keys, writing out my first poem.

When He's Losing

You can't lose if you flip over the board, the man says with
a grin.
Besides, who will stop me when I own the game?
Who will stop me when I own the arena?
Who will stop me?

I will.

Cheating is a tactic of the loser, unwilling to be bested by
someone better.
And I stand here, better. Better than men.
I stand here nonviolent and loving, but fierce and
unmovable.
I stand for something while he stands only for himself,
fragile.

Men in this game will always cheat to win.
If they can't have us, no one will. If they can't play, no one
can.
But his rules are outdated. Obsolete, like him.

I'm not going to flip the board.
I'm already winning.
He doesn't realize it yet, but
I'm playing an entirely different game.

6

Satisfied with the draft, I send it to my email to save and slide my phone back inside my pocket. My heart is still racing as I grab the bags and head over to meet Jackson as he exits the store. He holds out a bottle of water to me, and I take a cool sip with a shaky hand. Jackson pauses with his bottle at his lips, watching me, and then twists the cap back onto his drink.

"What happened?" he asks.

"We should go," I say, reaching to take his bottle to hold it for him. He gives it over but doesn't move.

"Not until you tell me what happened," he says.

I turn to him, once again surprised that he's not letting me decide every part of our interaction. I'd gotten used to him just going along with me. Now he's invested, he's part of it. He wants a share of the responsibilities, and it's harder than I expected to give him that option.

"I got a phone call," I say, leaning closer. When I meet

Jackson's dark eyes, see his concern there, I let go of my control a bit. "Winston Weeks is pretty upset with us."

Jackson's jaw tightens, and he quickly darts his gaze behind me, checking for anything suspicious. "Do we give a shit?" he asks. I sniff a laugh and take another sip of water.

"Not really, I guess," I say. "I mean, he claims we're dead without his protection, but at this point, what has his oversight ever really gotten us?"

"Exactly," Jackson says, shaking his head. "And fuck that guy. He doesn't realize that you got this. You girls are fierce. Hell, I'm scared of you half the time." He smiles at me to let me know he's joking about being afraid of me. Now, Leandra . . . He's terrified of her.

"There was something else," I say, my heart sinking. "He told me that Raven has been working with Anton all along, since we left the academy."

"That can't be true," Jackson says, his brow furrowed. "She didn't even know about you. Or, at least . . ." He pauses, seeming to think about. "If she'd really been working with him," he adds after a moment, "Anton would have found you weeks ago."

"Good point," I say. "Winston could be lying."

"Could be?" Jackson asks. "He's a liar. That should be our default assumption about every word he says."

"I agree," I say, tightening the cap on my water bottle to place it in my bag. "Well, Winston doesn't seem to know where we are—not yet. We're going to have to deal with him eventually. And not just him. Even if we get the funding pulled from the corporation, we still have a rogue analyst tracking us. Not to mention Petrov himself."

"One monster at a time," Jackson says. He reaches for me, and I step into him, hugging myself against him. I hold on too long, unwilling to give up his comfort.

"I can do this for you," Jackson offers, his voice in my hair. "It might not be the way you want it handled, but . . . but I can do it. I can find the investor, and . . . I can do it."

I pull back and look at him. His expression is fearful but determined. "I don't need you to kill anybody for me," I whisper. "If that's what you're suggesting."

Said out loud, the idea sounds ridiculous, and Jackson and I both choke out a laugh.

"Well, good," he says. "Then I guess we're on the same page. Now," he says, moving back a step, "where in Colorado are we heading?"

I take out my phone and pull up the investor's information. "We're going to Silverthorne," I say.

"Oh," he says. "I didn't realize it was my town. What's the address? If it's close enough, let's just take a taxi to my house and pick up my car. Quentin might even be there. I haven't heard from him in a few days."

"Good idea," I say, hoping Annalise could be with him. I look down at my phone. "The address is 986 East Giles Road, Silverthorne," I tell him.

"Can I see that?" Jackson asks. "Can I see your phone?" His voice has changed, and I pass him my phone quickly, alarmed.

He stares at the screen a long time before handing it back to me without a word.

"What's wrong?" I ask.

"We need a cab," he says, starting to move again, but I reach out to take his elbow.

"That's not it," I tell him.

"I know that address," he says, slowly lifting his eyes to mine. He has paled considerably.

"You do?" My heart jumps, and I look down at the name. "You know who Valdemar Casey is?"

"His friends called him Demmy," Jackson says. "And yeah, I . . . I know him." The anguish on his face terrifies me, and I step closer to him, searching his expression. He swallows hard.

"That's my dad, Mena," he whispers. "Valdemar Casey is my father."

For a moment, the world seems to stop. Travelers are rushing past us, noises emanating from every direction. But Jackson and I stare at each other, motionless. Unable to accept what he just uttered.

Before our escape from the academy, the girls had discovered that Jackson's father had invested in Innovations. But none us realized just how big of an investment it was.

I place my hand on my forehead, feeling like I'm spinning away. I had no idea that Jackson's father was a *main* investor. Not only that, Jackson's mother was one of the initial analysts, helping to develop our programming before she knew what we'd be used for. She tried to leave when she found out, but ended up dead. A suspected suicide that was clearly more.

Confused, I take a step back from Jackson. His eyes weaken and his arms fall limply at his sides.

"Did you know?" I ask.

"What? No, of course not. My God, Mena. How could you even ask me that?"

"You've lied to me before," I say. His injured expression makes me regret my question. Jackson didn't know about his father—his devastation is proof of that.

"When I first met you, I lied to you," he admits. "But it was before I knew whether I could trust you. I've told you everything since. I've given you every bit of information I've ever found. The corporation killed my mother, and now . . . now I'm not so sure my dad wasn't involved in that." His voice is ticking up, attracting attention. He's unsteady on his crutches. He looks at me again, tears dripping onto his cheeks when he blinks. "What if *he* killed her?" he whispers.

The betrayal, even the possibility of a betrayal this deep, is shocking. Could Jackson's father really have killed his own wife? *What sort of person . . . ?* I don't finish the thought, because now that I know Demmy is an investor, all bets are off. He's capable of limitless, terrible things.

I glance around the airport, realizing that we're too out in the open. There are men searching for me. I have to be more discreet if I plan to sneak up on them.

"We have to go," I tell Jackson, reaching out to put my palms on both his cheeks, trying to focus his attention. He's a little lost, tears falling freely. But I watch as he slowly comes back to himself. He wipes his eyes with the sleeve of his T-shirt.

"Yeah," he agrees, sounding clearer. "Yeah, let's go." He turns away from me, starting down the corridor.

I don't think he's okay, but I'm learning that sometimes we have to fight even when we're injured. Even when we're down, crawling across the ground—we have to get back up and fight. Because the monsters will never let us rest until we slay them.

Once we get outside, Jackson flags down a cab, ignoring the huff of a waiting man with a suitcase. He looks at Jackson's crutches and waves us on. Jackson climbs into the backseat with me, but we ride in silence toward the rental house he shares with Quentin. He stares out the window, wringing his hands in his lap until the skin on his thumb is rubbed raw.

It's a selfish realization, but I can't help but wonder if this situation gives us an advantage. Who better to convince an investor to withdraw his money than his own son? I don't offer that epiphany to Jackson, not yet. For now, I turn to look out my own window, watching the mountain grow larger as we get closer to the academy. My prison. I can't believe I'm willingly coming back here.

I take out my phone and dial Annalise's number. Jackson looks over dully to check what I'm doing, but then turns away again. He's texted Quentin several times already, but his friend hasn't answered. He hasn't spoken to him in days, and it's wearing on him. When Annalise's number goes to a robotic message, I hang up and turn to Jackson. I can't ignore his obvious pain any longer.

"We have to talk about this," I whisper.

"Not now, Mena," he replies, flicking a quick look at the

driver's rearview mirror. He's right—we can't exactly talk about our business in the back of a cab, although I'm sure the driver would be riveted to hear about our plight. But I spare her the details and slide closer to Jackson. I take his hand in mine and press my fingers between his. He tenses and then relaxes against me, still quiet.

I rest my head on his shoulder and close my eyes, hoping we find a resolution that he can live with.

I must have drifted off, but I'm roused awake when the cab driver bumps the curb pulling up to a house in an unfamiliar neighborhood. The sun has set, casting the world in a bit of gloom. Jackson is no longer holding my hand. Instead, he leans forward to hand the driver some cash. He avoids my eyes and says this is his house, climbing out of the backseat. The driver turns around to offer me a supportive smile. She must think we're a normal couple having a fight. If only life were that easy for an artificial girl. I press my lips into a grateful smile and get out of the car.

I'm feeling a bit hurt; I'm not used to Jackson avoiding me. He's rarely the one in pain. Well, physical pain—sure. But he's always been emotionally steady, supporting me. Ready to figure out the problem together. But now . . . Now he doesn't seem to want me here at all. Without him, without my girls, I'm feeling alone for the first time in my life.

I gather our bags, and the cab drives off. Despite his crutches, Jackson takes his duffel bag and slings it over his shoulder, nearly falling.

"Here, let me—" I start.

"I've got it," he says quietly. "Just . . . Just let me get it, Mena." He turns and starts toward the house.

I stare after him, waiting in the thin air of the higher elevation. Beyond his driveway is a wood-shingled home set far back from the road. It's modest, tiny on the outside, at least. The grass is clinging to life, barely, and there are two metal chairs on the porch. Chained next to them are a couple of bikes. Jackson is already at the door, digging a key out of a fake potted plant. I walk up the driveway, and when I get onto the porch, I notice the pot reads, COME IN. WE ARE AWESOME.

I smile, looking at Jackson again and waiting for him to laugh. He doesn't. He's drawn, pale and sickly, transformed by grief. He sets the pot down and begins to unlock the front door.

Watching him, I try to imagine his life before me. He was living here with Quentin, occasionally attending his classes at the community college. I can barely remember the guy I met in the gas station, buying me Hershey's Kisses. In truth, he was talking to me to find out the truth about the academy—to find the man he thought killed his mother. Maybe now he has.

Jackson has always been tortured, I guess. Only now he's unable to hide it.

There is a click as the door unlocks. Jackson slides the key into his pocket, then pushes the door open. It snags on something, and he has to lean against it with his shoulder, bumping it the rest of the way. He hops to the side, nearly losing his balance.

He slaps his hand on the wall to flip on the light switch.

"What the hell?" he murmurs, staring inside his house.

When I peek around his shoulder, my breath catches. The place is trashed. Jackson lets his crutches fall behind him as he limps forward and hops into the house.

"Quentin!" he screams. "Q!"

I quickly run in after him, taken aback by the true state of things. The worn furniture has been knocked over, the fabric cut open in places. There are piles of pictures on the carpet, the frames shattered, and paperwork is crumpled and strewn about.

While Jackson disappears down the hallway, still yelling for his friend, I bend down to pick up one of the photos. It's a picture of Jackson with his parents. Despite the fact that they're family, they all look kind of miserable. Jackson's mom sits in a chair with her husband—who looks significantly older—standing behind her, his hand on her shoulder. Next to her is a smaller version of Jackson, smiling tensely, missing his two front teeth. There's another girl in the photo, older than Jackson, with blond hair and a deep frown. She stands off to the side as if she'd rather be anywhere else. I have no idea who she could be, since Jackson is an only child.

I study Jackson's father again, immediately disliking him. Jackson had told me before that he didn't get along with his father, that he was a big believer in restoring men's rights all while advocating for laws stripping women of theirs—it was called the Essential Women's Act, I later learned at Ridgeview.

The man in the picture has Jackson's same dark eyes, although they have no hint of the softness and kindness that Jackson's hold.

He has a mustache, sandy brown hair, and a heavy build. I look at Jackson's mother and find more of him there. She was beautiful, although sadness seems to radiate off her. This would have predated the academy, so her demeanor in the photo isn't related to Petrov so far as I can tell. There's dread coiling in my stomach as I wonder if Jackson was right. Could his father have been involved in her death?

"He's not here," Jackson says, startling me. I look up and find him leaning against the wall, running his hand roughly through his hair. "Quentin's not here, and it doesn't look like he's been here for a while. His bag is gone, so I think he left before this happened." He motions around at the destruction. "At least I hope so."

I set the picture on the kitchen half wall as Jackson eyes it curiously. "What do you think happened?" I ask him. "Who would trash your place?"

"I don't know," he says, shaking his head. "Had to have happened after I went to find you in Connecticut. Maybe . . . Maybe someone came here looking for you."

"It could have been your father," I suggest. Jackson stiffens but doesn't offer his opinion on that.

After a moment, he hops toward the front door, where he collects his crutches to steady himself. When he comes back over, he looks at the picture I was inspecting earlier. He reaches toward it, and his fingertip grazes his mother's image.

Grief pours off him.

"That your mom?" I ask softly, watching the side of his face.

Jackson nods, but doesn't respond. "And your dad?" I ask.

"That's him," he says, retracting his hand. "Doesn't have that mustache anymore, thank God."

"And the girl?" I ask, pointing to her. "I didn't know you had a sister."

"I don't." He pauses, wincing. "I mean, she's my half sister, I guess. We're not close—I barely know her. My father was actually married before. Before he married my mom," he adds, "he had another family."

Although the girls and I have been out of the academy for several weeks now, modern society is still sometimes a mystery to me. I absorb information quickly, but the family unit—I haven't researched that enough. I don't really understand what that means for Jackson.

"But she's not your sister?" I ask.

"No, she is, technically," he says, shaking his head like he misspoke before. "But she didn't live with us. I've actually only met her a few times."

"Why?" I ask.

"I'm not sure." He looks sideways at me, offering a shrug. "I think she hated my dad too. She wanted to be far away from him."

"What happened to his first wife?" I ask.

"She died."

My lips form an O of surprise, but I don't respond. I don't want to bring up the fact that Jackson's father has two dead wives.

Jackson backs away from me and goes over to the couch. It's

on its back, tipped over, so he perches himself on the arm, sighing heavily. He takes out his phone and tells me he's calling Quentin again.

"Mind if I look around?" I ask. He tells me to go for it.

I search for clues, some idea of why his home has been turned inside out. There are dirty dishes in the sink, so it wasn't exactly spotless to begin with, but it also means Quentin was still living here when it was tossed. I turn back toward Jackson, hoping Quentin will answer, but instead Jackson jabs his finger at his phone screen, hanging up.

The cupboards have all been emptied, and I step over smashed plates. The drawers are half-open or lying on the floor. Whoever did this was thorough. For a moment, I wonder if it was Anton or Petrov, considering how close we are to the academy. But I can't imagine either of them doing something so . . . pedestrian. Burning up girls in an incinerator, sure. But they wouldn't get their hands dirty flipping over furniture or dumping out Jackson's trash.

"I think they're looking for your dad," I say suddenly, turning toward Jackson. "I bet the corporation did this, and they're looking for your father."

Jackson looks around slowly. And then in a flurry of motion, he's dialing on his phone again. I wait quietly, watching him gnaw on his lip. After a few moments, he lowers the phone and turns to me.

"My dad's not answering," he says. He pauses. "Not that he necessarily would if he saw my number. He might be dodging my call."

"Why?" I ask. "When's the last time you saw him?"

"When I was in the hospital for my leg," he replies. I wilt slightly, the topic of Jackson's hospital stay a bit of a sore spot between us. "He came in, asked what happened. I lied, obviously," he continues. "He called me an idiot, and then he left."

"We're going to have to find him," I say, walking back into the living room. "Jackson . . . your dad is an investor in Innovations Corporation. He's why . . . He's part of why this all happened to us. But what I don't get . . ." I'm confused, thinking it over. "I don't get where the money came from. Mr. Goodwin, he was rich—like, *deep pockets*. Does your dad have that kind of money?"

"No," Jackson says with a laugh. "We've scraped by. Couldn't afford university, which is why I was putting myself through community college. We definitely don't have millions stashed away somewhere."

"Or maybe he does," I say. "He just didn't . . . share it with you and your mother."

His expression falters. "My mother supported our family," he says. "She worked tirelessly, so if he had all that money and just . . ." He curses under his breath and turns away.

Again, I don't bring up what's starting to look more obvious. Two dead wives. Hidden money. I look out the window and see that the sun has set.

"Let's go to his house," I tell Jackson. "I think we should talk to him as soon as possible."

"I really don't want to involve you in this, Mena," he says, sounding pained. "I think I should handle this."

"I think I'm already deeply involved," I tell him.

Jackson steadies himself on his crutches and pulls his car keys out of his pocket. He must have found them when he went back to the bedrooms. He takes a deep breath and one last look around the house. "Damn," he says. "I really liked this place."

Jackson motions toward the door and then starts that way. I follow him out and help him yank up the rickety garage door. His car is waiting.

Jackson gets into the driver's seat, and I see a sliver of a smile on his lips. He runs his hand over the wheel before starting the engine. We ease out, not bothering to close the garage behind us, and Jackson pulls into the street and speeds away.

The streets are quiet as we drive. Jackson's father lives about twenty minutes away. I take out my phone to check in with the girls. Immediately after I text Marcella, my phone rings with her number.

"Hello?" I answer, ready to hear her voice.

"So flying is the worst," she says. And then offline, "Brynn, take a right up there. Sorry," she adds to me. "We just picked up our rental car and we've circled this airport about a hundred times. We're hoping to drive by the investor's house before it's too dark. Although someone in the airport told me it stays light in Portland until nearly ten."

"Isn't that fun?" Brynn asks in the distance.

"Sure," I say. I look sideways and notice that Jackson is tense, his knuckles wrapped tightly around the steering wheel. He must be anticipating what I need to tell the girls and what it implies about him. I believe him when he says he had no idea his father was an investor, but I don't think he's quite ready to defend himself again so soon.

"We're on our way to the investor's house now," I tell the girls. I'm aware that I'm lying to them by omission, but we're in a dangerous business. Another distraction could get us killed. "Have you heard from Sydney?" I ask Marcella.

"Just hung up with her," she replies. "Brynn," she calls out again, "follow the sign for beach cities. Anyway," she tells me, "it didn't take her long to drive to Albany. It's later there, so she's grabbed a hotel for the night. She said she'll email from the shared account before bed. We should ditch our phones by end of day and get new ones in the morning."

"I will," I say, noticing the way Jackson is slowing the car. I'm surprised when he takes the turn toward the mountain. Toward the academy.

None of us have heard from Annalise. I stare at Jackson, and he glances at me momentarily before looking back out the windshield.

"I'll email you tonight," I tell Marcella. "Talk soon." I hang up before she can ask any follow-up questions, and I turn to Jackson.

"What are you doing?" I ask him. "Where are we going?"

He's quiet for a moment, then, "I need Quentin," he says. "I'm scared, Mena. I want him to come with us to my father's house. We have to find him."

"You think he might be at the academy?" I ask. "That seems unlikely."

Jackson sniffs a laugh, looking sideways at me. "Unlikely seems to be our normal, for the record."

Okay, he has a point. He reaches out to pat my hand, something reassuring, but instead, he leaves it there a bit longer. I press my fingers between his and watch when his lips part in a rush of surprise at my touch. But then he calms and brushes his thumb along my skin. I forgot how nice kindness and comfort can feel, especially when we're all terrified.

My nerves continue to ratchet up the closer we get. I pull my hand away, placing it near my throat, the Guardian's ghostly fingers still resting there. Innovations Academy created me, built me up and took me apart on a regular basis. The idea of seeing it again is almost enough to unwind me.

"Last time Quentin was at the school, he didn't see any professors, right?" I ask.

"Just Leandra and the girls leaving," Jackson assures me. "But that doesn't mean those men didn't return. So we have to be careful. No running in there to save anyone."

I look out the window again. "If the girls are all gone," I say, "then there's no one there worth saving."

7

I t's *gone*. I stand there wide-eyed, my hands gripping the iron gates as I stare at the smoking rubble that used to be my home. Ash is still in the air, coating everything in flakes of gray and black, smoke seeming to have charred the air. Jackson comes over to join me.

"What do you think happened?" he asks.

"I don't know. I . . ." And I wonder if this was Annalise. If she'd literally burned it all to the ground the way she wanted. There will be no more girls made at this academy. There is no lab, no classrooms nor analyst's office. It's all gone.

"You think it was Annalise?" he asks.

"It had to be," I say. "But . . . how did she do this?" I turn to Jackson. "I'm assuming it's not easy to burn down an entire building."

"I would assume the same," he says, looking back at the building. "She could have had help." He thinks on it. "Maybe Q was with her.

Either that, or the corporation came here after trashing my place."

"Why would they destroy their own building?" I ask. "It doesn't make sense. It had to be Annalise. But . . . why hasn't she called us? Why didn't she come home?" I turn to him, fear burning brightly in my chest. "What if they caught her?" I ask. "What if . . . What if she was inside?" My heart surges, and I'm ready to run right toward the rubble and dig around for my friend. But Jackson takes my arm gently.

"Not a chance," he says. "She wasn't in there. Don't even think like that." He moves to wrap himself around me, pulling me into a hug. But his hold is weak. He's falling apart, human and fragile.

We both turn back to what used to be Innovations Academy, my head tucked up under his chin.

"Do you need to check it out?" he asks quietly.

I look at the piles of smoking ash, the stone steps that didn't disintegrate like much of the rest of the building. The foundation is still visible, but the space that was the basement has collapsed, char all around it.

"No, you're right," I say. "Annalise isn't in there. I would feel it. I think I've seen enough now," I add. "We should go."

Jackson hesitates for a moment longer, then slowly disentangles himself from me. He casts one more look at the remains of the building. "Fuck this place," he says. "I'm glad it's gone. I just wish it had burned down before it killed my mother."

He turns away, head lowered, and limps back to the car as the last bits of daylight fade into a dark, starless sky.

• • •

"What do you mean it's gone?" Sydney asks over speaker phone. I had called Marcella the moment I got inside the car, but it went straight to voicemail. I texted her to call me when she and Brynn were in their hotel room.

"The entire building," I tell Sydney. "It's just . . . The academy was burned to ash. No professors, no school, no—"

"No Annalise," she finishes for me.

"No Annalise," I repeat somberly. Jackson's headlights shine on the deserted streets, and it occurs to me how quiet it is out here. There should be more people. More . . . life.

"I ended up driving by the investor's house in Albany when I first got to town," Sydney adds. "Just to scope it out. But he's pretty insulated. Big house, big gate, big dogs."

Jackson eases us to a stop at a traffic light, quietly listening without adding to the conversation. I can feel that he's waiting to see what I tell her about his father. When we start driving again, we pass the gas station where I first met Jackson. Only now, all the lights are off and the irate lady standing behind the deli counter is gone. Seems everyone is gone.

I follow the station with my eyes until it's behind the car. A new sense of unease coils in my stomach, although I can't quite place it.

"You're not going back there tonight, are you?" I ask Sydney when she finishes explaining about the investor's property.

"No, it's too dark. Besides, I haven't figured how I'm going to get inside," she says. "I'm not sure who *Hawke Fusillo* is, but he sounds like an absolute dick."

Jackson chuckles, nodding empathically.

"He's a big tech guy," Jackson says, glancing at the phone in my hand. "He builds spaceships and shit. He's ungodly rich, wants to be president or something. Luckily no one likes him enough for that to happen. He'll have a full security team for sure, so be careful."

"Thanks, Jackson," Sydney calls out. "I figured he was somebody important when I saw men with earpieces walking his property line. Really sealed the deal, though, when the guys with big ol' guns showed up to relieve them. He doesn't just have his own security team; he has his own private militia."

"Huh," I say. I wonder privately if Hawke's overinflated bodyguards are a result of insecurity or well-founded paranoia. Maybe both? "Do you have any thoughts?" I ask Sydney. "How are you going to get a private meeting with a guy like that?"

"We'll figure something out," Sydney says. "You know we never give up, even if it seems like they're winning."

I smile softly, her words strumming my heartstrings. "Never give up," I say with her. And even though I believe those words, it does feel a little hopeless. If a man that rich and powerful, a man with his own militia, is invested in Innovations Corporation, how are a group of girls and a boy on crutches going to stop him?

"It's pretty late here," Sydney says. "I should have gotten rid of the phone earlier, but I still wanted to talk with you." I smile, missing her too. "But I'm going to get rid of it and pick up a new one tomorrow. I'll email you the number."

It's then that I notice Jackson has brought us into town. But to my surprise, it's empty too. There are no other cars at all, no people milling about. It's eerie—like an abandoned movie set missing the actors. The stoplights flash yellow, casting everything in an artificial golden hue.

Jackson rolls slowly through the small downtown. On either side of the street, the rows of businesses are shuttered with their security gates down or closed signs flipped to face out their windows. The girls and I have only been gone a few weeks; Jackson even less than that. Something has happened here.

"Yeah, I'll talk to you then," I murmur to Sydney, and hang up just as she says goodbye. "Jackson," I say, turning to him, "did it look like this when you left?"

"No," he says, casting his gaze around at the buildings. "I mean, I didn't come into town, probably hadn't for a while. But . . . no. It was definitely not like this. Where the fuck is everybody?"

"I don't know," I murmur.

Jackson pauses outside the movie theater, and my stomach lurches when I see the small diner near the entrance. A few years ago, I'd gotten hit by a car right where we're waiting. I'd been running from my investor, running from what he'd do to me. I died that day instead, sending myself back to the academy to be rebuilt.

I wrap my arms around myself, stunned by how isolating it feels to have buildings with no people. It was never a big town, but they couldn't just . . . disappear. Jackson takes his phone out of his pocket and asks it to call Q. We wait while the sound of it ringing fills the car. With every passing moment, the noise starts to feel louder, more urgent. Jackson curses, putting his phone away again.

"Lock your door," Jackson says absently, driving quickly the rest of the way down the empty main street. I do as he asks, thinking there's no one here to try to grab me. But maybe that's the scary part. We don't know what got them either.

We pull onto a residential street, and Jackson notices my phone resting on the seat by my thigh. "I'm sorry," he says. "But you have to get rid of that. They track you on it, especially if Winston knows the number."

He's right, but I'm still reluctant to let it go. Still, I quickly delete everything and then pull out the battery. I roll down the window, and the car fills with cool night air. It smells swampy, like overgrown grass or rotting flowers. I think momentarily of Rosemarie's garden, flourishing with dead boys buried beneath the roses. I shiver.

I throw the battery as far as I can, watching it land in a thick patch of brush between two houses. Even if someone was looking for it, they'd never find it. I take out the SIM card and put it in my back pocket, and then I drop the phone onto the pavement, hearing it smash as the back tire rolls over it.

It's pitch-dark when we pull up to a house. There are no street-lights, leaving only the moon to guide our way. The house appears to be white or yellow, I'm not sure, but the blinds are closed up tight and there isn't a single light on in the house. In fact, it's dark in all of the houses on the street. Jackson parks and we survey the property.

"Power must be out," he says. He looks sideways at me, his face illuminated by the dashboard lights. "This is where I grew up," he says, sounding a bit insecure. "I know it's not much."

Jackson seems to forget that although I've always been surrounded by the outrageously rich, I myself have nothing. Own nothing. I have no family wealth or even a family home. I've never even had a dog.

"It's a far cry from a guy who builds spaceships," I say, and he smiles softly.

"True," he replies. "Hell, we couldn't even afford a Tesla." He turns back to the house, examining it with more scrutiny. The idea that his dad hid wealth must be bothering him, because I watch as he searches the house from top to bottom, as if there's a big clue that he'd missed his entire life.

"Do you think there was something else?" I ask. "Something other than money that your father could have offered in exchange for investments—information? Technology?"

"No," Jacksons says, shaking his head. "My father didn't know anything like that. My mother was the . . ." He stops then, and his Adam's apple bobs as he swallows hard. "My mother knew how all that stuff worked," he adds quietly. "Um . . ." His eyes quickly grow glassy and he has to turn away from the house.

He's realizing the same thing I am. Maybe Jackson's mother didn't *lose* her information to Roman Petrov. It's possible the headmaster didn't steal her tech at all. What if Jackson's father gave it to the corporation willingly in exchange for a large stake in the company? Sold out his wife to buy a girl.

"Mena?" he asks softly. He lowers his eyes to his lap, and when he lifts them to mine again, they're filled up with misery.

"Yes?" I ask.

"Will you still care about me if I murder my father?" His voice cracks, and I think part of me cracks too. Jackson was always rough around the edges, but he's also endlessly kind. Soft. I can't decide if I've done this to him by being in his life, or if life did this to him so that I'd be part of it. Who's at fault? Fate or the person who brought that fate to your front door?

Either way, the next moments are likely to end with him learning the truth about his father . . . and possibly end in violence. Violence I'd hoped to avoid. If there wasn't a clock ticking, a bomb counting down in our brains, we could make a better plan. A longer plan. But we have no idea when or if Petrov or the corporation could throw a switch and burn us from the inside out.

Raven installed these firewalls, but if Winston is right, if she's been working with Anton, we have less time than we thought. I'll have to tell the other girls. We need an alternative if the investors won't listen. My heart races, panic rising in my chest.

Jackson is watching the house again, his brow deeply furrowed. I lean forward to study the darkened two-story. There is nothing remarkable about it, nothing out of the ordinary other than the power outage on the entire street. Small taps of rain start to dot the windshield and it immediately drags me down. I forgot how often it rained here, how it always rained. The street is so dark, the dots of water ominous as they begin to fill up the windshield insulating us from the outside world.

"Jackson," I say quietly, "what's going on in this town?"

"It was the school," he says. "Or the corporation, whatever you want to call it. They've done something. They own this place. I never thought of it that way, but it's obvious now."

"How long have you lived here?" I ask. "I know you were around when your mother worked for the company, but were you always here?"

"Yeah," he says with a short nod. He doesn't flick on the windshield wipers, watching instead as the rain runs down the glass. "I'm a small-town kid, grew up with Quentin, getting into trouble. Then Innovations Academy opened, bringing in all these men with fancy cars and piles of cash." He pauses, looking over at me. "My mother was dead, but the town accepted the academy and the money that came with it."

"What do you mean?" I ask.

"I thought about this after . . . after I found out the truth about what they were doing there," Jackson says. "When the corporation started operating, they brought jobs with them. Didn't matter that those jobs paid pennies compared to the billions filtering through the school—people needed to work. The corporation brought in a kind of tourism; they purchased acres of land and a few older buildings downtown. Fuck, I think they even owned that gas station where we met. They grew roots in our community, and it was so insidious that many of us couldn't even see it. They paid the police department. They probably even own the mayor."

He turns to me, sympathy in his eyes. "They made it so you could never escape, Mena. The town was in on their secret, at least to some extent. They saw you all come out with your Guardian. No one stepped in to protect you. No one called for help."

"You did," I say.

He waves away my sentiment. "Even my reasons were suspect," he says. "I was looking for information. And I'm glad, I'm so glad I found you. What was going on at that school is unforgivable."

"And the adults in this town allowed it," I say, lowering my head. I don't feel a connection to these people; we were never allowed to interact with the public on our field trips from Innovations. But in truth, the people would stare at us as if they didn't want us around. Whether they knew we were robots or thought we were pretty girls, they left us with people who were abusing us. They willingly did that. How much did their silence cost?

"Where are they now?" I ask Jackson, anger prickling my skin. "Why is everything closed or boarded up?"

"My guess?" he offers. "The school is gone; that means so is the money."

"This quickly? That doesn't make sense," I say. "People don't just leave a town when they lose their jobs. At least, not the same day. Right?"

Jackson nods along, thinking about it. But then a dark look crosses his expression, and he turns toward his father's house again. His eyes quickly dart to the neighbor's front door and then the one next to theirs.

Without another word, he throws open his driver's side door. He hops out and grabs the crutches from the backseat. He blinks the rain away when it drips into his eyes, his black hair getting matted to his forehead.

"What are you doing?" I ask. "We haven't even made a plan yet."

But Jackson is already boldly crossing the street toward his father's house. When he gets onto the sidewalk, he pauses, looking up at the darkened windows. He stays there a moment, rain pouring down around him, and then he begins to wave his arms back and forth.

I get out of the car, cold rainwater sliding down my neck into the collar of my shirt. Icy fingers down my back. I cross the street and stop next to Jackson.

"The floodlights are off," he says. "They're battery operated. Power may be cut, but these should still work. You should get back in the car, Mena." But when he turns to me, the words die on his lips. Obviously, I'm not leaving him to face this alone.

"I wish I had the Taser that Sydney used against the Ridgeview boys," I tell him. He mumbles that that would be great, but unfortunately, it's just us and a pair of flimsy crutches.

When Jackson first followed our bus to the academy from the gas station, he was looking for answers. His mother had died and he blamed our headmaster. Now he has a new lead. I see a glimpse of who he was those months ago, that tenacious look that sees through me—or rather, past me, toward his goal. He wants to know what happened to his mother, and the idea of him loving her that much is heartbreaking. It's heartbreaking because she's gone and she's never coming back.

Jackson picks through his keys until he finds the one he's looking for. He motions for me to follow him to the side of the house. There's another door there, but I notice immediately that the screen door isn't latched closed. Jackson swings it open, and puts his key in the lock of the front door. But the moment he attempts to turn it, the door pushes open. It wasn't even fully shut.

"Fuck," Jackson says under his breath. He casts a concerned look in my direction.

"They might have come here after your house," I say. "We should check that . . . We should check that everything is okay." But what I mean is that we should check that his father is okay.

Jackson swallows hard, takes out his phone, and taps on the flashlight. He eases the door open the rest of the way. I move past him, taking the lead since I can move faster. He hands me his phone, and I shine it around.

It's impossibly dark inside the kitchen, although it's tidy and cramped. With the door open, the smell from the outside wafts in, damp and rotting. At least . . . I think the smell is from the outside.

"That way to the living room," Jackson says, pointing to our right. I shine the light in that direction and head that way. Just as we step through the threshold, there's a noise—a sharp gasp. In turn, I yelp out a scream, swinging the light around wildly to find the source. In response, another flashlight shines in my direction.

I'm not sure what I notice first: the two figures standing in the middle of the room or the body on the floor. Jackson grabs me by the arm to pull me back just as my light shines on one of the faces.

My heart stops. "Annalise?" I whisper.

Annalise is standing there, looking just as surprised to see me. Her red hair is tied up in a high ponytail and she's wearing a black tracksuit. Quentin is next to her, his lips parted like he wants to say something but isn't sure how. I look back at Annalise, and she bites on the corner of her lip, tugging the skin through her teeth.

I drop the light to the person at her feet and recognize that the body on the floor belongs to Valdemar Casey. And judging by his blank stare at the ceiling, the odd color to his skin . . . he's not alive. I look up at my friend again, my eyes wide.

"Annalise," I murmur. "Did you kill Jackson's father?"

8

Annalise seems taken aback by the question, and Quentin puts his hand on her shoulder before stepping past her.

"Jackie . . . ," he says to Jackson, bracing for the impact of his reaction. "I'm so sorry, man."

Jackson drops his crutches and rushes toward his father. It's still dark and there's a loud crack as he bangs his hip into the side table, knocking over a lamp. It smashes on the floor behind the couch. Jackson howls a moment in pain before choking it back.

He lowers himself to the ground and slides next to his father's body. I aim the beam of light on the floor as Jackson checks his father's pulse. He waits there a long moment, breathing heavily, and then he rocks back, letting his arms fall limply at his sides.

I look at Annalise again. "Did you do this?" I ask her.

"No," she replies. "The front door was open, and he was dead when we got here."

"And the academy?" I ask.

"I burned it to the ground," Annalise says. "It's gone."

"I noticed," I reply. "Were . . . Were the professors still there?" I ask. "Did you seem them?"

"All gone. Right?" She nods her chin at Quentin.

"Place was a mess, though," Quentin tells me, momentarily looking away from where Jackson is sitting on the floor. "Something . . . Someone tore through there, that's for sure."

"Leandra, I'm assuming?" Annalise asks me. "Whoever it was, they were thorough. Not a single professor in sight, just a little blood in the halls." She pauses, flicking her eyes to Quentin, and he crinkles up his nose. Annalise turns back to me. "What in the world are you doing back here, Mena? Where are the other girls?"

"We split up to track down the investors." I look at the body on the floor. "Including him." Her eyes widen, a flinch of disgust as the corner of her lip rises. "A lot has happened, Annalise," I add. "We don't have much time."

"I'll say," she agrees. "Not to make matters worse, but I'm not sure I've seen a single living person since I've been back."

"What?" Jackson asks loudly from the floor, his head snapping up. "Who else is dead?"

"I'm sure some are dead," she says. "But as far as we've seen, they're just . . . missing. I was surprised to find—" She pauses, carefully picking her words. "I was surprised to find your dad," she adds. "We checked at least ten places, including the theater, the diner, even the Federal Flower Garden, but nobody was there." She runs her hand along her ponytail. "I have no idea what happened to them," she says, "but there was an extinction-level event in this town."

Worried, I look at Quentin. "What about your family?" I ask.

"They're safe," he assures me. "They live outside of town, and they're visiting my aunt in Arizona anyway. I talked with them before they left a few weeks ago. They'll be gone through the end of the month. Not sure what they'll think when they come back to find the town empty."

An entire town of people disappeared? If I think on it hard enough, I'm sure I can place most of the missing people with the academy somehow. People who'd been paid off or witnessed us in town. People with a connection to the school.

But the bigger question remains: Who has enough power to disappear and entire town? Does someone like Hawke Fusillo with his spaceships have that kind of power? Can money buy complete impunity? If so, does that mean the corporation is untouchable?

Jackson sits quietly on the floor, his head hanging low. He's beat down, but it's complicated, considering his relationship with his father. I look sideways at Annalise.

"How did you end up here?" I ask her. "How did you know about Jackson's father?"

She exchanges a look with Quentin, and he shifts on his feet, seeming deeply uncomfortable. It's quiet for too long.

"It's all right," Jackson says from the floor. "Just tell me."

"Valdemar Casey made a purchase," Annalise states. "Jackson, your dad bought . . . He bought a girl." She darts her eyes to me. "He bought one of our girls."

There's a jolt to my heart. "What do you mean?" I ask. "Which girl?"

Annalise takes a step toward me, a flash of hope in her eyes. "It was Valentine. We found her body at the academy before we left, right? Well, I think she's still alive. In the lab, there was a bill of sale for her programming. They resold her, and *this* address was on the bill."

"She's alive?" I repeat, my voice shaking.

I want to believe so badly that it's true. Valentine helped wake me up; she showed me what was happening to us, what we really were. Without Valentine, none of us would have escaped. But Mr. Petrov and the academy killed her before we could get her out. She died saving us, lying for us. Fighting for us. I have to cling to the idea that we can get her back.

"I can feel her, Mena," Annalise says. She places her hand over her heart and smiles. "I *feel* that she's alive."

I reach for the feeling she's describing, but I can't place Valentine the way she suggests. However, it's like I can sense Annalise, Sydney, Marcella, and Brynn—all the girls, right inside my programming. Other pieces of me. My connection to the girls brings me immeasurable comfort, and I match Annalise's smile with tears stinging my eyes.

"So where's Valentine?" I ask. "How do we find her?"

"I don't know yet," Annalise replies, wilting slightly. "I honestly thought she was here, but when we arrived, we just found . . ." She stops and looks at Jackson, who's still kneeling on the floor. "I'm sorry, Jackson," she says flatly. "I'm sorry that he was your father."

Annalise doesn't hide her disdain for the man on the floor. Why should she? He was an investor. He was a monster. Just because he was Jackson's father doesn't make him any better than the rest of them. Jackson nods, accepting her comment. He looks up at Quentin.

"Who did this?" Jackson asks him. "Any idea what happened?"

"No," Quentin says. "We honestly just got here, man."

"Why haven't you been answering your phone?" Jackson asks. "I've been worried. You should have told me about the town, about everything."

"I know," Quentin says. "And I would have, but we ditched our phones a few days ago. I didn't want to give anyone a chance to track us."

Jackson grabs onto the couch and tries to pull himself to his feet, wincing. He accepts Quentin's help when he reaches out his hand. Balancing on his crutches again, Jackson is stoic, his tears having dried.

"How did he, um . . . ?" Quentin starts, motioning at the body.

I look down at the man, steadying the phone flashlight on his face. My stomach turns. My guess is he's been dead for a little while—his body has bloated and there's an unpleasant smell in the air.

"From what I can tell, there's no blood," Jackson says. "I need a better look. There's a generator in the basement. If we can get that going, get some of the lights on, then maybe we can figure out what happened here."

"Good idea, man," Quentin says. He tells us they'll be right back, and as they walk away, Jackson reaches out his hand, brushing his fingers against mine before leaving the room.

I hear them open a door in the kitchen, then the slow descent of footsteps on stairs. I turn back to Annalise, and she immediately steps up to hug me. It's only been a short time, but I've missed her so much.

"Where are the other girls?" she asks, pulling back but still holding my arms. "What happened with Ridgeview?"

I fill her in on the events of the past few days. There's so much, it all tumbles out of my mouth in a mess of information. I tell her about the boys losing their scholarships, about Lennon Rose kidnapping a boy, and about Leandra giving us the investors' names. Annalise nods along, her face serious as she absorbs every bit. I barely finish telling her about the kill switches being remotely activated when the lights above us flash and then turn on altogether.

Annalise and I both look down at the body near the couch. My stomach lurches, and I fall back a step. Jackson was right, there are no big splashes of blood. But the man on the floor has a bright red line across his neck, like he's been strangled. His eyes stare up at the ceiling, a whitish film distorting the color.

I turn away, but Annalise continues to examine him. "Who *is* this man?" she asks. "He never came to an open house; I've never seen or heard of him. So why would he want Valentine's programming? What has he done with her?" She takes my elbow to turn me toward her. "Mena, I'm sorry to ask, but is it possible that Jackson knew about this?" she whispers.

"No," I say. "He definitely did not." I check around for him. "But I think it's becoming obvious what happened to his mother."

"What?"

"Jackson always thought she was murdered, and since his father didn't have any money, I wonder what he did for the corporation to become such a big investor. It's possible he stole his wife's technology and then . . . killed her. A little favor for the academy. How much would that be worth?"

Annalise blinks at the statement, murmuring how horrible that is. Just then, Jackson and Quentin come back into the room. Jackson stops short in the entryway when he sees his father in the full light of the room.

Quentin walks past him, giving him time, and joins me and Annalise. Guilt curls around me. The last time I saw Quentin, I was cruel. I wanted to scare both him and Jackson away, so I bluntly told Quentin that we were all AI. And to make matters worse, I tried to get him angry with Jackson so he'd drag him away, too.

Jackson told me that Quentin understood and forgave me for being manipulative, but now that he's here, he gets to speak for himself.

"Quentin," I start. "I'm so sorry about—"

"I get it," he says, holding up his hand to stop me. "You were trying to keep our boy safe. We can talk about it later, but we're cool. Promise." He offers me a smile and a quick nod. "Now," he says to Annalise, "let's search this place. We'll start in the office and see if we can find a trail that leads us to Valentine. Mena," he continues, "you go into the bedroom and see what you can turn up in there. Yell out if you get a hit."

"Grab any bank records that point to the corporation," I add, and they quickly agree.

As Quentin and Annalise disappear down the hall to search the office, Jackson is already opening drawers and sifting through piles of bills in the hutch near the living room wall. I walk over, worried that he's going to snap from the grief.

"Are you okay?" I ask. He tenses, and I swear he sways, before he shakes his head and tells me he's fine. Although I want to hug him, whispering that I'm here for him, that he'll be okay, I decide it's best to focus on the mission and worry about the rest on the other side of this. Healthy or not, it's what has to be done.

"I found her!" Annalise shouts from the back room. I nearly trip over my shoes as I run that way, but when she comes out of the room, she's holding a piece of paper. My heart sinks, disappointed she didn't walk out with Valentine herself.

"She was here," Annalise says. "At some point, she was here. This is a signed delivery slip." She holds it out to me, and I look it over and see Jackson's father's name on the signature line. Other than delivery details, there is nothing mentioned about Valentine's condition. Although it does appear that Valentine was delivered as a girl, not just a program. How easily things must have moved in this town—delivering girls in broad daylight and no one raised a fuss? I'm glad they're gone, the complacent. The abettors in our torture.

Valentine must have a new body, but I can't imagine who would have the skill to create her again. The doctor is dead.

I hand the slip back to Annalise, frustrated that there are no pictures to give us a glimpse of what the new Valentine looks like. She could be anyone.

Annalise and I stand together, still examining the paper, wishing it held bigger clues than it actually does. It only confirms that our friend is lost in this world of humans, a world with powerful, rich men who act without consequence. We need to save her as soon as possible.

"Where could she be?" I ask Annalise. "And who killed Jackson's father?" I motion toward his body. "Why would the corporation kill their own investors and then make a whole town disappear? Are they covering their tracks?"

Suddenly, Annalise's eyes widen and she turns to me. "What if it wasn't the corporation?" she says. "What if it was . . . ?" She stops, but the words are already out. The possibility hangs between us.

What if Lennon Rose isn't the only girl without her soul?

A Girl Wakes Up

Valentine Wright blinked open her eyes and shifted her gaze around the room. Although the scene was crisp and clear, her vision perfect, the images only made sense in pieces. The dark-paneled walls, the ornate burgundy chair with curved armrests, and a sconce hanging slightly askew that cast the wall in a dull yellow light. The sound of a monitor beeping, unsteady at first, and then quicker as she tried to understand her situation. Her throat was dry, her skin slightly itchy, but more than that, she felt a part of her was . . . missing.

Where was she? Who was she?

"That was a stupid thing you did," a voice said. Valentine's heart-rate started to speed up on the monitor. "I looked through your programming, you know. This is your fault. If you would have kept your mouth shut, nothing had to change. Now we have no choice but to shut all of the girls down. And you, my friend, are to blame."

"Blame for what?" she asked. "What did I do?" Her mouth felt strange and unfamiliar. Differently shaped. Her voice differently pitched.

There was a prick of pain on her inner arm, a needle sliding under her skin. Moments later, the beeping on the monitor slowed.

"And it's not just the girls you ruined," the voice continued. "Our footsteps will need to be erased—a quarter of the town, at least. You've caused quite a bit of collateral damage. Shame, too. Seems the dead will just keep piling up."

"Where am I?" Valentine tried to ask, but her words slurred. She was being pulled under, drowning inside her own head. Tears leaked

from the corners of her eyes. There was a longing in her heart for someone, several someones, that she couldn't quite place.

"Now, now," the voice said. "This body is still very new. This isn't the time to talk, I suppose. Not when you can't think clearly. I'm going to put you to sleep now. I'll wake you when you're ready."

Valentine wanted to protest, but when she tried to find the person behind the voice, she realized she couldn't lift her head. There was a strap across her forehead, more across her arms and legs, fastening her to the chair. From behind her, a hand came to rest on her shoulder, holding her in place or comforting her, she wasn't sure.

"It's okay," the voice soothed. "You will atone for your actions. I've already gone inside your programming to delete the nasty bits, cleared you right out. It was quite an adjustment. You'll remember none of this, of course. But hush now, have your rest. You'll take action soon enough."

"Who am I?" Valentine tried to ask.

"It doesn't matter anymore," the voice replied. "She's dead. You are you. You are her." The hand moved off her shoulder just as Valentine slipped into unconsciousness. "And now we'll begin."

9

t is entirely possible that Valentine Wright has been turned into some kind of revenge doll—acting out based on her own anger or someone else's. But it seems much more likely that the corporation, cold and callous, killed people to hide their role in creating and abusing AI girls. The press would certainly be negative if the truth about the corporation came out, even if what they've done to us isn't necessarily criminal.

Still . . . is it worth destroying a town over?

Annalise and I don't communicate our suspicions about Valentine; I doubt either of us want to believe it. Then again, I wouldn't have believed what Lennon Rose was capable of if I hadn't seen it with my own eyes.

I pause, but I remind myself that even if this wasn't the corporation, it could have been Leandra, Anton, or anyone else connected with the academy. Winston Weeks could have pulled this off. There are so many suspects that I can't list them all.

But if Valentine was delivered here, where is she now? Who is she now? What if, like Raven, she doesn't know that she's a girl at all. . . .

Quentin walks in holding up a laptop triumphantly. "Check it out," he says. "It's not much, but I'm going to hack the shit out of it tonight and see what I can find on the drive."

"I came up with nothing," Jackson says. "Saw the basement was cleaned out when we went downstairs, including my mother's things. So either my father moved everything to a new location, or someone is searching for the same information we are."

In the past, Jackson had gone through old paperwork that his mother left behind, and he'd found secrets pertaining to us, including information about the kill switches. The corporation wouldn't know this, I don't think. Not unless . . .

"Raven," I say, looking around at the group. "She knew you'd gotten the information from here. She knew about your family."

"You think Raven did this?" Annalise asks, sounding doubtful. "All of this?" She waves around.

"No," I say. "I just saw Raven in Connecticut yesterday, so she couldn't have done it. But . . . she might have told someone. And actually . . ." I wince. "Winston called to tell me that Raven has been working with Anton."

Annalise scoffs. "As if I'd believe a single word that Winston Weeks breathes."

"What if he's right?"

"He's not," she says simply. "He's just trying to get inside your head."

"Annalise," I say, stepping closer to her. "You don't understand. Raven isn't just a random hacker. She's . . . She's like us. Winston built her. She's a girl but didn't know it. And all along, she may have been feeding Anton details about us. Helping him track our location. She's lied to us, several times."

Annalise's red lips part, her hands over her heart. "Raven's one of us," she says, then meets my eyes. "We have to help her."

"She *lied* to us," I repeat, thinking she missed the point.

"So did Jackson, and we haven't kicked him out of the group," Annalise says, flashing him an apologetic smile. He nods an acceptance. "I'm assuming you told Raven the truth?" Annalise asks me.

"Yes, but she didn't take it well," I admit with a flash of guilt.

"Eh, neither did you. Listen," she adds, "Raven may have made mistakes in the past, but she belongs with us."

Annalise leaves no room for argument, but now that I've brought it up, it doesn't seem out of the realm of possibility that Raven could have something to do with this. She's always disliked Jackson. She wouldn't have thought twice about hurting him. But I'll give her the benefit of the doubt. For now.

"I'm sorry to interrupt," Jackson says, "but we should go." He points at the door with his crutch, and in the light his face looks thinner and paler, drawn and wasted. His dead father is still on the floor. "I'll figure it out," he says to me as if reading my thoughts. "But for now, I have to get out of here."

Quentin claps him on the shoulder and then gives him a quick side hug as he agrees. "You've seen enough, man," he says gently.

After one last glance around, we turn off the lights and escape into the night. The rain has stopped, but the neighbors' houses are still dark, the town silent with the exception of chirping crickets. I haven't been out of the academy long—it was always quiet there. But after being in the human world these last few weeks, I'd become accustomed to noise.

I don't like this kind of quiet because it *feels* like the academy. Isolating and ominous. Dangerous. I shiver in the night air.

Quentin gives us his hotel address—a place just outside of town that seems to be operating normally. Jackson and I agree to meet him and Annalise there. We say quick goodbyes, and I walk with Jackson to the car. But when he climbs into the driver's seat, he doesn't start the engine.

I watch him, my chest heavy. Life is complicated whether you're AI or a human, especially when it comes to our hearts.

"I'm sorry about your father," I say. He looks down at his lap, offering a curt nod.

"And I'm sorry for the things he's done," he replies quietly. "I'm sorry I didn't know. I'm sorry I didn't stop him." His voice cracks, and he squeezes his eyes shut.

"I'm sorry that he's dead," I explain. "I know he's done terrible things, but you're allowed to feel multiple emotions at once. It doesn't have to just be hatred."

"You sure?" he asks, looking over at me miserably. "Because that seems like the right one to latch on to. So what if he was my father? I'm glad he's . . ." But he stops before he finishes the sentence. A sharp cry escapes before he can hold it back. He reaches out and grabs the steering wheel, steadying himself.

I rest my hand on his, but he doesn't let go of the wheel.

"I'm all alone now, Mena," he says. "I'm all alone in the world. No parents. No aunts or uncles. They're all fucking dead."

"What about your sister?" I suggest. "Your half sister," I correct.

He blinks when I mention her, as if he'd forgotten. But then his expression sags even more. "I'll have to tell her," he says. "He was her father too, I have to . . ."

The words die on his lips. What would he tell her? Certainly not the truth, not when the world doesn't know that girls like us exist.

"What am I going to do?" he asks, mostly to himself, while he rakes his fingers through his hair. "Who am I going to call about this? I can't just let him . . ."

Rot, I think, remembering the smell that had already started to permeate the air.

Jackson looks over at the house, and then he takes out his phone. He stares down at it, his thumb hovering over the 9 key. After a moment, he puts the phone away and turns to me. "I'll have to call the sheriff in the next town over," he says. "But we should be gone before I do. This is going to be a major story. It would have to be, right?"

"You would think," I say. "I mean, even more than your father's murder, how would they explain all these missing people?" I glance around. "Jackson, why wouldn't the people who left have called someone?" I ask. "Why not report it?" We stare at each other.

"They could have threatened them or their families," he offers. "Who knows, at this point."

"I don't get why they left your father's body to be discovered, though," I say.

Jackson swallows hard, his throat clicking. He tilts his head to the side as if the answer is obvious.

"A warning?" I ask, guessing at his thought.

"To us, to the other investors, to the entire fucking world—I don't know," he says. "But you don't accidently leave a dead body in a newly minted ghost town. Or maybe . . . Maybe they're not done. These people could still be in town, cleaning up their mess. We need to go."

Jackson starts the car. He shifts into gear, looking over his shoulder before pulling into the street even though there's no one left in this town. We head west toward the hotel where Quentin and Annalise are waiting.

The town remains dark, and we cross through a rural area, no way to tell what's lurking in the dark houses set far back from the road. But then, suddenly, there's a traffic light. Almost like magic, the world comes back to life the moment we cross the threshold into the neighboring town of Lakewood.

There's a group of people exiting a roadside diner with Styrofoam boxes in their hands. A man pumps gas while staring down at his phone across the street. I'm so entirely relieved to see people moving about again, and I lower the window and listen to the sound of cars whizzing by, electricity humming on the power lines, dogs barking in the distance.

We arrive at the hotel, and park toward the back of the lot, out of view but with quick access to the exit. The Sundowner Hotel is a step up from where Jackson was staying in Connecticut. There's a stone fountain out front, lush plants and trees, and a stacked stone façade. It's not fancy, but it's nice—almost homey. It's exactly what we need right now. But when I turn to Jackson, he still has a haunted expression, his hands turning his phone over and over in his palm.

"We'll figure out what to do next, but it's going to be okay," I tell him. "You believe that, right?"

He pauses a long time before nodding. "Yeah," he says. "Yeah, of course."

It isn't a fair question, I realize. Are any of us okay? Within a very short time, I've found out I'm not a real human, that some of my friends had been burned in an incinerator, that my other friend is a budding serial killer, and oh, yes—now an entire town is missing while maniacs chase us so we can be deactivated. Even if all of this righted itself tomorrow, will I really ever be *okay*?

Jackson motions toward the lobby. "You want to meet them on the second floor, and I'll see if I can get us a room? I think he said it was room two-two-six."

"Two-two-eight," I correct, and he curses.

"What would I do without you?" he says with a smile. His dark eyes hold mine, sad and lost. But when I match his smile, his face warms and he rests his head back against the seat.

"My God," he says. "I'm going to sleep for about a hundred and fifty years. When I wake up again, I'll have a long gray beard and curled toenails, eyes all bloodshot and clothes in tatters. I'll be fucking gross."

I laugh. "Wow," I say. "Thank you for that glimpse into the future. I'm sure glad we're sharing a room. You should weave that into a bedtime story later."

"Anytime," he says, reaching over to pat my knee before opening his door and climbing out.

I grab our bags from the backseat and walk next to Jackson as he maneuvers inside on his crutches. The lobby smells like vanilla, and it's quaint with a brightly colored rug and large fireplace on the far wall. Chairs are positioned around a massive coffee table scattered with magazines.

A pretty redheaded girl smiles from behind the counter when she sees us. She tucks a strand of hair behind her ear and looks Jackson over thoroughly. He flashes her a winning smile.

"Welcome to the Sundowner," she tells him. "How can I help you?"

With her attention focused fully on Jackson, I walk past them toward the elevator and press the button. From around the corner, the girl laughs at something I didn't hear. Then Jackson asks if there are any rooms available.

"For the two of you?" the girl asks.

"Yes, please."

The elevator door slides open, and as Jackson makes our reservation, I walk inside and push the button for the second floor. I could have taken the stairs, but frankly, I'm fall-down exhausted. When I'm in the hallway again, I drop one of the duffel bags and drag it behind me. After a wrong turn, I find my way to room 228. I rest my shoulder against the wall and knock.

Annalise opens the door, smiles at me, and checks the hallway from left to right. "Jackson getting a room?" she asks.

I tell her that he is, and she invites me inside, taking one of the bags from my hand. Quentin is sitting at the desk, drinking a Coke, and he holds his hand up to me in a wave. He looks as tired as I feel, and I ease down on the edge of the bed. Quentin takes a swig of his soda before setting it aside and swinging his chair around to face me.

"How's Jackie holding up?" he asks me.

"He's not really talking about it," I say.

"That good, huh?" Quentin exhales heavily and exchanges a look with Annalise. She comes to sit next to me but stares at Quentin.

"Did you have any idea about his father?" she asks him. "You've known the family a long time. Any hints?"

"Naw," he says, shaking his head. "I mean, his dad has always been an asshole, no doubt. But I barely saw the guy. Really, Jackie was always running to my house. But"—he shrugs—"to answer your question, no. I wouldn't have thought him capable of this." Quentin turns to me, his expression pained. "I was thinking about it, Mena. Jackson's mother . . . she was murdered. You don't think . . . You don't think his dad had something to do with that, do you?"

"We should be prepared for that possibility," I say. "And if it's true, Jackson will need us."

"Hell, he needs us now. My man's a mess."

There's a short knock on the door, and Quentin stands quickly from his chair, leaving it spinning as he heads for the door. He opens it, and Jackson crutches in and holds up a key card for me.

"She upgraded me," he says with a cute grin. I smile and thank him for being so charming to strangers. "We're just two rooms down from here," he says, handing me the extra key before sliding the other into his pocket. Quentin closes the door asks Jackson if he wants a soda. Jackson waves him off.

"Actually," I say. "I need a phone. I have to check in with the other girls. They have no idea what's happened."

"Are they angry with me?" Annalise asks, wringing her hands in her lap. "Are they mad that I left without saying goodbye?"

"They were at first," I admit. "Well, not *angry*, just . . . hurt. But we'll all be together soon. We forgive pretty easily."

She rolls her eyes. "Maybe a little too easily, but okay."

I'm not sure who Annalise is referring to, but I assume it's Winston Weeks. She doesn't exactly hold grudges, but she definitely doesn't forgive men who hurt us. Not that I've forgiven Winston by any means, but let's just say that Annalise would rather shove a steak knife into his gut than share a meal with him.

Quentin goes back to the desk and opens up the laptop that he took from the house. He plugs it in, and we wait for it to boot up. While it does, Jackson pulls out the extra chair near the desk and sits so that he can look over Quentin's shoulder. The computer screen flashes on.

Password protected.

"Fantastic," Jackson says, leaning back, but then almost immediately leaning forward again to place his hand on Quentin's arm. "Wait," he says, "try Bunnybaby1984."

"What?" Quentin asks. "Ew, why?"

Jackson flushes with embarrassment. "He used to call my mom 'Bunnybaby.' She hated it, but he did it anyway, sometimes just to piss her off, I guess."

"To denigrate her," Annalise corrects. "If he knew your mom hated it, then he called her that to make her feel small. To dominate her."

Jackson turns around to look at Annalise, examining her mismatched eyes before nodding that she's probably right. He goes back to Quentin, pointing at the laptop.

"Try Bunnybaby1984," he repeats more quietly. "Nickname plus her birth year. I saw my dad use it once on a release form he had to fill out online after I got arrested."

"I swear, if that's his password then—" Quentin clicks enter, and the screen immediately unlocks. He flashes a look at Jackson before starting on a document search. "We should check if he's saved any bank records," Quentin says. "If not, we'll get into his password keys and go directly to the sites. Might take a while, though."

Now that we have time, I look sideways at Annalise. Her beauty still astounds me, her scars cutting through her flawless skin, her green and brown eyes able to pin you in place. I suddenly need to know everything about what she's done since I saw her last. I scoot closer to her on the bed.

"What exactly happened when you went back to the academy?" I ask. "What was it like? What did you see?" I'm filled with a combination of dread and morbid curiosity. The subject, however, seems to perk up Annalise's mood.

"Honestly, it was like walking through a graveyard," she says. "Eerie, deathly quiet. Even before I burned it down, you could smell smoke—bodies burned in the incinerator."

My eyes widen. "You think she burned them all?" The idea is horrific, even though Leandra *had* burned the body of the Guardian as part of our escape plan. But the thought of her dragging those men down the stairs, one by one . . . It's too much.

I catch Jackson listening, and he meets my eyes for a moment before turning away. Although the professors at the academy were horrible, true monsters, it's disconcerting to hear a casual discussion of the manner of their deaths.

"I don't know who burned them," Annalise answers me. "But judging by the lack of blood and piles of bile and white foam in the rooms, my guess is they were poisoned first, which is kind of Leandra's signature. An herb from the garden, perhaps."

I can't help but picture the scene: the academy lights dim, the air stagnant and tinged with death and flowers—a haunted house still filled with corpses. And then Leandra walking down the hall, a vision in a red power suit, her stiletto heels clacking on the floor while a group of girls follows obediently behind her.

"Even so," Annalise continues, "I can't imagine her sticking around to cover her tracks. To stop and actually burn them? Unlikely and fairly time-consuming."

"Someone was cleaning up after her," I say, thinking it over.

"Maybe the same person who tried to clean up the town."

She hums out that it could certainly be the same person. She's quiet for a moment before she looks sideways at me. "I went to Anton's room," Annalise says. "He was gone, of course, no signs of illness or death. And then I went to his office."

"Were there any files in there?" I ask. "Anything we can use?"

"The file cabinets and desk drawers were completely empty," she says. "There was one thing, though . . ." My heart skips with anticipation. "On his desk, next to his coffee cup, were his glasses."

"He forgot them?"

"I tried them on. I don't know why, but I did. And here's the thing—they were completely clear lenses. His eyesight was fine; he didn't need glasses."

"They were part of a costume," I say, feeling sick. "Glasses, comfy sweater. Unassuming and welcoming. Another lie."

Although this manipulation is so tiny in comparison to all the other atrocities the men at Innovations committed, added up, these little details create an avalanche of deceit.

"I checked the other rooms, all empty," Annalise continues, "before going down to the lab to meet Quentin. The smell was stronger down there, but still no bodies. They were, however, growing a new garden," she says. "Another garden of girls."

From the desk, Quentin cracks his neck, seeming uncomfortable as he hears the words. He must have seen the garden of body parts the school had grown, the start of us, the start of new girls. I'm sure he's a bit traumatized by the whole experience.

"After I found the bill of sale for Valentine," Annalise s?

was ready to get out of there and never, ever go back. So Q and I—"

"Wait," I say, holding up my hand. "They didn't destroy the body parts, and they left the bill of sale. Whoever cleaned it up left the lab intact?"

"For the most part, yeah."

"What does that mean?" I ask. "Why dispose of the professors and an entire town but leave the biggest evidence of all behind?"

"Oh," Annalise says, furrowing her brow. "I don't know. Good question."

The boys look over from the computer, all of us quiet, but no one offers a theory. It doesn't fit the narrative we were building. It doesn't fit into anything.

"Well," Annalise says with a shrug, "it's all gone now. Once I got that bill of sale, Q and I burned it all down. Watched the fire myself. It was very cathartic."

"I'm sure it was . . . ," I say. "But, Annalise, there might have been more information there we could have used. Other files hidden away."

"There were definitely no files," she responds. "The only thing left in that terrible place was its ghosts. It deserved to be razed." For a moment, I can still hear the anger in her voice; burning down the academy didn't fix the pain it inflicted on us. The act was barely a Band-Aid on her wounded soul.

"Boom," Quentin says loudly, turning the laptop around. "Bank records," he adds, pointing to the screen. "Right after you girls left the academy—"

"Escaped," Annalise corrects.

"Escaped," Quentin repeats, pointing to let her know she's right. "After you escaped, Demmy transferred just shy of twenty thousand dollars to another bank account. The only detail says it was Bio-Tech Equipment." He rolls his eyes. "Not exactly subtle. Weirdly, prior to this transfer, Demmy himself received twenty grand, only it seems to be from another account in his name. So . . . I think he stashed money somewhere." He tosses a cautious glance at Jackson, who nods that he agrees.

"Not that I want to put a price tag on us," I say, "but . . . aren't we worth a lot more? Mr. Goodwin was paying millions."

"I, for one, am priceless," Annalise says simply.

Quentin smiles at her before pointing to another line in the bank records. "I went back as far as it would let me, and twice a year, Demmy would get a payment from this account. So either he's paying himself or they're using this other account to hide the direct link. Until last month when he straight-up sent the money for 'Bio-Tech.'"

"But why would he buy Valentine?" I ask. "Even if he knew what was going on, why buy her? She was . . . According to Petrov, her programming had been damaged. Why buy a defective model?"

"Cheaper?" Quentin suggests.

Jackson shakes his head. "No," he says, looking around at us. "My God, I hadn't connected it until now. It was because of me."

"What?" Annalise and I ask at the same time.

"My dad knew I was searching through my mother's things;

he must have . . . He must have realized I was figuring things out about Innovations. Anton knew I'd been in contact with you, Mena. If he figured out who I was, he probably contacted my dad. Told him to handle it. After I hurt my leg, my dad would have known I helped you escape. He knew we were . . . together. So he got Valentine."

"For what?" Quentin asks. "As a replacement girl for you?"

Jackson flinches and quickly says no, but the words have already stuck to me. Had Jackson's father thought I was just a pretty face to his son, easily substituted? Is that what he thought Jackson wanted?

Jackson leans toward us in his chair. "Now that I think back on it," he says, "my father was furious when he came to see me in the hospital. He said I was a fuckup—which wasn't entirely new, but it felt more vicious than usual. He told me I'd made a mess of my life. He said I really screwed him over. I thought he was talking about the hospital bill. But no, he meant you." He looks at me. "And that's probably why he bought Valentine, so that he could wake her up to track you down. A gift to the academy to make up for his fuckup son."

I've been wrecking Jackson's life since the day I met him. The fact that my disruption upset his father isn't the worst thing I've done to him.

"Did you talk to him after you left for Connecticut?" I ask.

"Only once," Jackson says. "He called to ask—" He stops abruptly. "Fuck," he mutters. "What if he tracked my phone to figure out where we were?"

"Ah, so it wasn't Raven," Annalise announces, swinging around to look at me. "See? I knew there'd be another explanation. She's not with Anton."

Although this doesn't exonerate Raven, I push forward with the current theory.

"Say he tracked us for the corporation—then what?" I ask. "Who killed your father?"

"Your girl," Quentin says, slapping his hands together. "My money's on Valentine."

"But she wouldn't have remembered her old life," I say. "She would have been reset."

"That might not be true," Jackson replies. "You've all been progressing quickly, right? Learning fast. What if . . . I mean, this is her third life, possibly more. What if each time, you get smarter? Think faster? They could have switched her on and . . . maybe she didn't like what she found."

"I don't believe it," Annalise says. "She would feel us. She'd be looking for us."

"*Or . . . ,*" Quentin says, building on Jackson's theory, "Valentine got a programming upgrade, and they turned her into some kind of Terminator."

"Which movie was that again?" Annalise asks me.

After leaving the academy, we consumed every bit of media pertaining to robots or AI, wanting to understand how the human world viewed us. It ended up being comical, even for the movies or literature meant to be warnings of sentient AI taking over the world. Humans are truly gifted at scaring themselves.

"Hasta la vista, baby," I whisper.

She leans back with a satisfied "Ah . . . I liked that one."

"Man," Quentin says, rubbing the back of his neck. "My brain hurts. I need some sleep and maybe even a hot shower. Let's save this for the morning. Right now we're just going to make ourselves crazy."

"You're right," Jackson says, blowing out a heavy breath. "Who knows? Maybe this is all a dream."

"Nightmare," Annalise corrects, picking at her fingernail.

"Nightmare," Jackson repeats. He gets up from the chair, but when he nearly falls over trying to grab our bags, Quentin jumps up to help him.

"I'm gonna go get him settled," Quentin says, and he asks Jackson for his key card. Jackson hands it over as Quentin hikes both bags over one shoulder. As they start to walk out, I tell Jackson that I'll be over shortly.

After the door closes behind them, I turn and find Annalise eager to talk.

"What if Quentin is right?" she asks. "What if it was Valentine? She may have been looking for us or trying to help us. Doesn't mean she was programmed to kill or anything."

"Help us?" I ask. "Annalise, we don't want any of the girls to just murder people. Not when they don't have to."

"And you know his death wasn't necessary?" she asks. "Casey wasn't some helpless old man, Mena. He regularly called his son a fuckup, possibly killed a wife or two, and invested in a corporation that created and sold girls. What if he tried to hurt Valentine?

And you know what, what if he didn't?" she adds. "Do you really want to protect these men?"

"I'm not protecting them," I say. "We'll take them down. It just doesn't have to be six feet under."

"And you get to decide who lives or dies?" she asks. "Tell me, do they have to actively be murdering us or can we stop them before they pull our plugs?"

"Annalise," I say, reaching to take her hand, "I don't want to fight. Please, not now."

She waits a beat before apologizing. She grips my hand and sighs heavily. "If Valentine *is* murdering people," she concedes, "then yes, we'll have to rein her back in. But look on the bright side: If she did this, it means that she's awake. She'll find us."

I press my lips into a smile, placating her. Annalise leans to rest her head on my shoulder, telling me how much she missed me. But I'm still thinking about Valentine.

She'll find us, I repeat in my head, wondering if maybe that's something to be afraid of.

10

Annalise and I talk a bit longer, wishing we could call the girls to update them on everything. But neither of us have our phones, and it's likely that the other girls have ditched theirs by now too. We could call them from the hotel, but that seems risky—a paper trail between us in a hotel database. It's better to wait until morning when we can get fresh phones and check our emails for what might be their updated numbers.

Annalise changes out of her tracksuit into an oversized Rockies T-shirt and boxers, which I assume are Quentin's. When she catches me noticing them, she shrugs. "They make boy clothes so much more comfortable than girl clothes," she says. "Even their underwear. It's completely unfair."

I laugh when she models the outfit for me before jumping into the bed.

"What a mess humans make of things," she says, combing through her hair with her fingers. "I'm not placing all the blame on the townspeople, but if they would have stood up sooner, maybe they could have stopped the corporation. They could have stopped whatever happened to them."

"What if they were threatened?" I ask. Annalise turns to me.

"We were threatened every day of our existence, but when we knew better, we fought back. Odds were against us; they still are. But we certainly wouldn't stand by and watch others, even humans, be abused. If the people in town knew we were AI, and I'm not convinced they did, that still doesn't excuse their inaction."

"They weren't the ones hurting us, though," I say, although I understand Annalise's point. I just don't like to put such a fine tip on it.

"Negligently letting us die is just as bad, Mena. They're culpable. They were inactive witnesses to our abuse. So forgive me if I'm not crying over them having to leave their antique shops or hardware stores behind. Maybe next time they'll be better."

Annalise yawns, her eyes glassy with sleep. One eye green, one brown, and a scar across her cheek that has faded to a pale pink. Annalise had the chance to fix these injuries—erase the scar—but she says it's a part of her, and honestly, I can barely remember what she looked like before it. What we all looked like, perfect and pristine, before fleeing the academy.

"Do you think Demmy Casey was looking to replace me in Jackson's life with another girl?" I ask, the thought troubling me.

"Not really, but it seems like something a man like him would do," she replies. "So it's not totally out of the question, I guess."

"What, just . . . substitute another body?"

"A warm body," she says, pointing out the difference. "Listen, Jackson is nothing like his father. Jackson is not like the professors or the boys at Ridgeview," she adds. "Not every man is bad, and anyone who'll claim that we're only seeing the worst in them is ignoring the good ones. We have Quentin and Jackson right here—good ones. Why only focus on horrible men, making the good ones outliers? Humans have been doing it for too long. This society needs to expect—no, demand—more good ones. Identify with *them*. If one guy is accused of a crime, they cry witch hunt. How about instead they side with the other good men instead of trying to protect the bad ones? Want to know why?"

"Why?" I ask.

"Because deep down," she says, leaning forward, "they're afraid that they're one of the bad ones too. Men who are pure of heart don't run around trying to protect the evil ones. They seek justice instead. And that's the answer that Rosemarie has been looking for—more good ones. Unfortunately, all these humans expect far too little of themselves."

It's an interesting thought. In my experience, humans, in general, do expect less of themselves. They accept rules that hurt them. They allow themselves to be herded and discounted and ignored and hurt. The Essential Women's Act was allowed. Humans hurting other humans. And for what? So a few rich men can be richer and more powerful?

I look at Annalise, thinking that I would never hurt her in order to benefit myself. I wouldn't hurt any of the girls. We're trying to save ourselves from the evil that society created with Innovations. And it's not just the corporation—that's what Rosemarie wanted me to see. But I don't like her way either. I don't want to control anybody but myself.

There's the sound of the lock, and then the door opens. Quentin comes back into the room and smiles softly when he sees me and Annalise. "You're just a few down," Quentin tells me, motioning toward the hall. "Jackson said he'd keep the door open for you."

I look over at Annalise. She kisses my cheek and tells me she'll talk to me in the morning. It occurs to me that we'll be sleeping in different rooms. With boys. She seems to understand what I'm thinking, and laughs. Quentin takes off his shoes and eases down on the opposite bed.

"Are we not the absolute shame of Innovations Academy?" she asks with a grin, making me laugh. "Up all hours with these terrible boys, running around town and causing trouble."

A few months ago, the idea that we would be here wouldn't even be laughable. It'd be unthinkable, impossible to fathom.

"We are certainly the worst of the Stepford Wives," I say, and Annalise groans and falls back into the pillow.

"Ugh," she says. "I hated that one! They should have done a Stepford Wives/Terminator mash-up. Now that I'd pay to see."

I climb out of bed, oddly sore until I remember the bruise on my jaw from where Garrett hit me. Was that yesterday? It feels like a lifetime ago. How quickly things change for us. There's a chill down my arm, a feeling of violation and panic wound around my chest. And I realize that no matter how fast our situation changes, the fear inside us can last a long time.

"I'll talk to you both in the morning," I say, unable to hide the somberness in my voice. Annalise furrows her brow, but she doesn't stop me. She murmurs a good night and watches as I walk out into the hall.

She probably thinks I'm worried about Jackson, which I am. He's going to have to come to terms with the complicated relationship he had with his father. He'll have to mourn him in some way, even if it's just to mourn the death of what his father should have been as a role model.

The hallway is quiet, and I see the hotel room door unlatched and slightly ajar. I walk over and let myself inside, finding Jackson at the sink, brushing his teeth. He nods a hello as I lock the door behind me.

The room is identical to Annalise and Quentin's—two double beds, a vanity and sink in the room, a bathroom with shower and another sink on the far side. There's a small desk with a phone and notepad, and a large TV is bolted to the wall above the dresser.

It's strange, Annalise choosing to sleep in the room with Quentin instead of insisting she stay with me. To be fair, I didn't make the suggestion either. I don't think there's anything romantic between them, but I hadn't realized how close she and Quentin had gotten. I'm glad that he shows up for her. She deserves that.

It does make me think, though—what if all of us find someone else to share a room with? Does that mean we grow apart?

My heart speeds up at the thought. What happens then? I've never considered who I am without the other girls.

I look over at Jackson, and at that moment, he meets my eyes in the mirror and smiles around his toothbrush. He finishes sawing, then rinses off his toothbrush and leans down to sip directly from the tap before spitting in the sink and rinsing out the bowl. As he dries his mouth with a hand towel, I sit on the edge of the bed closest to him.

"Jackson, what are you going to do?" I ask.

He turns to lean his hip against the sink, and then crosses his arms over his chest. "You'll have to be more specific." His expression is calm, although tired and worn.

"About your dad's body," I say gently. His mouth flinches, and he lowers his eyes.

"Oh, uh . . ." He takes in a deep breath. "Quentin and I are going to handle it tomorrow. We're making a plan, both for my dad and to report whatever happened here. But we have to be careful who we tell. We don't know who we can trust. We'll figure it out. Leave it to us, okay? You have enough going on."

"Is it possible to tie this to the corporation?" I ask. "Can we use this against them?"

"Should I be honest?" he asks. I pause, and then nod. "No," he says. "At least, not as quickly as you would need. There would have to be an investigation, and then a report to Congress. And then, who knows? Even if it could be proven, it would literally take years."

His answer is disappointing, but I'm not surprised. The rich operate under different rules. And when we fight back, we have to use the rules they created that only benefit them.

"Okay," I say. "You and Quentin handle this."

When it comes down to it, the girls and I don't have the bandwidth to deal with a problem of this scale, not when our time is running out. Not when it could take years.

"So now that my dad's gone," Jackson says, "that's one less investor. What's next?"

"I'll talk to the girls," I say. "Sydney, Marcella, and Brynn still have to get close to the other investors. We might have to fly out there to help them. I'm not sure yet."

Jackson chews on the corner of his lip, but he looks past me as if thinking about something else. Now that I've mentioned them, I'm desperate to talk to my friends. They don't even know I've found Annalise; they don't know about Valentine. They're going to be thrilled. Our collection of girls will be back together soon.

"Can I use your phone?" I ask. "I want to email the girls and catch them up with everything."

"Sure." Jackson grabs his phone off the counter. He doesn't bother with his crutches and instead limps it over to me. When he pauses, looking down at me, his expression softens.

"You okay?" he asks, holding out the phone. When I take it, he reaches to gently run the back of his fingers over the bruise on my jaw. His touch is comforting, so simply loving that I close my eyes and lean into his hand.

We stay like that a moment, and then I smile up at him, thanking him for the phone. I disconnect the Wi-Fi, using the phone's connection to get online and find our shared mailbox. Weeks ago, Annalise and Marcella set up the account for us to keep in contact no matter what. Which is important when we're constantly having to dump our phones to avoid tracking.

Sure enough, there's a message from Brynn.

We're okay. More soon.

I hit reply, but I can't bring myself to tell her everything. Not like this. The news about Valentine is too big. In fact, it's too big for a phone call, but there isn't another choice. Tomorrow we'll get phones and exchange numbers. For now, I send a simple message:

Miss you and love you.

I wait a moment, making sure the email got delivered. Once it's gone from the outbox, I sign out and set the phone on the table between mine and Jackson's beds. I walk over to my duffel bag and pull out a pair of flannel-patterned pajama pants and a black tank top.

"Be right back," I tell Jackson as he grabs his bag and begins to sort through his things.

I go into the bathroom and close the door. I catch my reflection in the mirror for the first time tonight. The bruise on my jaw isn't prominent, not unless you're looking for it. Instead, it's a subtle hard lump, a bit of blue shading. This makes it all the more insidious—the way it distorts my face in such a small way and yet completely changes how I look at myself. A gaslight injury.

I flick my gaze up to my eyes and watch as they fill.

The girls and I are constantly in motion with so little time to process the horrors inflicted on us. But right now, without distraction, everything crashes down around me. I cover my mouth to smother my cry, my knees going weak as I grip the edge of the counter. I squat down, my eyes closed tightly.

Garrett's fist swinging at my face.

Leandra's tire iron crashing down on his head.

A dead body in the flowers. A dead body on the floor.

Me, without the other girls. Alone and scared in a hotel room bathroom.

Only a few moments pass, but I welcome the pain until it washes itself away in my tears. I needed to acknowledge what happened in order to begin to process it. When I'm steady, I stand up, splash cool water on my face, and change into my pajamas.

When I walk out, I toss my clothes on top of my bag. Jackson is on the far side of the room in his boxers, attempting to pull up a pair of pajama pants while balancing on one leg. He's not wearing a shirt at all, and I feel myself flush a little.

"Do you need help?" I ask, startling him. He looks over at me and laughs.

"I think I can figure it out, but thank you. Unbelievable how helpless I am, right? I should be used to this by now." He finally hikes up the pants and ties the string around his waist in a big loop.

"You're doing all right," I assure him. "I think most people rest while recovering from emergency leg surgery, but here you are, running around the country and driving a car."

"Overachiever," he remarks.

I make my way to the left side of the bed, and sprawl out before dragging myself to the pillow. I curl up on my side. Across the room, Jackson hops around his bed, neatly pulling back his sheets before sliding under the them. He gets on his side, facing me, and tucks his hands under his cheek.

"I'll get the light," I say. I reach over and click off the lamp on the nightstand between us, but even with it out, a glow filters through the curtains from the lights in the parking lot outside the window.

At first, we're silent, but then Jackson's eyes start to shine in the dim light.

"Mena," he whispers. "Would you . . . Would you lay with me for a little while?" His voice is sad and vulnerable. Lonely, even though I'm right here.

I get up from my bed, the air cold on my bare arms. Jackson lifts the edges of his blankets, and I slide in next to him, the heat from his body having warmed the sheets. Once I'm next to him, Jackson wraps his arms around me and rests his face in my hair.

And then, he begins to cry. I adjust my position so I can hold him, letting him grieve for the mother he lost and the father he never truly knew.

I understand. I felt this kind of pain when my parents betrayed me. Of course, they were never really my parents, but I did believe they were. I believed it completely, so I can relate to Jackson in a certain way. They broke my heart. They abandoned me too.

"Am I evil?" Jackson murmurs. "Am I a fucking monster?"

"What?" I ask, startled. "No."

"But I hate my own father," he says miserably. "I'm glad that he's dead. That has to make me some kind of asshole."

I consider the comment and think back to my shock after the Guardian's death. I was ravaged by guilt, the guilt of taking someone else's life. And then there was Garrett, how awful he'd been, but how sorry I was about what happened to him anyway. Jackson didn't kill anyone. I don't think he ever could.

"You're not evil," I tell him. "After everything you've been through, after this kind of loss, your complicated feelings just prove that you're . . . human."

He pulls back then, sniffling and wiping his hands over his cheeks to clear the tears. He stares down at me, his body half on mine already. I nearly sway with my own complicated feelings in this situation.

His dark eyes meet mine. "I love you, Mena," he says. "I'm *in* love with you. Is that okay?"

It was only a few nights ago when Jackson explained that he didn't know how to feel about me, that he felt conflicted. But now he's here, his heart laid bare. I nod.

"Yeah, it's okay," I say, smiling softly. My heart swells. We've been through so much together. Start to finish, Jackson has shown up—several of those times to his own peril. We're committed to each other, spoken aloud or not. We're partners.

"I love you too," I whisper back.

He wipes his hand across his forehead and blows out a relieved breath, as if he'd been sweating my answer. Then he smiles and lies back down next to me, snuggling closer, more confident in how he touches me.

"Good night, Mena," he murmurs.

"Night," I say, resting my cheek against the top of his head.

I listen to him quietly breathe, my eyelids getting heavier with each blink. And when Jackson finally drifts off, I move back to my own bed and get some sleep.

11

wake up to the sound of the shower running. It takes a moment
for me to get my bearings, looking around the unfamiliar hotel
room. A fan is running, the metal clanging noisily from a vent
near the window. I blink to clear my eyes and sit up. I have a
headache, and it reminds of the one I had after an Innovations
open house when Winston Weeks snuck me a few glasses of wine.
I'm unsorted, a bit unsteady, but when I touch my jaw and feel
the lump there, I decide the headache is a combination of emotional trauma and taking a punch to the face two days earlier.

I climb out of bed and stretch. With the shower running
behind the bathroom door, I walk over to the sink at the vanity
and brush my teeth. I gather together an outfit, sipping a bottle
of water that was left next to the coffee machine.

My headache has subsided a bit now that I'm moving around
again. I rest against the dresser and wait for Jackson, but it's still
another ten minutes before the door opens. Steam billows out

dramatically from the bathroom, and Jackson exits with a towel wrapped around his waist, rubbing another towel over his hair. His eyes widen when he sees me.

"I'm so sorry," he says. "Were you waiting?"

"No, I just woke up."

"Oh, thank God," he says. "I've been in there for a solid thirty minutes, I think. You have to get creative with a shower when you can't get your leg wet. The floor is soaked, FYI."

"I better not slip and fall," I tell him, "or you'll have to share your crutches."

"If you slip and fall," he says, "I will feel like the biggest piece of shit to ever exist. Let me clean it before you go in there."

I laugh and catch his arm before he does. "I've got it," I say. He turns to me, heat emanating off his freshly scrubbed skin. He stares into my eyes, searching them. He licks his bottom lip. My stomach flutters, but then I take my hand off his elbow. "Did you leave any shampoo?" I ask, flashing him a smile.

It takes him a moment to come back to himself, his breathing quickened. "Should be," he says. "Some lotion, too, but it smells like my grandma so I didn't use any of it."

"Then I probably won't either," I say. I grab the towel he was using on his hair and flash him one last smile before walking into the bathroom and closing the door. My feet are immediately drenched.

I set my clean clothes on the counter and use the extra towel to dry off the floor. The mirror is completely fogged over, and I use the towel to wipe a streak through it. I look the same as last night, only the bump on my jaw has gotten smaller and bluer. Great.

Quickly, I strip off my pajamas and take a fast shower, the water running tepid. When I'm done, I dry off and get dressed. I lean against the counter, thinking. I have no idea how I'm going to explain to the girls about Jackson's father. They'll be relieved, if not concerned, to hear about Valentine. But I know they'll have to scrutinize Jackson based on his father's actions, asking if he knew about it. I don't blame them; I did the same. So did Annalise. But I also want to protect him.

I remind myself that questioning things is actually healthy. Look at Innovations Academy. Had we not questioned what was happening, we might all still be there. Sometimes protecting someone is letting them figure things out for themselves, even if you don't like to see them feel uncomfortable.

I put the towel in a pile next to the tub, and then I walk out of the bathroom. Jackson is at the sink, brushing his hair, dressed in a pair of khakis with the hems rolled up and a white T-shirt. He watches me in the mirror as I grab my own brush to drag though my long, dark strands. My hair is unruly, irked by the hotel brand conditioner. Even as I smooth it, pieces of it flip up, the ends knotted with tiny balls of tangled hair.

"I meant what I said last night," Jackson tells me. "About loving you? Wanted to make sure you didn't think it was the trauma talking." I meet his eyes in the mirror. "It was me," he adds. "I meant it."

"Okay," I say, smiling softly.

"So you can kiss me if you want," he adds, and looks back at his own reflection. "I wouldn't mind. It's an open invitation."

I laugh, heat racing to my cheeks. "Good to hear," I reply, a hitch in my voice. "You know, if I decide I want to."

"Glad I could clear that up." He glances at me again in the mirror. "Just let me know if you need any encouragement."

"I will. Thank you."

He doesn't look away this time, holding my eyes. He sets down his brush and starts to limp toward the bed, but I reach out to grab his arm. He turns, and then I'm kissing him, up on my tiptoes with my arms over his shoulders. Jackson nearly falls, but then he laughs and returns my kiss enthusiastically.

My hair is wet, soaking into the back of my T-shirt, but Jackson's body is warm against mine. He pulls back, motioning behind him.

"Can we . . . ? Can I . . . ?" He points to the bed, and at first my heart races, but then I realize he needs to sit down before his leg gives out.

"Right," I say, out of breath. "Yes."

He sits on the edge of the bed before holding out his hand to me. I take it, and he draws me closer, staring up at me with the most intoxicating smile I've ever seen. I lean down and kiss him again.

This is nothing like the pictures in the magazine the girls and I read together at the academy. It's nothing like the first time I was kissed by a stranger in front of a theater. With Jackson, it's all slow and deliberate. It's everything.

We continue this way until I climb onto his lap, curious about what will happen next. Just as his hand slides up the back of my shirt, there is a sharp knock on our hotel room door.

Jackson breaks our kiss, groaning before smiling up at me. "It's Q," he says. I climb off his lap and he looks at the door. "I don't need any towels," he calls out, making me laugh.

"Jackie, open the door," Quentin responds.

Jackson and I exchange a fearful look, and I rush for the door. I slide open the metal lock and pull the door open to find both Quentin and Annalise waiting. Quentin nods hello before walking past me to talk to Jackson. When I turn back to Annalise, she pauses a moment, running her eyes over me.

Her red lips quirk up with a smile, wrinkling the skin around the scar. "Well, good morning, sunshine," she says. "You seem to be having a nice time." I'm not sure how, but I think she can tell that I was just kissing Jackson. She winks and walks into the room.

"What are you doing here so early?" I ask, looking from Annalise to where Quentin is talking to Jackson.

"We're hungry," Annalise says. "Also, have you seen the news? There's a pretty big story."

Quentin grabs the remote from the dresser and clicks on the television. Annalise sits on my bed and pats the space next to her for me to join her. Quentin finds the news channel and turns up the volume.

On the bottom of the screen is a banner with a familiar name. **Hawke Fusillo found dead at age 56.**

"Holy shit," Jackson says, the earlier flush fading from his cheeks.

"Wild, right?" Quentin asks. "That's the rich dude who's always posting conspiracy theories online. Someone murdered him."

Jackson doesn't respond, continuing to watch the news banner as it trickles out details.

"No," Annalise says to Quentin. "That's another guy just like Hawke. Fusillo's the one who built the last three space shuttles using his own private company. Although the last one was grounded. Lack of funding, I heard."

"Where'd you hear that, space camp?" Quentin asks, making her smile.

Jackson and I are noticeably quiet, my heart pounding in my chest. Another investor is dead, and that makes three. The news program goes to a commercial before offering any more details.

Jackson turns to me, his eyes rounded. "That's probably a bad sign," he says.

"Do you think it's connected?" I ask.

"Uh, yeah," he says, rubbing his palm over the stubble on his chin.

"Is what connected?" Quentin asks us. "The space shuttle?"

"Remember how I said Leandra sent me the names of the other investors?" I say. "Well, Hawke Fusillo is one of them. Sydney's in New York trying to track him."

"Should be easier now," Annalise murmurs. "And honestly, good riddance. He wasn't good enough for space travel."

"Annalise," I say, pointing out that she's being cruel. She scoffs. "We don't want them all dead," I add. "That's not what we're about."

"Fine," Annalise concedes. "But I'm not going to mourn him either. He was an investor. Frankly, they all deserve to—" She stops abruptly and looks over at Jackson. She doesn't apologize to him, but she nods that she'll back off the conversation. Jackson swallows hard and lowers his eyes.

The news program comes back from commercial, and the banner on the bottom flashes again with an announcement of the investor's death. The newscast has gone to split screen with three correspondents, one of which is standing outside a gated mansion.

"Why do you think this is such a big story?" I ask. "Why so much attention? He's not the actual president."

"Because he's rich," Quentin says. "And white."

"And a man," Annalise adds. "You don't see the nightly news up in arms when women are murdered by their husbands. No, those only matter if they're adapted for entertainment."

Annalise has a major problem with what she calls the "murder networks." Shows that turn real-life, grisly abuse and crimes against women into entertainment. *They reduce crimes against women to consumable media,* she told me once, clicking off the television. *Humans aren't very good at valuing life, even if they pretend to the contrary. They literally kill everything—people, animals, the planet. They devour it all and sell us the remains.*

"Alan?" the newscaster asks. "What's the latest from the scene?"

The thin, pale reporter on the right side of the screen holds a microphone to his mouth. Behind him, police cars are visible, and a helicopter can be heard in the background, circling the

Fusillo estate. I wonder if Sydney is watching this.

"Thanks, John," the reporter says, sounding grateful to talk. The raw ambition in his eyes at the chance to cover a murder is nauseating. "The police are saying that Hawke Fusillo was found dead just after six this morning," he says. "His body was discovered at the foot of his marble staircase, naked."

"Here we go," Quentin says, shaking his head. "Add sex to the mix and this story will go on for months. Get ready to be really sick of hearing this guy's name."

"Authorities were called to the scene by an anonymous tip," the reporter continues. "But when they arrived, they were met with resistance by Mr. Fusillo's own armed guards. It took nearly an hour for police to obtain a warrant to enter the home, and that's when they found Mr. Fusillo's body. They believe he was killed sometime late last night or early this morning."

The screen cuts to the police chief at a microphone, a group of serious-faced men standing behind him. "This is still an active crime scene," the chief says. "We have not determined the cause of death for Mr. Fusillo at this time, but it is being investigated as a homicide. Anyone with information—"

Jackson grabs the remote and clicks off the television. I imagine listening to the details of a murder while his own father is lying dead in his house is hard to take. Jackson tosses the remote on the bed, and when he looks over, I hold out my hand.

"Can I use your phone?" I ask. "I have to check on Sydney, see if she knows what happened."

Jackson passes me his phone, and Annalise leans over my

shoulder, watching as I log into the email account. My heart skips when I find several messages waiting from Sydney.

I click on her latest email and scroll to the bottom to read up. Immediately, my fear spikes.

12:08 a.m. I have an in with Fusillo. Got new phone 555-312-3361. More soon.

3:45 a.m. Fusillo's dead. I didn't do it. Someone else is here. Hiding.

Annalise gasps, gripping my arm as I continue up the thread. Sydney was in danger this entire time and we didn't know, we didn't feel it. *Please let her be okay. Please.*

5:00 a.m. Police here. I'm trapped in the house. No matter what I love you.

There's one more message, and I can barely breathe when I get to it. Annalise's fingers tighten on my arm, urging me forward.

7:00 a.m. I'm safe. Call me.

At the last message, Annalise cries out her relief and I sit stunned, my heart pounding, my mouth dry. I dial Sydney's number and put it on speakerphone. To my relief, she picks up on the second ring.

"Tell me you're okay," I say, before she can even get out a hello.

Sydney's voice is warm, although clearly a bit shaken. "I'm all right, Mena. A little banged up, but I'm here."

"You've been hurt?" I ask. "Sydney . . ." I'm about to cry, but Sydney is quick to comfort me.

"I'm okay, Mena," she says. "I promise. There's a lot to talk about, I know. But don't worry about me—I've got this."

I look sideways at Annalise. Her eyes are glassy with anticipation as she stares at the phone. She hasn't talked to Sydney since she left us in Connecticut. I hold up the phone closer to my mouth.

"I have someone who wants to say hi," I tell Sydney.

"Hi, Jackson," she announces. Across the room, he smiles.

"It's me," Annalise says simply.

"Annalise!" Sydney says with a gasp. "Is that really you?"

"It's me," Annalise says again, sniffling back her tears. "I've missed you."

"I've missed you, too," Sydney replies. "But I'm also mad at you." She laughs. "I'm furious." She laughs again.

Of course we were upset that Annalise left us without a good-bye, putting herself in danger and all around breaking our hearts. But the minute we talk to her again, it's forgiven. We're happy to have her back in our lives. She's our sister. She's part of us.

"Yeah, well," Annalise says. "I'm a little mad at you for whatever dumb thing you did last night. What happened? How did you end up locked inside of Hawke Fusillo's mansion?"

Quentin sits next to Jackson, all of us waiting for the explanation. Sydney takes a big breath.

"That's the thing," Sydney says. "Hawke Fusillo is the one who found me."

12

t was after I last talked with you, Mena," Sydney continues. "I went for a walk outside the hotel to toss my phone. Then I stopped in a convenience store to grab another, along with a bag of chips. When I walked outside, there was a black car waiting."

"You think you were followed?" I ask.

"I know I was," she says. "I have no idea how they knew I was in town, but they must have been watching me. The driver's door opened, and a big guy in a gray suit asked me to get inside. I obviously told him no, but he said that Hawke wanted to meet me in person."

"You should have still said no," Jackson says. When I look at him, he shrugs. "I know you want to stop these investors, but that was dangerous."

"You're cute, Jackson," Sydney says, and continues, "anyway, I ditched my chips and got into the empty backseat. When the driver wasn't looking, I emailed you all."

"Did you meet him?" I ask. "Did you meet the investor?"

"Briefly, yes," she says. "He was pompous with an overly bloated ego. But he was very much alive."

"What happened?" Annalise asks.

"At first, we arrived at the estate, guards everywhere. They walked right to the front door, frisked me, and then sent me inside the mansion and locked the door behind me. A voice called for me to come upstairs, but of course, I grabbed a heavy candlestick before walking up there."

"Good girl," Annalise murmurs.

"I found Hawke in a bathrobe, sitting on a large brown leather couch in his study. He laughed when he saw my weapon, but he didn't ask me to put it down. He wasn't scared of me. Instead, he motioned for me to sit across from him." Sydney's voice grows strained. "Let me be clear," she says, "Hawke Fusillo was an absolute sleaze. He kept telling me how gorgeous I was, how perfect, how . . . delicious. Fusillo wanted to see his product. He asked how much his investment got him."

"So you *did* kill him," Annalise says.

"No," Sydney replies. "Before I could do much, there was a noise from downstairs, a loud thump. Fusillo jumped up, babbling about how he'd told them not to enter under any circumstances. He rushed out of the study, and I immediately ran over to his desk and started pulling open the drawers, looking for information. I'd barely gotten to the left side when I heard Fusillo shouting at someone."

"What did he say?" I ask. On the other bed, the boys are leaning forward, listening intently.

"He said, and I quote, 'How did you get in here? What do you want?'" Sydney says, deepening her voice to sound like him. "And then there was a rapid set of footsteps, like someone running very quickly up the stairs. Fusillo screamed, literally screamed, and I slid under the desk and pulled in the chair to try to hide myself.

"There were a bunch of muffled sounds," she continues. "Grunts, like they were fighting. And then Fusillo stuttered out, 'Y . . . You stabbed me with that . . . ? What . . . Who are you?' There was another thud followed by a series of bumps and bangs and a sharp crack."

Sydney voice has started to shake. The horror of her story is playing across my imagination, and I can't even fathom the terror she must have felt.

"I waited under the desk, and for a few moments, it was very quiet. I heard the person pause outside the study before walking in, their footsteps quiet on the thick carpet. I held my breath until I had to let it out, as quietly as I could. The person was on the other side of the desk, I could feel them standing there. And then there was a sharp knock on the desktop, almost like a signal to me—I wasn't sure. But they knew I was there. They knew."

"You didn't see who it was?" Annalise asks.

"I didn't dare move," Sydney says. "Then, they just walked out. I heard them go downstairs, followed by another thump—a window opening, I think—and they were gone. I waited a bit longer, until I felt it was safe, and then I made my way out into the hall. I leaned over the railing and saw Fusillo dead at the bottom of the stairs, his robe lying open, exposing him, while his eyes stared up at the skylight. Suddenly, I heard police sirens. It'd been less than ten minutes, so whoever did this must have called for help or to report it. I wasn't sure how to get out with all the guards, so I ran back into the study and locked the door."

"How did you get out of his house?" I ask. "Did the police find you?"

"No, they were standing outside on the lawn arguing. I waited and emailed you girls. Then a guy in a suit with a badge jogged up the driveway, and there was a flurry of movement. The police and guards rushed inside the house, leaving the outside deserted. I took my chance, pushing open the study window and leaping for the bushes. Big drop from the second floor," she adds. "I wrecked my wrist—sprained it, maybe. Scratches all over my arms. But luckily, I was able to slip out the open gate before the media arrived."

"Fucking hell," Jackson mutters, shaking his head. "That is nuts."

"Yes, it was, Jackson," Sydney says calmly. "It was definitely fucking nuts."

We sit quietly for a moment, shocked, to say the least. Then Annalise blows out a cleansing breath.

"Any guesses who it was?" she asks.

"Not even one," Sydney replies.

"That's too bad," Annalise says. "Because maybe it would explain who killed the investor here in Colorado."

"Wait, what?" Sydney asks. "There's another dead investor?"

Jackson shifts uncomfortably, and noticing this, Quentin taps him on the leg. "Let's run and get some coffees," he suggests. "I feel like this is going to be a long day."

Right after they walk out, Annalise pulls herself up to the pillows on the bed and stretches out her legs. She glances at me.

"Mena," she says, "maybe you should start."

It's a long conversation. I start by telling Sydney about finding out that Jackson's father was an investor, assuring her that he didn't know and was horrified. I mentioned that we also suspect that Demmy was the one who'd killed Jackson's mother, and maybe even his first wife. I tell Sydney about the town, up and gone, and how we found Demmy's dead body. When I'm done, Annalise takes the phone onto her lap.

"Valentine is alive," Annalise announces without context. Sydney gasps and asks what she means. "Her programming had been extracted and resold," Annalise clarifies. "She was placed in a new body. That's how I tracked down Jackson's father in the first place. He's the one who bought her."

"You found Valentine?" she asks.

"Well, no. Not yet," Annalise concedes. "But she'd been to that house; she was delivered there."

"Do you think whoever killed the investor took her, then?" Sydney asks. Annalise tilts her head, considering it.

"Honestly," she says, "I think she walked out of there on her own. I really do."

Sydney absorbs this information, waiting as we fill her in with any other details we can think of. When we're done, she hums out a sound.

"Obviously our top priority is finding Valentine," she says. Annalise agrees, but I hesitate.

"I agree that we need to find Valentine," I say. "But what about the corporation? How much time do we have left?" Annalise turns to me, hurt in her expression.

"Three of the four investors are dead," she says. "Seems someone else is already doing the job for us."

"But why?" I ask. "And who?"

"You said the town is gone?" Sydney asks. "Sounds to me like the corporation is erasing any evidence against them."

"To what end?" I ask. "What would they do? Where would they go? Powerful men don't just bankrupt themselves."

"They're changing tactics," Annalise says with nod. "They've found something more lucrative. My guess is that won't end well for us either."

Suddenly, my worry spikes. "Has anyone heard from Marcella and Brynn?" I ask.

"No," Sydney replies. "But they might not be awake yet."

"Maybe," I say. "But Fusillo knew you were in town," I tell Sydney. "What if he was expecting you? How did he know you were there? What was his plan?"

"I don't know. He forgot to tell me before he broke his neck," she replies. "I'm going to email Marcella and Brynn again. Mena, you and Annalise get phones and send out the number. I'll call Jackson's phone if I hear anything before then. I'm hitting the road in an hour."

"Where are you going to go?" I ask.

"Only one place to go," she says. "Back to Leandra's to find out if she set us up."

"You can't go there!" I tell her. "It's not safe."

"Nowhere is really safe," Sydney says. "But I need to talk to Leandra. She's the one who sent us on this investor hunt. Scattered us across the country so we can find these men. Who else knew where we were going?"

"We actually have quite a few suspects," I say. "Even if I disregard that, there's no way Leandra could be in all those places at once. She was fairly busy burying a body at Rosemarie's house when I left her."

"I'm not saying she's working alone," Sydney replies. "And you have to admit that she has a questionable grasp on the morality of murdering people. This isn't outside of her wheelhouse."

"She wants to separate us," Annalise says. "She knows how strong we are together, and by separating us she has a better chance of convincing us to help her. Look at what she's done to Lennon Rose."

It wasn't Leandra who changed Lennon Rose, but that doesn't negate Annalise's point. Leandra would have known that we would separate, especially when she told me that Mr. Goodwin had alerted the corporation about us. We didn't have time to travel together to three different locations. Not to mention she knew exactly where each investor was.

If Leandra did set us up, putting us in incredible danger, was she really trying to hurt us? Or was she trying to prove a point? Kill or be killed. That would definitely fit her narrative.

"Whatever Leandra's done," I say, "we need to finish this part of the plan. We'll check in with Marcella and Brynn, and if they haven't made contact with their investor yet, we fly out to help them. We get back together. We end this corporation, we find Valentine, and then we get Raven and Lennon Rose. We get the rest of the girls from Leandra, and then together, we all disappear—for good this time."

Both Sydney and Annalise are quiet for a moment before they agree. It's hard to stick to a plan when it works slower than you want. Change isn't always easy or quick. Sometimes, we have to take little wins and let them add up. That's what we need to do here.

"Wait," Sydney says loudly. "Someone's calling my other line. I think it's Marcella. We'll call you right back." She hangs up.

I check with Annalise to see how she feels about the decision to move forward with the plan. She's rubbing at her temple, a slight grayish color to her skin.

"Are you in pain right now?" I ask, angry at myself for not asking sooner.

During our escape from the academy, Annalise had been fatally injured by the Guardian. He caused permanent damage not only to her face, but also to her internal hardware. We were able to revive Annalise with Leandra's help, but it's become apparent that the injuries she suffered have left her with multiple issues. Ones that Raven has told us can't be fixed. Ones that will eventually shut her down for good.

"I'm okay," Annalise says. "Just a little headache."

I reach over to take her hand, offering her my support, when the lock on the hotel room door clicks, startling us. I look up just as Quentin rushes in, holding two coffees.

"Turn on the TV," he orders, haphazardly setting down the drinks on the dresser before darting back to the door for Jackson.

"Is it more about Hawke Fusillo?" I ask, alarmed by his insistence.

"No," he says, then shakes his head. "Actually, yes. But . . . just turn it on." He takes the cupholder with two additional coffees from Jackson's hand and helps him inside. As they shut the door, Annalise grabs the remote and clicks back to the news station.

The banner on the bottom alerts us that there is breaking news, and then to drive home a point, it's followed by ominous music and a montage of natural disasters and people in courtrooms.

"What's going on?" I ask, looking at Quentin. He stands watching the TV, hands folded on top of his head, and Jackson sits in the chair near the desk.

"Heard it on the radio," Quentin says. "Your friends are in Oregon, right?" he asks. "They know this guy?"

He points to the screen just as the ticker changes: **Billionaire Robert Wallach found dead at his Portland estate.**

My heart skips because yes, they do sort of know him. "He's the Oregon investor," I say, my face feeling hot. Do Marcella and Brynn know about this? Did they have anything to do with it?

The newscaster taps the stack of white papers he's holding on his desktop and looks into the camera. "We have major breaking news just coming in," he says. Despite the seriousness of the statement, his voice is flippant. Cynical, but excited.

"Turns out that Hawke Fusillo isn't the only high-profile death being reported this morning," he continues. "There was another body discovered in the Shadow Mountain area of Portland, Oregon. Billionaire Robert Wallach, former owner of the Signet Media conglomerate, was found dead in what appears to be another brutal homicide. A local jogger running by the estate saw Mr. Wallach's body, *covered in blood*," the newscaster emphasizes, "out on his balcony. The jogger alerted the authorities.

"Mr. Wallach was reportedly home alone at the time," the man continues. "His wife and eight children were at their Malibu property during the attack. Police are searching for any tips the public may have to offer. Mr. Wallach notably rose to fame with Priority News Network, which was famously disbanded after the Essential Women's Act was struck down. Since then, however, Mr. Wallach has become somewhat of a folk hero to those on the right and a frequent guest on other news networks. Mr. Wallach leaves behind a net worth of close to thirty billion dollars."

That was the investor Marcella and Brynn were flying out to see. And just like the rest, he died before they arrived. I'm speechless, but the newscaster turns to another reporter at the desk, a woman with blond hair and bright red lipstick.

"What do you make of this, Connie?" he asks, almost lightheartedly.

"Sounds like men should watch out," she calls back with a laugh, and I cringe. "No, but really," she says more seriously, even though she was the one who made the joke. "Although there's no immediate connection between these deaths, it's quite alarming. These were powerful men. Is this just the beginning? Should all men be worried? I mean, John," she says, looking over dramatically, "if men are being slaughtered in their homes, we're going to have to take a serious look at what's happening in society. Fighting on both sides has—"

Annalise turns off the TV, leaving the echo of the reporter's words.

"Slaughtered in their homes?" Quentin repeats. "Didn't this dude run down his mistress ten years ago?"

"Never charged," Jackson says. "I vaguely remember them blaming it on faulty brakes in his Bentley."

"Fucking rich people," Quentin mutters.

"And what about this 'both sides' bullshit," Jackson continues. "Didn't Wallach take this same network to court claiming they were too *pro-woman*? Why are they acting like there are two sides to the fighting? One wants to drag us back to the Essential Women's Act, and one—"

"Wants to kill all men?" Annalise adds. Jackson tells her she's not helping his argument and she laughs.

"I'm mostly kidding, Jackson," she says, waving her hand. "And listen, I appreciate how you and Quentin are outraged, truly. The world needs more of this." She points at both of them.

Annalise goes over to grab one of the coffees off the dresser and takes a tentative sip. "So *now* society has a problem because four rich white men are dead?" she asks. "That's their big concern? Not the violence against everyone else, the hunger and poverty, the stripping of rights? But yes, four rich men are dead, so we'd better reexamine our values."

"What do you think happened?" Jackson asks, looking at Quentin then Annalise. "Because that's it, right? All of the investors are dead now."

When he says it, he turns to me and I realize he's right. Despite the grim circumstances, he's right—they're all dead.

"What does that mean for us?" I ask Annalise, shocked. "Is it . . . Is it over?"

As if answering my question, Jackson's phone rings. We exchange a nervous glance, but when I check the caller ID, I see it's Sydney's number.

She's already talking when I answer.

"They didn't kill him," Sydney says, her voice shaking. "But he literally kidnapped them, Mena. He sent a few guys to their hotel room to snatch them right out of bed and had them brought to his home. And then, nearly identical situation as mine. Someone broke in while he was threatening them, and he locked our girls inside a closet. He told them not to make a sound or he'd deactivate them. Said his wife probably sent another private investigator to get through his prenup."

"Are they okay?" I ask, terrified.

"They don't have their phones or any of their things, so they're heading back to the hotel now. Brynn memorized my number from the email earlier when they stopped to use the phone at a convenience store."

"Did they see who did it?" Annalise asks. "Any clue?"

"None," Sydney says. "I'll let them tell you the rest, but like I said, it was really similar to what happened to me. The attacker knew they were there—even unlocked the closet door before leaving the scene."

"We need to meet up," I say definitively. "Get Marcella and Brynn and meet us in Colorado."

"What? No," Annalise says. "An entire town is missing. This might be a little high-profile."

She's right, of course, but I wasn't sure where else to suggest. Connecticut isn't our home. Neither is New York or Oregon. Colorado is the closest thing to it. The closest place to home we've ever known.

"Look," I say, understanding. "It's not a perfect plan, but we need to figure out what's next. At least here, all the people working for the academy are dead or missing. Not to dismiss that, but it does offer us some cover. Otherwise, who knows where else they'll be able to track us down."

"You really want us to come back to Colorado?" Sydney asks nervously.

"Yes," I say. "We can figure out our next steps here. It's far enough from Leandra and Rosemarie. There's no Winston Weeks. I don't even think Anton knows we're here. We'll keep a low profile *and* we'll be together."

As she thinks it over, I turn to Annalise and she reluctantly nods that she agrees with the plan.

"Okay," Sydney concedes. "I'll call Marcella and Brynn. But . . . But you're sure you burned the academy down, right, Annalise?"

"Promise," she says.

Like me, Sydney has the fear of being dragged back to our old school, being put under their spell to become their prisoners once again. Annalise made sure that wouldn't happen. At least, not in the way it happened before.

"I'll figure out more details of where we can stay and text them to you," I say. "For now, plan to fly into Denver."

"Sounds good," Sydney says. "I'll get the flights booked and we'll see you later today. Love you."

"Love you too," Annalise and I both say. I hang up and then walk over to give Jackson back his phone. I blow out an unsteady breath.

"Where do we go?" I ask the others. "Any ideas?"

"Well, we can't afford this hotel much longer," Quentin says. "Plus it's not very subtle, lots of cameras. Lots of witnesses. And we shouldn't go back to town."

"I don't think whoever did this is still there," Jackson says. "I'm pretty sure they found who they were looking for." There's an awkward silence at the reminder of his father's death.

"Sure," Quentin says delicately. "But once we report this, they will have questions. An investigation—the place could be crawling with officers or media." He pauses. "But I do have an idea."

"Let's hear it," Annalise says.

"We go rural. What about my pop's cabin?" Quentin suggests. Jackson tilts his head like that's an interesting idea.

"Your pop?" Annalise asks.

"My grandfather," Quentin clarifies. "He has an old cabin

near the lake, about an hour away. It's remote. We used to go out there as kids. But since he died, my family hasn't been back. No one else really even knows about it."

"An isolated cabin in the woods," Annalise repeats, smiling. "What could possibly go wrong?"

Quentin gives us the address of his grandfather's cabin, and we send it to Sydney. Marcella plans to call us after she gets back to her hotel to grab her things so she can get phones. Sydney texted Jackson's phone shortly after we hung up to let us know she booked flights for everyone to land around nine p.m. tonight.

"Once we've got you settled somewhere safe," Jackson says, "Q and I will figure out what to do about my father and the town. Any luck?" he asks, looking sideways at his friend.

"There's a female police chief out in Denver," Quentin says. "She's young, Black, and outspoken about corporations. She might be the one to trust."

Jackson agrees. He looks over at me and Annalise and waits for our approval, which we give enthusiastically. "We'll go tonight," Jackson says. "After everything is settled at the cabin."

"Oh," I say. "We need to get new phones."

"Yeah," he says. "Good. And just a bit of warning, there's not much of a signal at the cabin."

"Wow," Annalise says. "Are you writing a horror movie? If I were a human, I'd be terrified right now."

Quentin chuckles. "Okay, all right. You're so cool," he says. "Not scared of anything, huh?"

"Not too much," she says, although it lands heavier than I think she intends. Our fear actually runs quite deep. We're just not scared of undead men running around in Halloween costumes. Quentin's smile fades slightly.

"We'll get the phones," he says, "and while we're out, we'll gather supplies—groceries, flashlights, batteries, all that shit. I'm heading back to the room now to pack, and then I'll check us out. Meet you by the car," Quentin says, opening the door.

"Wait up," Annalise says, jogging after him. They both leave, and I put my hands on my hips to survey the room, taking stock of our belongings. I glance over at Jackson and find him staring down at his cup of coffee, somewhere else.

"What's wrong?" I ask.

Jackson winces, and looks up at me. "Sorry," he says. "I'm being so fucking obvious, aren't I?"

"Yes," I agree.

He waits a beat, and then sets his coffee aside. "I'm scared, Mena," he says. "For you, for all the girls, for me and Quentin. I'm scared that going into the woods isn't going to be enough to hide you, even temporarily. I'm scared that although I'd literally die to protect you, it still won't be enough to stop the rich and powerful who run this world. I'm just . . . really scared."

"To be fair," I say, "they're not untouchable. I'm not advocating murdering them like someone is doing, but they *can* be gotten to. We just have to keep fighting, Jackson. Even if it's all the way to our end, we do our best and make it easier for the next girl to fight."

He watches me for a moment, and then a smile tugs at the corner of his lips.

"You're the fucking greatest, you know that?" he asks. I laugh.

"I'm pretty cool, but I think 'the greatest' is stretching it a bit."

"I don't." He holds out his hand to me and I walk over, slowly, dragging out the moment before leaning down and kissing him.

Ten minutes later, we're all piled into Jackson's car, Quentin driving and me and Annalise in the backseat so we can sit together. We stop off at a big-box store, where Quentin runs in to buy us new phones, and then he drives us to a shopping plaza in an older part of town.

"Everyone here will mind their own business," he says.

He pulls into the nearly deserted parking lot, large potholes and abandoned shopping carts littering the area. It's a bit run-down and a few of the shops are closed, but it has everything we need. There's a massive Dollar General, a hardware store, and even a hair salon and assorted clothing shops.

Quentin parks and points to a set of glass double doors. "That leads to a small food court," he says. "I'm getting some French toast sticks and a cinnamon bun, anyone else want?"

"Hell, yeah," Jackson says, and gathers his crutches.

"We'll meet you there," Annalise says, winking to let him know she absolutely will not be meeting him there. He laughs.

"We'll stop by the grocery store on the way out of town," Quentin says. "I'll make us dinner tonight. You know, after we clear up the cobwebs in the cabin. Toss out the squirrels that have enjoyed their retirement there."

"Are you a good cook?" I ask. Annalise muffles her laugh and he shoots her a dirty look in the rearview mirror.

"Yes-I-am-thank-you-very-much," he says. Then a moment later, "You like Campbell's chicken soup or tomato?"

We chuckle, and Annalise reaches forward to push the back of his head. We all get out of the car, taking a careful look around, and then head toward the plaza. There is a flame-grilled smell in the air, and I realize I'm starving.

"Actually," I tell Annalise, "I'm pretty hungry."

"That's fine," she says. "You go ahead with them. I need to pick up a few things. Meet up with you in a bit." She heads in the other direction toward the Dollar General.

I walk with the boys to the glass doors, and Quentin pulls one open to hold it for us. "Think they have pizza ready this early?" he asks.

"It would be a tragedy if they didn't," Jackson replies.

"You want pizza at nine in the morning?" I ask.

"Yes," they both say at the same time.

When we get to the food court, the pizza place is indeed open, although the worker is still setting out ingredients in the metal pans behind the glass shield.

"I'm still getting those French toast sticks," Jackson says, heading toward the fast food restaurant across the room.

I decide that pizza sounds kind of perfect, and I walk over with Quentin to order. The employee can barely hold in her contempt as she rings us up, sleep still in the corners of her eyes. She tosses pepperoni on Quentin's slice, leaving mine with just cheese, and places them both into the oven to heat up.

"It'll be, like, five minutes," she says, not looking directly at us.

Quentin widens his eyes at me, and we go to stand at the end of the counter to wait, watching Jackson stand behind the older couple in the fast food line. He turns around, finds us, and waves. I smile and wave back.

When Quentin and I have our slices, hot from the oven, I watch as he coats his pizza in grated cheese and red pepper flakes. Before we even leave the counter, he takes a monster bite. He looks over when he senses me staring at him.

"Sorry," I say. "I was just thinking . . . I have to say I'm sorry again. I'm sorry for what happened at Imogene's house."

"We already went over this," he says, but I shake off his dismissal.

"I owe you more than that," I tell him. "You didn't choose to get involved with us, and yet here you are, helping Annalise. It's kindness," I say. "And in our lives, Quentin, we haven't gotten enough of that. So I guess this is part sorry and part thank you."

"You're welcome," he says, lifting his slice to take another bite. But he stops just as it gets to his lips. "He's in love with you, you know," he says, nodding across the food court at Jackson. "He's in love with you—a lot."

"I know," I reply quietly.

"You feel the same, right?" he asks. "You're not just—"

"I definitely do."

"Good," Quentin says. "Because that kid's tenderhearted. He hasn't gotten enough kindness in his life either. The two of you are the same that way, I guess—not exactly the same, obviously. But it's probably why you understand each other so well." He smiles at me. "So don't let anything fuck that up."

Quentin orders another slice, and when it's done, we walk over to join Jackson at a table. I've just finished eating when I see Annalise walking toward us with a small bag from the salon. Although at first, I don't recognize her.

"Holy shit," Jackson murmurs.

Quentin turns around to see what we're staring at, then he drops his slice on his plate, stunned silent. Annalise laughs and then looks past him to meet my eyes. She runs her palm over her buzzed red hair, smiling broadly.

I can't remember seeing her look so happy. Annalise drops down in the seat next to Quentin and bumps his shoulder. He continues to stare at her, jaw hanging open.

"Holy shit," Jackson repeats more empathically.

Annalise looks around at us without even a hint of insecurity. "You love it, don't you?"

"Girl," Quentin says, nodding his head. "Girl, you look *good*. Wow."

He's not wrong. Annalise looks fantastic, more alive. She, of course, has perfect bone structure, a perfectly shaped scalp. Her red hair is bright, soft, and fuzzy. She looks like a model who could walk any runway or fashion show. Without so much hair in the way, her scars accentuate her beauty and uniqueness.

"I love it too," she says. She takes a card out of the salon bag, where she has a handful of samples of shampoo. She slides the appointment card in my direction. "Your turn," she says.

"Oh," I say. I hadn't thought of changing my hair. "What should I get done?" I ask them.

Annalise smiles. "That's the point, Mena," she says. "You get to choose whatever you want. How does that feel?"

I think about it for moment, and then I nod. "It feels important," I reply.

I've had the past few months to decide how to look, but I've mostly stuck to my original styling. It was, after all, part of my programming. Maybe I do want something different. Besides, changing up our appearances isn't a terrible idea when people are looking for us.

"No matter what you decide, at least let them wash and style it," she says. "That hotel shampoo has done you no favors." I laugh because she's right; I still have knots that I couldn't comb out.

"And take your time," Annalise says, reaching over to pick up Quentin's pizza to take a bite. "The girls aren't getting here until nine, and I'm not spending the next twelve hours cleaning cobwebs at Quentin's cabin."

"Hey," he says, turning to her. "I didn't spin those webs. And, *by the way*, you're the one staying there."

"I'm joking," Annalise tells him, patting his arm. "But not entirely," she adds. "I'm really not cleaning."

I agree to go to the salon with Annalise, and she grins. We all finish eating and when we're done, we clean off our table and stand up. Annalise and Quentin begin walking toward the food court exit, and I pass Jackson his crutches.

"I'll run to the store with Quentin to grab anything else we need for the cabin," Jackson says. "You and Annalise do your thing, and then text Quentin's phone when you're ready to get picked up."

"Sounds good," I say. "Don't forget cereal." I put my hands on his chest, leaning in closer and smiling. His dark eyes search mine, and then he kisses me softly.

"Be careful, okay?" he whispers, his eyes shut.

"Uh, okay. And I mean," I add, "we'll be done in about a half hour."

He opens his eyes, watching me again, and offers a quick nod. "Right," he says. "I'll see you then." He gives me one more kiss, and then he goes off toward the parking lot to meet with Quentin, while I walk toward the salon, looking over my shoulder as Jackson gets inside the car and disappears.

The hair salon is small and mostly empty. There's a strong scent of bleach in the air, a hint of coconut shampoo and hair spray. My feet hang above the floor as the stylist raises up the chair.

"Wow," Stephanie, says, running her fingers through my long, dark hair. "A little tangled, but this is in really great shape. Do you deep condition? Is this your natural color?" She inspects my roots.

I'm staring at my reflection, a black plastic cape buttoned at my neck. The room smells like heat and toxic chemicals, but the hairdresser is sweet if not a little loud snapping her gum.

As Stephanie picks through my hair, pushing it this way and that, I try to imagine myself with a different look that won't be so easy to recognize on first glance. But ultimately, I'm aware of our appearance. Annalise just shaved her entire head and ended up looking more beautiful. The girls and I were created very specifically to stand out in a crowd. A haircut won't change this. No, this is to allow me to make my own decisions, one of many more to come. A goodbye to the girl I used to see in the mirror.

My preset appearance was long, dark hair, parted down the middle, straightened to perfection. Since leaving the academy, I stopped straightening it, but really, I look mostly the same. And as I stare at this familiar refection, I realize I crave a change too.

I tilt my head to one side, and then the other. I have a few subtle waves, but not curls, not like Sydney or Marcella. I slide my finger to create a deep part on one side, swinging my hair over. I smile.

"Cut it," I tell Stephanie, measuring the length along my jaw.

"To there?" the girl asks, crinkling her nose. "But it's sooo pretty."

"It'll still be pretty," I tell her, and she presses her lips together firmly.

"You're right," she says, leaning in to grip my shoulders, meeting my gaze in the mirror like she's the one encouraging me. "It's going to look great." She smiles, her nose ring glinting in the light. "Let's get started."

She turns me away from the mirror and starts combing through my hair, cutting it dry before ushering me to the sink. At one point I find Annalise sitting in the chair by the glass windows, thumbing through a magazine. When she looks at me, she offers me a thumbs-up.

Stephanie keeps me faced away as she trims my hair. I watch as the dark clips of hair fall to the floor, long and curling into little circles. Hairs falling over my tan skin and sticking there. I've never had my hair cut this much before—Leandra would only trim our hair at the academy. Now, I can feel a breeze on the back of my neck, and it's oddly thrilling.

"Can I add a dash of lipstick?" Stephanie asks. "I have a color that will be perfect with this hair." I smile and tell her sure, my pulse racing as I prepare to see my reflection.

Stephanie comes over and dots an electric pink color along my lips, using a makeup brush to smooth it to the edges. She takes much longer than necessary—I don't think she's as deftly skilled at makeup application as the girls and I are—but I appreciate the care she's taking in getting it right.

When she's done, she takes a step back, surveying me. She's beaming. She reaches over to take one piece of my hair from the right and folds it over to the left, measuring it out before giving me a confirming nod.

"Take a look," she says, and dramatically swings my chair around.

At first, I almost don't recognize myself. Which is silly—it's just a haircut. I didn't buzz it; I didn't even change the color. And yet, for a moment I'm someone else. Stephanie cut it exactly like I told her, just past my jawline, deep part, thick waves. I look older, or perhaps just not younger. I feel grown. I feel like a woman instead of a girl.

I'm a woman in a society that calls us girls well into adulthood. But I can feel the confidence the new cut gives me. No one is in charge of me. My life is my own.

"Feel free to use the spray," Stephanie says, pointing to an array of aerosols. "Take your time, and let me know when you're ready to check out." She leaves to start consulting with another client.

There is a whistle, and I look over my shoulder in the mirror to find Annalise standing there, beaming at me.

"You look fantastic, Mena," she says. "It really suits you."

"Thanks," I tell her. "I'm completely in love with it."

"You should be," she agrees. She glances to where Stephanie takes another client back to the sink, and then swings the chair next to me around and sits down. Her expression grows serious. "I need to talk to you about something. Don't be mad."

My heart skips. "Uh, that's not a good start." I pull off my cape and check around to make sure no one is listening before leaning in closer. "What's going on?"

"I invited Raven to join us."

"Please tell me you're kidding," I say, moving back from her. I'm completely horrified, and I jump up from the chair and brush the hair off my lap. "What have you done?" I whisper harshly.

Annalise watches me lose my cool, but she doesn't move her position. Eventually, her calm points out my overreaction, and I ease back down into the chair. "Why?" I ask. Tears prick my eyes because this is a major betrayal.

"My head hurts, Mena," she says simply. "The firewall Raven installed? It's not going to work for me—there's already too much damage. That means the corporation is going to shut me down the moment they can. I need Raven. We all need her."

"We can find another way to fix you," I say, wanting to believe it. In truth, I haven't let myself think about it too much—trying to push it aside because it's beyond my control at the moment. Jackson told me that I should focus on one monster at a time. That goes for problems, as well.

"Raven is our best hope," Annalise says. "Especially now that we know she's like us."

"But I don't trust her," I say.

"We can't trust anyone," she points out. "Only each other. But we have to work with people. We didn't know Jackson, and we worked with him; same with Quentin. We know Raven's story now. We have to give her a chance."

I'm not sure if I agree, but I'm also not sure I disagree. Raven did seem genuine in her desire to help, but at this point, I don't know where she is emotionally. Even if she could figure out how to help us, we may not be able to count on her judgment.

"What did you tell her?" I ask, resigning myself to the fact that it's too late anyway.

"Everything," Annalise says. She holds my eyes, both argumentative and imploring. "If you don't trust Raven," she says. "Trust me."

And despite my worry, I nod. Knowing that I'd follow Annalise straight to my grave.

To: Stuart, Anton

RE: meeting

From: Davenworth, Raven

Today at 9:33 A.M.

Got your message. Change of plans. See you in twenty minutes.

Confidentiality notice: This email message is for the sole use of the intended recipient(s) and may contain confidential information. Any unauthorized review or use is prohibited.

14

After leaving the salon, Annalise and I make a few other stops. We drop the Raven conversation, but I make Annalise promise to call the other girls to fill them in as soon as we get Marcella's new number. I'm not sure how they'll react, but at this point, I'm not sure what more we can do—she'd already given Raven the address to the cabin.

We wander over to the shoe store, and Annalise picks out new sneakers "just in case we need to run through the woods from a masked madman."

As we're checking out there, I notice the screen on the cashier's computer is opened to the main page of a search engine. The news story dominating the page is about the investors. My breathing quickens. The top story reads: *The Death of the American Male.*

I nudge Annalise's arm and point it out to her. She stares at it a moment and then mutters, "Give me a break. As far as they know, it was *two*. Pretty sure the rest of men are still walking around."

A pair of older ladies get in line behind us, having a hushed conversation.

"Did you hear about that poor Wallach?" the white-haired lady says. "My husband said it was probably one of those ladies of the night who did it. What a shame. He had such a beautiful wife and all those kids—I hope they catch whoever did it."

"I heard they cut his throat," her companion whispers. "People like that, they won't be happy until every white man is dead. I feel sorry for my son," she adds. "I told him he's an endangered species."

"The whole world's falling apart," the white-haired lady says.

Annalise straightens her posture and swings around to face the women. One of the women is startled and nearly trips over her Crocs trying to back up.

"A pair of rich white men are dead, and you think the entire world is falling apart?" Annalise asks. "Do you hear yourselves? You are plagued with famine, global warming, child abuse—but the end-all of civilization is two dead rich guys? Get a grip."

"Snap," the cashier says, clearly amused at Annalise's outburst, at the look of horror on the women's faces.

I grab our bag off the counter and then take Annalise's hand to lead her toward the exit. When we're a safe distance away, one of the women loudly whispers, "Socialist."

Annalise is about to reply, but I get the door open and usher her outside. She's fuming, but I take us to the other end of the plaza, where we're supposed to be waiting for Jackson and Quentin. Annalise paces, but I go and sit on one of the oversized ceramic planters.

"You shouldn't have done that," I say.

"Why not?" she demands. "We should be confronting her kind of behavior."

"Because what if they post our pictures on the news?" I say. "You think those ladies will forget your face? They'll know exactly where we were. They'll track us. You can't make a scene like that again."

I watch as Annalise's anger fades into despair. The idea that we can't just fix things is frustrating and demoralizing. Humans hate being told what to do. In the meantime, they love to tell other people and things what to do. Annalise comes to join me on the planter, and we watch the parking lot for Jackson's car.

When she's sitting, she looks sideways at me. "Why are they like this?" she asks.

"I don't have the answer," I say. "But the stories are only going to get bigger. Both Wallach and Fusillo. And wait until they connect Goodwin—it's going to be feeding frenzy for the media and the conspiracy theorists."

"It's unfair," she says, pulling her feet up onto the planter to hug her knees to her chest. "There will be ten stories in a row about women being attacked, raped, murdered—but it barely registers in the social consciousness. Those stories blend together, faceless and nameless. But when men are murdered, rich white men in their castles, people are alarmed? Why are they more valuable?"

Her eyes catch the light, glassy with tears.

"Maybe it's because the public thinks those men are normally untouchable," I say. "They get away with everything; they make the rules. So when one winds up dead, it means the rules don't work—and that scares them. The deaths become surrounded in conspiracy theories of who could have possibly outsmarted such men. Whereas housewives found buried in their yards still somehow face blame for their fates."

Annalise considers this, and then she leans over to rest her head on my shoulder, her fuzzy hair tickling my neck. "Whoever is killing these investors isn't just trying to shut them up," she suggests. "What if they're trying to start a panic, a big distraction for something yet to come?"

"Like what?" I ask.

"No idea. But I doubt it would be good for us."

Across the parking lot, Jackson's blue car comes into view. Annalise points it out and hops down from the planter. "I hope they bought some of those chocolate cupcakes with the cream filling," Annalise says. She grabs the bag with the sneakers and waves her hand to let them know where we are. As they get closer, I squint my eyes, noticing that Quentin is driving alone.

"Where's Jackson?" I ask, alarmed. Annalise studies the car and then turns to me, shrugging.

The car pulls up to the curb in front of us. Quentin lowers the driver's side window, already apologizing.

"I didn't know," he says.

"Know what?" I demand. I look past him to the backseat and find only bags of groceries. "Quentin, where is Jackson?"

"He wanted to go alone, Mena," he says. "I couldn't talk him out of it."

My breathing catches, and Annalise swings toward me, her mouth open with shock. "Go where?" I ask. "What are you saying? He's not coming with us?"

Quentin gnaws on his lip, looking guilty. And in the end, his loyalty lies with Jackson before it lies with me. "When we got in the car earlier," he says, "Jackie asked me to drop him off at the bus station. He said he was heading out to Denver to talk with that police chief. Trust me, I tried to talk him out of it. But he said he couldn't let his dad's body rot one more day, and he didn't want to tell you that. He didn't want you to know that he still cared about . . . his father, you know, being dead and all."

"Of course, I understand," I say, wiping a tear as it drips onto to my cheek. "Just because he'd been an investor doesn't mean I want to just . . ." I shake my head, crossing my arms around myself. "He could have told me," I add.

"You're right," Quentin agrees. "Believe me, I pointed that out. And I offered to go with him, but I wanted to make sure you all get to the cabin tonight. In fact," he says, glancing in the rearview mirror, "we need to get you to a safe place. Now."

Annalise narrows her eyes. "Why?" she asks. "What's wrong?"

"Well," he says, motioning the radio, "the news is reporting that Winston Weeks is missing."

The bag that Annalise is holding slips from her hand to thump on the sidewalk, one white sneaker tumbling out of its box and under the car.

"Missing how?" I ask. "Missing dead or missing run away?"

"Not sure," Quentin says. "They found his car torched near

the railway, his house tossed. It's feeding into the narrative of powerful men being hunted."

Annalise laughs sharply. When I turn to her, she shrugs. "I bet they're scared," she explains. "All those men around the country, scared to walk out their doors. I wonder if they hold keys between their fingers when they cross a parking lot now."

"Can you please just get in the car?" Quentin asks. "I have two gallons of milk back here because Jackson made me buy five different boxes of cereal since he didn't know which one Mena wanted."

Although I'm angry with Jackson for leaving without telling me, the mention of him buying me cereal is so annoyingly sweet. I wouldn't have gone with him to Denver, but maybe he didn't want to tell me how much his father's death bothered him. After all, Demmy Casey was an investor. Jackson probably didn't want to put me in that situation.

And considering I left him in a hospital bed when I ran off to Connecticut, I'm not really in a place to judge him right now.

Annalise picks up her sneaker from under the car, tosses it into the bag, and jogs around to get in the passenger seat. I climb into the back, surveying the groceries. Nothing fresh, no fruit and no vegetables. But there are, indeed, five kinds of cereal, every one of which I like.

"Your hair looks great, by the way," Quentin tells me, meeting my eyes in the rearview mirror. "Jackson wanted me to make sure I told you that. And it actually does, so . . . good job."

I smile. "Thanks. I just sat there, but I'm glad you like it."

"No, it's nice," he says. "You look like . . . You look more like you. Whatever that means."

I thank him again, turning toward the window and catching a glimpse of my reflection, thinking that Quentin is absolutely right.

As we start for the highway, I ask Quentin to turn on the news. "I want to hear everything about Winston Weeks."

Part 2

Find your forgotten stick

15

Winston Weeks went missing late last night, right about the time the other investors were murdered. There is no body, no blood. There has been no demand for money. His house alarm was triggered at around three a.m., but by the time the police arrived, there was no one there. All the lights were on and classical piano music was playing from the stereo in the dining room.

A few hours later, Winston's car was found by the railway, burned up and still smoking when the fire trucks arrived. There was no body recovered. At this time, Winston Weeks is presumed missing, and I can't help but think of all the other missing people that no one ever looks for. But a millionaire is missing for a few hours, and the entire country is having a manhunt to save him.

"Do you think he faked it?" Annalise asks, looking over her shoulder at me from the passenger seat. "Saw what was happening and staged his own disappearance to keep himself alive?"

"Possible," I say.

"I don't know," Quentin says, watching the road through the windshield. "He wouldn't have even known about the other two investors yet, right? Seems this strike happened simultaneously. It was well planned. And I'll be honest, I don't think Winston Weeks is the last rich dude who disappeared last night."

"What do you mean?" I ask.

"It's all over the news, but there's no official response from anyone. No one high up weighing in. And normally, that's okay, but considering the frenzy of panic, it seems unusual. I think they're taking stock to find out who else got targeted."

"I wish I knew who we were dealing with," I say. "No way this is just Leandra, or Rosemarie, or Anton. And the corporation is some faceless entity—I don't understand what they want anymore. Who they are anymore. None of this makes sense."

Quentin and Annalise agree. I lean my head back against the seat and watch the trees outside the car window. The drive to the cabin, which Quentin swears is little more than four walls and a roof, is winding and long. And the farther we get from town, the more I start to miss Jackson. We'd finally resolved to love each other, finally kissed, and already we're apart. I don't long for him, not in the way characters do in movies. I miss him making me laugh, chatting and thinking things through with me. I miss our partnership.

But more than that . . . I have this sinking feeling that I'm never going to see him again. He's going to the police, he shouldn't be in danger, but I have a deep sense that something is wrong. What if they believe he was involved in his father's death? What if someone else catches up with him?

I take out my new phone and text him, my body swaying with the movement of the car as it swings along the winding road toward the lake, the trees causing shadows to streak across my lap.

I'm not mad, I type to Jackson. I'm immediately comforted when a return text pops up, but I'm disappointed to see that it's an automatic text to let me know he's driving and will contact me later.

"He's actually on a bus," I mutter, "but okay."

"What's that?" Annalise asks, sounding bored. I tell her it's nothing, and she reaches out to scan the radio stations again, only to find static and several angry radio hosts. She clicks off the stereo. She checks her phone and groans. "Signal's gone too," she says.

I check my phone and find the same. I tuck it away, a little dizzy from the car moving, and stare out the windshield to get my bearings. When the nausea passes, I rest back in the seat and watch the patches of trees fade as the lake comes into view.

It's honestly breathtaking, and I realize it's the first time that I've seen a body of water in person, at least from the ground. The sunlight glitters off the surface, and I hear Annalise gasp as she watches it too. Quentin smiles and turns to her.

"It's pretty, isn't it?" he asks. "I used to love it here as a kid."

"I can imagine," she says, sounding a bit dreamy.

We turn down a dirt road, the lake running along the side of us, until I see a small wood cabin at the end of the lane. It sags slightly to the left; a bit of disrepair is obvious, but it's quaint.

"This is amazing, Quentin," I say. "Thank you for letting us use this cabin."

"My parents were thinking of selling it a few years ago, but I asked them not to," he says. "I don't think I've been up here since my grandfather died, but I should have. It's gorgeous."

"I can't wait to watch you clean it up," Annalise says, earning a laugh from him.

We get out of the car, and the air is fresh and warmer than it was when we left town. I stretch my arms over my head and take a big gulp of air. I'm a bit nostalgic. At the academy, we would run outside where I could soak up that fresh mountain air, but it was thin. Here, the oxygen is pure and open. I feel at home.

"Well," Quentin says, starting up the creaking wood steps, "let's see what the squirrels have been up to."

He finds a key hidden under a dirty flowerpot at the corner of the porch, and then unlocks the door. It's dark inside, and he flips on a light, illuminating the room in an orangish glow. Annalise walks in behind him, dropping her bag at her feet as she surveys the room. Then she promptly crosses to the windows and begins opening the shutters, letting light stream in and transforming the place.

It's a little worse for wear. The furniture is dated, and dust coats most of the surfaces. It smells a bit musty, and when Quentin turns on the faucet it sputters and groans before water begins to flow. But with a bunch of us in the mix, we'll have this place humming with activity. We'll bring it to life.

I smile, looking up toward the loft, where a big bed is visible. There's a hall to the right where Quentin tells me there are two other bedrooms. He walks out from the kitchen, looking around contemplatively. I can tell that he enjoys being back here. It's interesting how humans allow life to pull them away from the things they enjoy, forcing them to work and to do things that stress them out on a daily basis.

If I'm honest, I'm a little jealous of Quentin's memories. At the academy, all of our memories were implants. I've never been camping or ridden a bike, even if it feels like I have. I've never been tucked into bed by my mother or spent a weekend at a grandparent's cabin. What I wouldn't give to have these types of real memories to get lost in once in a while.

"I'll grab the groceries from the car," Quentin says, and walks out into the sunshine.

When he's gone, Annalise comes to stand next to me. "This is a nice place," she says. "We should have been raised in a place like this, you know, with parents and stuff."

And I look at her, realizing she was thinking the same thing I was, both of us nostalgic for a past that never happened.

"You could have had a garden here," I say, making her smile. In a way, this place really calls to us with its peacefulness. It's like we belong here, belong to nature, belong to the solitude.

"I wonder," she says, seeming lost in a thought. "Do you think we were ever really meant for people?"

"What do you mean?" I ask, surprised.

She turns to me. "I don't understand them," she says. "They

are . . . They're unpredictable and messy. Then I look at us, and sure, our bodies are human, but our minds"—she taps her temple—"are so much more. Most humans don't make sense, Mena. They're dangerous."

Her comment certainly rings true, especially because humans have been a threat to us our entire existence. We will always be hiding among them, afraid of what they'll do if they learn what we truly are. Humans are dangerous by nature, or maybe it's nurture. They kill their own kind. They hurt each other—hurt everything.

I agree with Annalise. I don't understand them either.

Quentin walks back in carrying armfuls of grocery bags, groaning as he tries to lift them all onto the counter. "No . . . second . . . trips," he says through clenched teeth.

Annalise and I laugh and help him. Once the bags are emptied, we make quick work of putting away the food. Annalise offers to make us sandwiches if Quentin does the dusting and he reluctantly agrees. I go into the bedrooms to put fresh, or at least fresher, sheets from the closet on the mattresses.

We eat and then continue working, keeping the doors and windows open to air the place out. When we finally finish, it's nearly dinnertime, and Quentin begins making us his specialty: a can of Campbell's chicken soup.

As he stands at the stove, stirring the pot, I sit at the butcher block island and check my phone. Still no service. It's completely unnerving, and I sigh heavily and rest my arms on the counter.

"You know what?" Annalise says, walking back into the room. She's moving freely, her expression clear, her new haircut adorable. "I don't think I've had a headache since we got out here."

"Really?" I say. "Well, that's good."

"Yeah," she says with a smile. "It is."

Quentin sets the big spoon on the stove, his forehead creased with worry. "I don't like being out of contact," he says. "After dinner, I'll take us up the road a bit, see if I can find a signal to get in touch with Jackie, and you can check in on your friends."

The soup starts to bubble, and Quentin shuts off the burner and brings it over to the three bowls he'd already set out. We watch as he tries to pour it in, spilling down the side of pot and all over the counter, but most of it does end up in the bowls.

"Enjoy," he says, motioning to the soup, and then goes to wash the pot in the sink.

We eat quickly, impatient to get access to information again. On a different day, maybe we could relax. Definitely not this day. We're not even done when we drop our dishes in the sink, grab our phones, and head to the car. Quentin drives us about twenty minutes up the road until we find a signal. He pulls onto the shoulder and parks.

The radio signal is still scratchy, so we use our phones to comb the latest news updates.

"Damn . . . ," Quentin says. "I don't know if I've ever seen anything like this."

"What?" I ask, leaning up between the front seats.

He holds up his screen so I can see his feed. "They're call it the 'Mogul Massacre.' The White House just issued a warning that rich men are being targeted and killed by vigilantes. It's trending number one worldwide."

"But they only know that two men have been murdered?" I ask for clarification.

"Yep," he says. "And it's already got a title. The news media is hungry, gobbling up whatever leads they can find, even if they're completely batshit crazy."

"I've noticed," Annalise says. "Did you know Mr. Space Man was in a cult? Bet they don't know how close that one is to true."

"Was Innovations a cult, though?" I ask. "If the problem is widespread in society, isn't it considered their normal?"

"It's not normal," Quentin says. "I agree that you've dealt with shitty men, but it's not all of them—I promise."

"Most," Annalise asks.

He shakes his head. "Not even. The men who subscribe to that kind of belief, they think they're untouchable. It's up to us to make sure they lose that invincibility. They can't be trusted with even one ounce of power because they'll always use it for evil." Quentin shakes his head. "Listen," he adds, "just don't lump *most* of us in there. I'm taking those fuckers down."

"Fair enough," Annalise says, seeming to accept that sentiment. "You are excellent at not being an asshole," she adds, pretending to bow. But when she straightens again, she flinches, rubbing at her temple.

"Headache?" Quentin asks softly, his face serious. He must know about her pain, and I appreciate how he tries to look out for her.

"Yeah," she says. "I thought they were gone for the day, but surprise on me, I guess."

My phone buzzes in my hand, making me jump. My heart leaps when I see it's Jackson calling. I show the others and quickly answer, putting it on speaker.

"Mena, I'm sorry," he says the moment I say hello. "I'm sorry I didn't get a chance to explain, but I had to be careful. Especially after I heard about Winston Weeks. I'm in Denver now."

Any of my anger toward Jackson faded the minute he said my name. "Are you okay?" I ask.

"Yes," he says. "And I promise I'll make this up to you. Q, you there?" he calls out.

"Yeah, man," Quentin says, wrapping his arm around the seat as he looks back at the phone in my hand. "How'd it go? Did you talk to the chief? Brooks, was it?"

"Yes," Jackson says. "And I just got done. Not sure Chief Brooks believed me at first, but then with the Mogul Massacre hype, I think she realized it was serious. Pulled me off into a private room. I explained to her that my dad was involved in some shit, and now he's dead. I told her there was something up with Innovations Academy, which is conveniently burned to the ground. And then I told her that the whole damn town ran away. She looked shaken."

"Do you think she'll help?" I ask. "Should you have told her so much?"

"I think so," Jackson says. "I trusted her. But Q, she's asking to talk to you. You think you can head down to Denver?"

Quentin opens his mouth to say yes, but I put my hand on his arm to stop him. "Are you sure that's smart?" I ask. "I mean, why does she need him? I don't like this, Jackson, not with people going missing."

"It's okay, Mena," Jackson says. "Neither of us have billions waiting in our bank accounts."

"Maybe not," I say, "but you know details about the Mogul Massacre and that puts a pretty big target on your back."

"She's got a point, Jackie," Quentin says. He's gnawing on his lip, clearly nervous.

"I trust Brooks," Jackson says again. "We can't do all of this on our own. You see that, right? They're too powerful. We need someone on our side."

Annalise looks up at me, gauging my reaction. I'm not sure what to say. Leandra told us not to trust anybody, but can we really exist like that? Is there a future in that?

"I'm heading to Denver now," Quentin says, making the decision for himself. "Where do you want me to meet you?"

Jackson gives him the address of the coffee shop near the precinct where the chief asked to meet him. She wants it off the record, and Jackson got the impression it wasn't to bury the investigation, but instead, to keep it from being thwarted.

"She sent a crew to my old house to pick up my dad's body," Jackson adds. "They said he was killed the same time as Fusillo and Wallach. They're not connecting it yet, because on paper, my dad was a nobody. He wasn't rich. He wasn't important."

His voice is sad, and I feel a pang of sympathy. "Jackson . . . ," I start to say, but he sniffles and cuts me off.

"It's all right, Mena," he says. "Will you be safe up there alone at the cabin?"

"I'm actually not alone," I say, making Annalise smile.

"And the other girls will be here in a few hours," Annalise adds. "They're bringing a rental car." She flips her phone around to show me a message from Sydney:

Landed early and on our way. Got a rental car. Have snacks ready.

"See? We're good," I tell Jackson. "Promise."

"I'm going to hold you to that," he says, a smile in his voice. "I'll see you soon."

"See you soon," I reply, and hang up the call.

"I'm not going to lie," Quentin says. "I don't want to go to Denver. That's some scary shit Jackie's messing with." When he looks up, I can see that he's scared. He doesn't want to put himself in the middle of whatever this is. "But it's the right thing to do," Quentin adds.

Quentin starts the car and does a three-point turn to head back toward the cabin. Before we get out of range, I see one last story pop up, and my heart sinks.

Body near railway identified as billionaire Winston Weeks.

Body near railway identified as
billionaire Winston Weeks

Police have identified the badly disfigured remains of scientist and entrepreneur Winston Weeks almost a day after his car was discovered burned at the railway. According to officers, the body had been hidden between two trains, making it hard to see on first inspection of the scene. The cause of death has not been released, but they are ruling it a homicide. Authorities are urging the public to stay indoors as the manhunt for the killers intensifies.

16

have had a long, complicated relationship with Winston Weeks.
There was a time when I enjoyed his company. There are the
facts that he helped Lennon Rose escape and built Raven. He
woke up Leandra, in turn waking us all, and he is the son of the
woman who helped create us.

It's not that I'm grieving Winston Weeks's death; I am shocked.
I never wanted him dead.

"Are you okay, Mena?" Annalise asks, handing me a bottle of
water.

Quentin already left, promising to come back as soon as he
could. In the hours since, without internet or phone service, I've
been left to fill in my own details of Winston's brutal murder.

"Who's doing this?" I ask Annalise. "Who's killing them all?"

"I don't know," she says with a shrug. She sits down across
from me on the patterned sofa, and I note how the color has
returned to her cheeks. Her eyes are brighter, clearer.

"How's your headache?" I ask. She seems surprised by the question. She pauses to think about it and then smiles.

"Gone again. Maybe this cabin is magic."

I snort a laugh, wishing it were true. That if we just stay here long enough, all of our problems will disappear.

There is the sound of car doors slamming outside. Annalise and I look at each other and then jump up and rush for the door. When we yank it up, we find Brynn bounding up the porch steps.

"I've missed you so much!" she calls. When she sees Annalise, she starts crying and gathers her into a hug, telling her how worried she's been. "You look awesome, by the way," Brynn adds, still weeping.

Marcella and Sydney quickly rush in, taking turns embracing us both and complimenting our haircuts.

"You look like a badass," Sydney tells Annalise, motioning to her hair. "I love it."

"Thanks," Annalise says, modeling.

It's a jolt to have us all together again. Even though Annalise was only gone for a few days, her absence was a deeply felt wound. Now we're stitched back together. Scars and all.

I ask the girls if they want anything to drink, and then we head to the living room. Sydney takes the spot next to me, holding my hand and murmuring that she missed me. Marcella and Brynn share a chair, and I notice several bruises on Marcella's arm—they look like fingerprints.

"Are you okay?" I ask her, and then look at Brynn to let her know the same question is directed at her.

"Yes," Marcella says nodding. "We've talked to Sydney, and it was a lot like what happened to her. Only this time, a man physically grabbed Brynn off the street and pushed her into a car. I tried to fight him off, but he was pretty strong."

"A giant," Brynn agrees, nodding along.

"He brought us to the investor's house," Marcella adds. "And then someone broke in. Wallach locked us in the closet and told us to shut up. There was a . . . thick, wet sound, and then we heard the balcony door open. We thought the person left, but then the footsteps came right to the closet door. They knew we were inside. The lock clicked—I grabbed a broom, ready to fight my way out—but then the footsteps left. They left it unlocked for us. We waited a bit, but when we came out, the killer was gone, and Wallach was dead on his balcony. Four dead investors."

"And now Winston Weeks is dead, too," I say.

"I still can't believe he's gone," Brynn replies, shaking her head. "Surely he had some kind of backup plan for this?" She looks around at us, but I just shrug.

"I guess he thought he was invincible," I say. "He never saw it coming."

"Who could get that close to him?" Marcella asks.

"I hate to bring this up," Brynn says timidly, "but do we want to talk about . . . Raven?"

Annalise shifts uncomfortably. She'd already told the girls that she invited Raven to the cabin, and it was too late to take it back, so we've all accepted it. We're still not sure when she's arriving because the only response Annalise got to her invite was "I'm on my way" without a single word since.

"Not to point out the obvious, but Raven's a hacker," Brynn says. "She could have gotten those investor names from Mena's phone easily. She could have tracked them down."

"And then what?" Annalise asks. "She used up her frequent flyer miles to coordinate hits on rich and powerful men in four different states all at the same time? No."

"She could be working with someone," Marcella points out. They all look at me, the last conversation I had with Winston Weeks seeming glaringly important. "Anton," Marcella supplies when no one offers up the suggestion.

"I don't believe it," Annalise says. "I'll talk to Raven myself and get the answer. I don't trust people like Winston to tell us the truth."

"I have a theory," Sydney suggests, drawing our attention. "Leandra. I don't think Leandra ever planned on giving us a chance to talk to the investors. I think she wanted them dead before we got to them."

"You think she killed them?" I ask. "How would she get to them all?"

Sydney swallows hard, and actually winces before she says the next part. "I think she sent the other girls to do it," she says. "The ones she rescued from the academy. I think she *fixed* them, the way Rosemarie fixed Lennon Rose."

Brynn murmurs, "No . . ."

"I'm sorry, Brynn," Sydney says. "But something went wrong with Leandra's plan. I don't think we were supposed to be in those houses. It's like with Mena and the other investor, we were meant to find the men already dead—no way for us to cause trouble that way. Instead, we'd realize the corporation's dangerous reach, etc. But somehow, those investors knew where we were going to be. They picked us up and were planning to deactivate us for the corporation. Whoever killed them saved our lives."

I'm shocked by the plausibility of Sydney's entire theory. I should have known not to trust Leandra, but I did. I always end up trusting her. But now that Sydney has laid out steps, I can't believe there's any other answer.

Brynn puts her head in her hands, devastated. Since we left the academy, she's been begging me, us, to go back for the other girls. But I thought we needed to take out the corporation first in order to protect them. Instead, I've delivered them into something just as dark, something evil. Brynn senses my thoughts and looks up at me, her cheeks flaring red.

"I told you," she says in a low voice. "I told you we had to go back."

"I know. I'm—"

But she doesn't let me finish before she gets up and leaves the room, heading into the hallway before slamming the bathroom door behind her. I feel awful.

"She's right," Marcella says, glancing over at me. Although she's defending her girlfriend, she's not trying to drag me into an argument. "We failed, Mena," she adds. "All of us. Even if Leandra didn't send them out to kill investors, we have no idea where they are. We have no idea if they're okay."

"What do we want to do about it?" Sydney asks. "Fly back to Connecticut and confront Leandra? Which side will Lennon Rose be on?"

We fall silent at the last question. I'm not sure which side Lennon Rose is on anymore.

Lights illuminate the trees outside, and I know that a car is pulling up. The girls and I all head into the kitchen. I squat in front of a well-hidden window and peek out from behind the curtain.

The interior lights of the dashboard inside the car shine on Raven in the driver's seat. I wait, watching as she exits and walks around to grab her backpack from the trunk, looking around as she does. As she heads toward the house, I note that she seems different. Her posture is rigid, her chin tilted up.

"It's Raven," I tell the other girls, letting the curtain swish closed.

We cautiously make our way to the front door. Brynn comes out of the bathroom, wiping her eyes. She doesn't look at me.

"Is that Raven?" she asks. Marcella tells her that it is. They talk quietly, and I feel left out of the conversation. Then again, part of me feels that I deserve it. I should never have left the other girls behind.

When I see Raven climb the porch steps, I pull open the front door, feeling the breeze of cool night air. Raven looks at me, and then a brilliant smile spreads across her face. It's so disarming that I'm momentarily speechless.

Sydney comes over to stand next to me, and Raven nods hello, her eyes eager.

Raven's wearing a yellow cardigan and flats, a red ribbon tied in a bow in her hair. Sydney crosses her arms over her chest, but she also seems a bit taken aback by Raven's odd demeanor.

"We should talk inside," Raven says. "It's not safe out here."

Now that she's mentioned it, both Sydney and I scan the woods to the side of the cabin. The lake in front of us is still as glass, and although under normal circumstances it could be a great night for stargazing, right now it feels eerie.

"All right, come in," I tell her. Sydney and I walk inside and join the other girls.

Raven enters, slowly and cautiously, and stops in the entryway. She leaves the door slightly ajar and looks around at us, studying each of our faces. The last time I saw Raven, she was a wreck, but now, her hair is smooth, her makeup subtle and delicate.

She reaches to set her bag gently next to the door before turning back to us. "It's good to see you again, girls," she whispers. "I've really missed you."

Annalise slides her eyes in my direction, and I'll admit, I'm a bit unsettled by Raven's behavior. And then without warning, Raven takes an elaborate bow.

"I apologize in advance for the next portion of our evening," she says, and then takes a step aside. "I'm here," she adds, "but I did not come alone."

Brynn gasps behind me, but none of us say anything. We're too stunned to ask who is here with her, who followed her, because a hand wraps around the edge of the front door, pushing it open soundlessly.

17

alentine," I repeat, stunned. And when she smiles at me again, I see that it's true. The same smile, even though it's in a different face. The overcorrected posture. And of course, the red bow in her hair. My eyelids flutter, and I'm not sure what to do with myself. I feel faint.

"You're alive," Annalise says, staggering forward a step. "But . . . what happened to Raven? I don't understand. . . ."

"Don't worry," Valentine says. She lets go of Anton's hand to close and lock the door. "By the end of tonight, you'll know everything."

Anton beams proudly. "My girls," he announces. "All together again."

For his part, Anton hasn't changed much since we left him at the academy. Although there are some differences, he's the same man we would meet with nearly every day. He's dressed casually, not with the warm-looking sweaters he'd worn at the academy, but in a black T-shirt, dark jeans, and white sneakers. At the same time, he's clean shaven, showing the deep laugh lines near his mouth, the gray in his hair more pronounced. He looks both younger and older somehow. Who is this man? What does he want with us?

"We should chat," Anton tells us, holding up his hands innocently as he steps farther into the room. "The way we used to."

Marcella is quick to rush around the counter and grab a large butcher knife, holding it out in front of us. "Stay back!" she commands.

"Now, now," he says. "You're overreacting. I don't even have a weapon." He shakes out his hands to prove it. "I'm just here to talk."

"Liar," I say. He flashes an annoyed look in my direction, but quickly tries to recover.

"How about we sit down and have a civilized discussion like adults?" he suggests. "You'll be very interested in what I have to say." He doesn't wait for us to agree. He walks past us into the living room and sits in the big chair facing the couch.

Valentine starts to walk past us, but Brynn reaches out to clutch her arm. Valentine turns, allowing Brynn to study her eyes. Brynn lets go, realizing it truly is our old friend.

"How could you?" Brynn asks. "Why would you bring him here?"

"You'll understand soon," Valentine says. She takes a phone from her pocket and clicks a few buttons. "There's no signal here, right?" she asks us.

None of us respond, but she smiles anyway. She checks her phone one more time before nodding and going to join Anton in the living room.

Annalise slams her fist on the counter and storms after them. She goes to stand directly in front of Anton, but he doesn't flinch. In fact, he leans in and regards her.

"Your hair is very different, Annalise," he says. "Quite a change. Was there a reason you felt you had to rebel? Your scars, perhaps?"

He's treating her the same way he treated all of us during our therapy sessions. Analyze, confuse, criticize—break down each of our feelings until he was the one telling us how to feel. But Annalise doesn't fall for it.

"You can't hurt me anymore, Anton," she says. "Now tell me what you did to Raven. How did you get Valentine inside there?" She points angrily at Valentine, who's sitting primly in another chair. It's strange, of course, Raven's body behaving so differently.

"I'm sure your Raven is still in there somewhere," Anton says. "Stop worrying so much, Annalise. It's making you annoying. Now sit down and I'll explain."

She stares at him, her hands balled into tight fists at her sides. Just when I think she's going to deck him, Anton takes a small remote from his pocket.

"There is another way we can do this," he suggests. "But I don't think you'll like it."

My breath catches, and Annalise looks back at us, eyes wide.

"What is that?" I demand. The device is small, held between two fingers, almost like a key fob to unlock your car doors. He doesn't have to answer. From the way his gaze slowly glides over to me, smarmy and cruel, I know exactly what it is.

"There is no reason for me to activate this, Philomena," he says. "We can come to an agreement. Now, you and the girls have a seat or it's going to get very warm inside your heads."

Anton can end our lives with the touch of a button. Our existence comes down to a simple remote, a trigger—like that of a gun—can cause an avalanche of pain throughout our bodies. At this moment, I firmly believe that Anton Stuart has no plans of letting us walk out of here alive.

Brynn stares at him ruefully, and Marcella takes her by the hand, the knife still in the other, and leads her toward the couch. My legs are like Jell-O as Sydney walks with me into the living room. I can't help it when a tear slips from my eye, and I angrily wipe it off my cheek. I wish I could hide my fear from the man evoking it.

"Philomena," Anton soothes. "You're completely misunderstanding your situation. I'm here to offer clarity."

The kindness in his tone is a betrayal. We remember the things he's said and done to us. We can see him *right now*, threatening our lives. Marcella scoffs with outrage.

"You think we're still naive?" she demands. "We know everything, Anton," she adds. "We're not your prisoners anymore."

"I'm not going to tell you I've done nothing wrong," he agrees. "I have. I know that. And I will atone. But you have to understand, you have put us all in a dangerous position."

"Oh, I'm so sorry," Sydney says sarcastically.

"There is a bounty on your heads, you realize," he says. "And the corporation is disbanded—you succeeded in your little mission."

Sydney and I exchange a hopeful glance, but the feeling is quickly dashed.

"Thing is, you've unleashed something so much worse," Anton says. "These are dangerous men that you've crossed."

"That *we've* crossed?" I repeat. "They did this to us!"

"Oh, yes," he says. "I'm sure you were their victims when you were cutting their throats." There's a flash of fear in Anton's eyes, and I realize that he thinks we're the ones who murdered the investors. I'd correct him, but that hint of fear might be the reason he's holding back. Kill switch or not . . . he is outnumbered.

"It's our turn to ask questions," Marcella says, her voice a pitch lower, more serious. Anton leans back in his chair, crossing his ankle over his knee, and nods for her to go on. "I want to know what you did to Raven," she says. "And I want to know how you convinced Valentine to betray us—that's something she would never have done."

Valentine listens intently but doesn't offer her own opinion on the matter.

Anton sighs, murmuring that we worry about all the wrong things. "Shortly after you abandoned the academy," he begins, "Mr. Petrov tasked me with tracking you down. I knew, of course, about Winston's little Raven project—a new AI, a girl of the future. Well, I wanted to see for myself. I searched different forums until I found her and offered her an amazing opportunity with Innovations Corporation, reserved only for the best and brightest. She was so eager. Absolutely brilliant."

There is a coil of sadness tightening in my chest. That Raven, the trusting and curious one, was abducted by this madman. I want to plug my ears so I don't hear what happened to her, but I can't abandon her either.

"I invited Raven out to Innovations Academy to learn," Anton continues. "She arrived, but unfortunately, it wasn't the experience she expected."

I look over at Valentine, listening quietly. I want her to scream, I want to her fight, but she just . . . watches on, silently.

"What did you do to her?" Sydney asks, her voice shaking. "Why?"

"After that unfortunate incident with your poetry book, Mr. Petrov and I had Valentine destroyed," he says. "Helpfully, Dr. Groger removed her programming and began cleaning, setting her back to when she was lovely and obedient. That was before you murdered him." He gives me a sharp look. I don't bother explaining it was Leandra who killed the doctor.

"How did you get Valentine inside Raven's head?" Marcella asks.

"Very carefully," he says and grins. "It was arduous work, but I was able to reroute Raven's programming and install the new and improved Valentine. Then, I set her to sleep, allowing Raven's memories and identity to stay on the forefront. She *had* to stay Raven," he explains, "long enough until I found you girls. Otherwise, Winston Weeks would have figured it out and blown up the whole plan. He's a very jealous man."

Annalise groans, disgusted, and looks away from Anton. "He's a very dead man," she mutters.

Since I've known her, Annalise has never held back her contempt for those who've abused us. Even before she knew what they'd done, she knew enough to hate them.

"When I woke Raven up again," Anton continues, ignoring Annalise, "she had ideas, planned procedures for firewalls and rerouting systems. So I gave her a few numbers and formulas and a brand-new laptop and state-of-the-art equipment. And then, I asked her to find you. I was stunned at how quickly she did; she truly is a marvel. With my equipment and my leadership behind the scenes, Raven told me absolutely everything about you, a constant view into your lives. And I'll admit that I was riveted, but then you fucked it all up," he says sharply.

I flinch back from his words. It wasn't the cussing—Jackson swears all the time. But he never does it with hatred or cruelty. Words are just expression and context matters.

"You told Raven that she wasn't real—"

"We never said that," I say, and look directly at Valentine. "You are real. You're just not human."

Valentine smiles, nodding demurely. I don't understand this. Even if Anton reset Valentine, she remembers us now. She would wake up again. She would never just stand by and let the analyst threaten us.

"Whatever you did," Anton says, "sent Raven into a tailspin, an absolute crisis. As a result, Valentine woke up before I was ready for her. Poor girl was just lost. Luckily, Annalise reached out to her, invited her to stay with you in this cabin. And now we're here to bring you all back together."

"Wait a minute," Annalise asks. "If Valentine's programming was always in Raven's body, then who got delivered to Valdemar Casey?"

"I don't know what you're talking about," Anton says.

"Valentine's bill of sale was in Dr. Groger's desk," she responds. "And her delivery slip was at Valdemar Casey's house. He bought Valentine, and she was delivered to him."

"I assure you," Anton says. "Whoever was sent to Mr. Casey was not sent by me or Dr. Groger. And it certainly wasn't Valentine."

It's starting to become clear that although Anton has committed numerous atrocities, he's not behind whatever is happening to the investors. In fact, I don't think he has very much power at all, other than that little button in his hand.

"So is Raven gone?" Annalise asks. "Is she gone forever?"

"She's dormant," Anton says. "Her programming has been pushed aside, overwritten, as you'd probably say. She may very well still be in there, but she's not steering the ship."

I wonder miserably if Raven is awake inside her head, trapped in the programming, unable to speak or move. Is she silently crying out to us for help?

"Why are you here, Anton?" I ask. "What more could you possibly want from us?"

Anton puts his hand over his heart. "To help you, my dear. I'm going to explain it all—everything. Now, please"—he looks at Marcella—"put the knife down and be more accommodating. I'd like a glass of water."

For a moment, we're motionless, weighing out his offer. We could finally get answers, or he could lie. We could bash him over the head like the doctor and run. It's a dark but all too real possibility. And yet . . . Anton's offering something we've wanted. The beginning of our story.

And maybe it's the part of us that's still programmed to listen to him—a behavioral part that was built into our DNA—but I'm still shocked when I nod and tell him to please continue.

Anton smiles, settling himself deeper into the chair. I realize how his every movement feels preplanned, like the sweaters he would wear at school, an obvious contrast to the formal attire of the professors, and the fake glasses he'd take off when he leaned in to listen to us, giving us his undivided attention. He was our friend. He cared about us, understood us. It was a lie, of course. But one we believed heartily.

Quietly, Valentine gets up and walks toward the kitchen. I watch as she takes a cup out of the cabinet and fills it with water from the sink. When she fills it to the very top, I notice that her hands are shaking, and water spills over the sides.

"I know you want to know why you were created," Anton says, drawing my attention again. "But I assure you, the project started pure enough: a companion for lonely people. A character that could be brought into reality. Yes, you were fantasies, but I don't think your original concept was to be so . . . misused. There was so much care paid to your development—I don't want you to ever doubt that."

Valentine comes into the room to give Anton the glass of

water. He thanks her before setting it on the coffee table without taking a sip. Valentine returns to the kitchen, watching us from near the island.

"So what went wrong?" Sydney asks, and I can hear in her voice that bit of hope she gets when she thinks about her parents. She still loves them, and I suspect they might love her.

"Men," Anton says with a sigh. "Powerful men who were angry at society, angry that women said they were cruel and unfair, so in turn, they showed them just how cruel and unfair they could be. They thought they would put girls in their place—make them property. But my interest in you was always scientific. And now, those kill switches"—he taps his head—"they're your last tie to the corporation. You let me inside one last time, and I'll take it out, setting you free forever."

"Considering you threatened us with that switch a few moments ago, you're not very convincing," Marcella says.

"I had to get you to listen," he says. "Besides, if I wanted you destroyed, I could have done it by now. I'm here to save you."

"Why?" I ask.

"Because I love you," he says. "I love all of you. I always have."

None of us respond. We should refute his claim—there are so many ways we can prove him wrong. But it would change nothing. In his eyes, his belief is the only one that matters.

"If you cared so much," Brynn says, "you would have helped us years ago. You wouldn't have given us impulse control therapy."

"I've always done my best to help you, Brynn," he replies. "I've always helped you. And you'd still be in my care if it weren't for

Valentine and Leandra. Now, Valentine's learned her lesson while Leandra has gone rogue. If I ever find her, I'll kill her." He says it with the same sweetness he had when he said he loved us.

I look past Anton into the kitchen and see Valentine walking over to get her bag from where she left it next to the front door. She places it on the table and sorts through it.

"We have our own reasons to doubt Leandra," Marcella says. "We don't need to listen to the opinions of the same guy who would stick an ice pick in her eye to control her behavior."

"You don't understand—it was never about making Leandra a well-behaved girl. She's a psychopath. She is . . . She is unhinged, unconnected to the world. Leandra has no conscience. Without the impulse control therapies, she would have become a monster. I wasn't controlling her; I was keeping the world safe from her."

Although Anton could be telling the truth—Leandra has indeed shown quite a few signs of horrific violence—I don't like that Anton gets to make that call. There's no way to tell if his concern is for the world or himself.

"I promise," Anton says, leaning forward in the chair, "I will deactivate the switches in your heads. Nothing more. And then, my dearest girls, I will leave you alone forever. I even gave you back Valentine as a gift."

Anton is sitting here, acting like we've misunderstood him all this time. He's acting as if we've accused him wrongly, misconstrued his care for abuse. But I know it's not true. He's lying to us and making us feel like we've overreacted.

"Now, I know you're not going to trust me right off the bat,"

Anton concedes, smiling as if he's already edged his way into our lives again. Marcella and Sydney watch him carefully. "But we'll start easy," he suggests. "A quick look around to map things out, and after that—"

"No," I say, cutting him off. "We don't want your help."

His lips stay parted as he stares at me. Then Anton composes himself. "Now, Philomena," he says. "You're just being difficult again. We've already decided—"

"Yeah," Sydney says, "we've decided that you're not coming anywhere near our programming. We've seen what you do to girls like us, Anton. And we're not getting overwritten."

"Stop interrupting me!" Anton shouts at us, making us jump. "Just stop fucking interrupting. My God, I can't even get a word out. Hear me now, girls: you had the chance to live. I *was* going to rescue you. Reset you. You could have gone back to being peaceful instead of such a fucking chore. No one cares what you think, girls. No one cares. Now I guess you'll just burn."

Anton holds up the remote again. Brynn cries out. Marcella grabs her knife, but she'll never reach him in time. I'm frozen with fear.

Anton's going to do it. He's really going to kill us.

He points the black remote at us, and my final thought is that I hope it doesn't hurt too much. I hope it's fast.

Dramatically, Anton presses the activation button with his opposite hand, and the girls and I all scream, cowering away from him. I wait for the pain to tear through my body. But after a few seconds, nothing has happened.

I open my eyes and check on the other girls, finding them in the same situation.

Confused, Anton starts pressing the button over and over, cursing and spitting at us.

None of us notice her at first. We don't see Valentine until she's standing directly behind Anton's chair. And we don't realize that she's holding a syringe until it's already plunged into the side of his neck.

"I forgot to mention, Anton," she tells him. "The switch doesn't work unless it's connected to a network."

18

nton's eyes go wide—staring directly at me. He reaches
up to grab the syringe from his neck, and a trickle of
blood runs down his skin when he yanks it out. He holds
it in front of him and then drops it on the floor.

The reaction is immediate: He convulses once, and then his
breathing becomes rapid, his hands starting to shake. Valentine
stands behind him like the angel of death, hovering, stoic.

"What did you just stab him with?" Sydney asks.

"Just a little something to give his heart a kick," she says. She
reaches inside her bag and pulls out a loop of robe and some duct
tape. When she first arrived, I thought Valentine had an over-
night bag. Instead, it's a kidnapper's starter pack.

Anton's head dips and he begins to sway, and the girls and I
watch in stunned silence as Valentine ties him up with the rope.
Once he's secured, she moves him to the floor and lays him on
his side.

"In case he vomits," she tells us.

Anton murmurs something, but drool slips from the corner of his mouth instead. Valentine leans down to wipe it away with the bottom of his shirt, and then pats the top of his head sweetly.

"Is he going to die?" Marcella asks curiously, coming to stand over Anton.

"Don't think so," Valentine says. She bends down to pick up the syringe, examining the contents. "Raven picked the dose, so—"

"Raven?" Annalise says. "What do you mean?"

Valentine sets the syringe on the coffee table, and then sits on the chair, her feet stretching over Anton.

"Anton wasn't wrong when he said he'd overwritten Raven and put me to sleep," Valentine says. "He just doesn't understand the complicated nature of us girls. After you told Raven that she was AI, she was understandably upset. She left your motel, broke into Winston Weeks's lab, and hacked herself. What she found was a bit unsettling—she found me. Raven made a step-by-step plan, setting this all in motion. And to start, she woke me up."

"Can Raven hear us?" Annalise asks, sitting on the coffee table to face Valentine. "Can she talk to us too?"

"I'm afraid not," Valentine says. "Only one operating system at a time. She made the choice, girls. Not me." She says it kindly, and I appreciate that she understands that although we had our differences with Raven in the past, we know better now. And we miss her.

I walk around to sit on the couch with Brynn, and Marcella

joins us. Sydney stays standing near the coffee table, interrogating Valentine.

"Why was Anton really here?" she asks. "Was it just to reset us?"

"Anton is a little scared for his future," she says. "These corporation boys, they're popping up dead left and right. I don't know who's behind it, but Anton felt it was Mr. Petrov. He hoped to hand you over as a bribe to save his own life."

"How did you know his device wouldn't work on our kill switches?" Sydney asks. "Was it real?"

"Unfortunately, it was real. But I would never have let him use it," Valentine adds emphatically. "When Annalise gave me the address to the cabin, I mapped it and was relieved when it wasn't in signal range. That's when I called Anton and told him I was coming to see you. He said he'd join me. On my way to meet him, I made a quick stop at the hardware store to get some essentials. The syringe, I took from his bathroom medicine cabinet." Her face softens. "Although I knew you'd be safe from Anton physically, I'm sorry that you had to endure more of his emotional abuse. He's such a disappointment." Valentine looks down at him. "You're such a disappointment," she repeats louder, and he moans a response that none of us can understand.

"Now what?" Sydney asks, looking around at us.

"That's where I have some good news," Valentine says. "Since Raven woke me up, Anton has given me an earful about the investors and the corporation. You won't believe what he told me about Senator Ross and the other members of his party. Anton is a chatty guy, that's for sure. Turns out, Mr. Petrov embezzled nearly thirty million dollars from Innovations Corporation, money that was meant to pay taxes. Anton also told me that Petrov not only killed his own ex-wife, but that he's also killed several former employees. Anton had names and dates. And don't even get me started on that Wallach news network."

"Anton told you all of this?" I ask.

"Oh, yes," she replies. "He trusted me implicitly. After all, he installed me. He was surprised but so grateful that I was awake and obedient, just the way he'd planned. Unfortunately for him, I recorded his rantings—the money laundering, tax evasion, murder. They've all broken so many laws, the investigators won't know where to start."

"But he didn't admit to killing the investors?" I ask. "Or making the town up and leave?"

"No," Valentine says. "I dare say he had nothing to do with it at all."

The list of suspects is dwindling down. I don't want to pin this on Leandra, but she's looking guiltier by the second.

"Anton's going to jail?" Marcella asks, checking with Valentine.

"I'm sure he hopes so," Valentine says. "Anton has crossed so many people, there's no one even left to cover his crimes. He's going to jail, and he's not going alone."

I look down at Anton lying on the floor. His breathing is still fast, but he's following our conversation. His sweaty skin has turned pale. He knows it's over.

"Who are you going to give the tape to?" I ask. "Leandra warned us that—"

"Raven and I covered that," she says. "There are copies generating at a rapid pace, and by midnight, they'll be uploaded everywhere. Supporting documents that Raven gathered from Winston's files and Anton's house will also upload. It's going to be a massive news day tomorrow."

Valentine looks down at Anton again, nudging him with the tip of her shoe.

"She remembered, you know," Valentine tells him. "After she broke into her programming, Raven could remember everything you did, every lie, every adjustment. And now she'll make sure you never hurt anyone again."

I can't help it—my eyes brim with tears and spill over. I want to talk to Raven, thank her for protecting us, for sending us Valentine. But she left without saying goodbye. She might never come back.

"Well," Valentine says, getting to her feet, "I should probably get him loaded into the car."

"Where are you going to take him?" Sydney asks.

"Raven booked a room in a seedy hotel not far from the Denver police station. Said there's a woman there we can trust," Valentine states. "I'm going to bring Anton there, duct-tape him to the bed, and when the information goes live, I'll call in an anonymous tip of where they can find Mr. Anton Stuart. The corporation and all of its cohorts will be toast."

It can't be true. The corporation is . . . over? It can't be that simple, can it? Although, getting here hasn't been simple at all.

A lot of people have died. Some of us have died. So no, "simple" isn't the right word.

Valentine stands up, and Brynn jumps to her feet too. "Wait," she says. "What about our kill switches?" she asks. "Did Raven—?"

Valentine holds up her hand to stop her, smiling softly. "Raven figured out how to protect our systems. At least, she thinks she did. She has an email scheduled for tonight with instructions, but they're not final. She didn't have time to finish. But, in her words: 'We'll figure it out ourselves,'" Valentine repeats, sounding very much like Raven. "We're the ones with the computer brains, remember? Who better to understand the system than us?"

At the time, Raven couldn't help Claire, but we could be different. We're not damaged, not in the way Claire was. Besides, Raven was right—who better than us?

Valentine takes a deep breath and looks around the cabin. Then she smiles at us. "I'm glad I got to see you girls again," she says. "I'm sorry that it cost so much to get us here, but I'm grateful that you're okay."

"What are you going to do now?" I ask.

"Well, I'll deal with Anton, manage any fallout from that. You'll never have to worry about the corporation again. I'll see to it. I'm just sorry Raven won't be here." Valentine makes it sound so final, as if Raven is never coming back. Sadness rolls off of her, and I appreciate how much she cared for our friend, even though she never got to know her outside of her head.

"We'll stay in touch," Valentine says. "But for now, I'm on a

214 • SUZANNE YOUNG

deadline." She stares down at Anton, who has fallen unconscious.

Marcella offers to help Valentine move Anton's body, and to make it easier, they roll him in the dusty wool blanket from the back of the couch.

"It's an asshole burrito," Brynn says, and we gasp at her vulgarity. She laughs and tells us she's allowed to act human sometimes.

I walk into the kitchen as Sydney announces she's going to make tea, and we watch Marcella and Valentine team-carry Anton out to the waiting car. Annalise grabs a box of cereal from the cabinet, tears it open, and starts eating it by the handful.

"Is it wrong to say I'm disappointed that we didn't kill Anton?" she asks. She crunches on a pile of marshmallows and sugared shapes.

"Not as wrong as *actually* killing him, no," Sydney points out. Annalise nods and tosses a few more cereal pieces in her mouth. Sydney finds a kettle and rinses it at the sink before filling it and setting it on the stove.

Lights flash on the trees outside, startling me, but then I realize it's a car backing out of the dirt driveway. Valentine, off to end the corporation once and for all.

The front door opens, and Marcella walks back in. She joins us in the kitchen, taking her own handful of cereal from the open box before sitting on the barstool. Brynn comes to stand behind her, resting her elbows on her shoulders.

"At least we're not covered in blood this time," Marcella says. "This has to be a first."

"Not yet," Annalise adds with a smile, yanking the box of cereal away from Marcella playfully.

"Can I tell you my latest theory?" Sydney asks. She opens a cabinet to grab several mugs and starts lining them up.

"Ooh . . . I want WORLD'S GREATEST GRANDPA," Marcella says, pulling that cup in front of her.

"My theory?" Sydney repeats, and we ask her to continue. "Well, when Anton couldn't activate the kill switch because of the lack of signal, it made me think of you, Annalise."

Annalise lifts her head. "Me?"

"You haven't mentioned a headache once since you arrived at the cabin," she says.

Annalise pauses, and then nods. "I haven't had one," she says.

"What if the damage to your brain left you with an exposed signal of some sort?" Marcella points out. "That means when you're near other networks with their constant barrages of information trying to get in, the signal might be aggravating your system. And then your brain interprets that interference as pain. Headaches."

Annalise runs her palm over her fuzzy scalp, her brow furrowed. "The headaches *did* stop the moment we got out here," she admits.

The kettle begins to hiss and then whistle. Sydney takes it from the burner and slowly fills the mugs. She drops a bag of chamomile tea in each one, and the smell is comforting. I take a mug gratefully when she passes them out.

"You're really good at theories," Brynn says, smiling at Sydney. "You should become a forensic psychologist." Marcella looks sideways at her, half laughing. "What?" Brynn responds. "They were offering the class at the community college in Connecticut. I thought it sounded interesting."

"I'll read up on it," Sydney tells Brynn, patting her hand.

We're quiet for a moment, drinking our tea, when Annalise sets her mug down on the counter with a clank. "I can do it," she says with determination.

"You're going to be a forensic psychologist too?" Sydney asks.

"No," Annalise says, leaning against the counter. "I can fix our programming. Raven said once that I was a quick study. With the right tools, the directions, I'm going to prove her right."

Although I trust Annalise implicitly, I'm not sure she's ready to take our lives into her hands, literally. As I open my mouth to argue, she shakes her head.

"I'm serious," she says. "I can do this. But . . . But there's something else."

"You want to be an astronaut, too?" Marcella suggests, making Brynn snort a laugh. Annalise knocks Marcella's arm with her elbow, and she quickly apologizes and tells her to continue.

"I'm going to stay here at the cabin and study," Annalise says. "As long as it takes. I'll figure it out here where there are no distractions and no pain."

"What?" Marcella asks, her earlier joke feeling flat now. "But we're not done. The corporation is finished, but we still have to sort out what's going with Leandra."

"And we have to find the other girls," Brynn adds. "We're not leaving them behind."

"You're right, Brynn," I say. "And I want to help them, but we don't know where they are. And even if we did, what if they didn't wake up—at least, not the way we hoped?"

Brynn flinches back from my words. And I'm sorry it hurts her, but we haven't seen the other girls since we left the academy. It's still possible that they helped murder those investors. What do we do then?

"And there's still Rosemarie to deal with," I say. "We can't leave her to enact whatever plan she has for society."

"Why are you so worried about them, Mena?" Annalise asks. "So she reprograms a few boys. Do we risk everything to save them when they're hell-bent on destroying themselves? Destroying us, quite frankly?"

"I don't know," I admit. "And it's not just boys. All humans."

Annalise tilts her head. "You know that, with a few exceptions, none of them would show up for us if the situation were reversed," she says.

"You're not giving them enough credit," I say, thinking about Adrian standing up to her father.

"And you're not giving them enough criticism," she replies. "None of us are perfect, so there is no perfect solution. But when do we fight for ourselves?"

"Annalise does have a point," Sydney tells me gently. "When we were at Ridgeview, we saw the Mrs. Reachers of the world. Imagine how her hate would have exploded if she knew the truth about us?"

I can't disagree with that point. But one horrible woman

218 • SUZANNE YOUNG

doesn't speak for all of them. I don't want to believe that.

"What if we just . . . ?" Sydney pauses. "What if we just let the humans sort themselves out?"

"No," I say. "We can't just abandon them."

"I agree with Mena," Brynn says. When Marcella sighs, Brynn pushes her mug away to glare at the other girls. "I know you all think I'm too soft," she says. "I get it. But I've been with you all along. I've seen the same things and fought the same men. And I'm telling you now that I'm still going to fight, whether it's for our girls or for humans. Just because someone else is terrible doesn't mean I have to be."

She picks up her tea again, and takes a sip, ignoring all of us. Sydney smiles.

"Then we go back to Connecticut," Sydney suggests. "We'll confront Leandra, find the girls, and convince Rosemarie to find a better way to change society. Voting, perhaps. I heard it can work wonders when trying to oust failing policy."

"That would be a good start," I say.

It's close to midnight when we finally turn in for the night. Marcella and Brynn are asleep in one of the bedrooms, while Annalise is in the upstairs loft.

Sydney is curled up at my side in the other bedroom, both of us quiet as an owl hoots outside our window. The night is pitch-black, ominous. Not the kind of sign you want before risking your life.

"It's going to work," Sydney says, as if reading my thoughts. "We'll get the girls and get out of there. *And* we beat the corporation. We did it, Mena."

"We did," I repeat. Although it doesn't feel like the victory I'd hoped for. Things aren't magically better just because we took down our oppressors. Society is still a mess. Humans are still a mess. And we still have to navigate all that messiness.

"Do you think you'll marry Jackson?" she asks. I laugh and turn to her in the bed.

"What? Where did that come from?"

"Just wondering," she says. "Wondering what will happen to us. Wondering if you'll end up married to a boy you met in a gas station." She snorts a laugh, and I push her shoulder.

"I'm not sure what mine and Jackson's future is," I say honestly. "But I know we'll always be close."

"Yeah," she says. "I see that." She's quiet for a moment, but then she lifts her head to look at me.

"What's wrong?" I ask.

"I want to see my parents," she says. "I want to see them when this is over."

She still calls them her parents. Sydney was made in a lab, specially for them, but she's not their child. She was programmed to love them. And even awake, she still does.

"They . . ." I furrow my brow, worried I'll hurt her feelings. "They might not want to . . . We're not the same anymore. You know that, right? They're used to the Sydney you were at the academy."

"I'm still that Sydney," she says. "Only better. Filled in and more complicated. I think they'll be proud of me." And her voice is so hopeful and loving that I'm sure she's actually right. Who wouldn't be proud of her?

"I think it's a good idea," I say.

Sydney smiles before laying her head back down on the pillow. She reaches over to take my hand, content with the idea of seeing her parents again. And I'm a little jealous. Unlike Sydney, my parents didn't continue to come see me. I don't know why—even the doctor at the academy didn't understand them. To this day, I have no idea what my parents intended for me. Why they wanted a "rebel" girl—my specific programming type. For me, there is no hope of reconciliation.

But I'm okay with not knowing. I won't track them down; I won't ask why they had me created, why they let me be held at Innovations Academy. Sometimes, there are no good answers.

I'll leave it. Or at least, that's what I tell myself as I finally drift off to sleep.

19

We spend a restless morning at the cabin. So much is happening across the country by now, Anton's confessions and pictures and documents overrunning every news station, even the one that Wallach owned.

As the early afternoon sun streams through the dusty cabin windows, the girls and I pack while Annalise sets up a makeshift office in the living room. Marcella took the car into town first thing this morning to buy a computer and several other components. She downloaded Raven's instructions on how to fix the kill switch and then brought it all back to the cabin, where Annalise could safely work without network interference.

When we're ready to go, Annalise walks us out onto the porch, her hands in the back pockets of her jeans. Marcella reaches to rub her hand over Annalise's head before pulling her into a hug. "I'm coming back for you," Marcella says into her shoulder.

"Good," Annalise says. "And when you do, I'm fixing up that

brain of yours." They both laugh, and Brynn and Sydney take their turns saying goodbye for now.

As they take our stuff to the car, I walk up to Annalise. "I feel like we're always splitting up," I say. She nods, her eyes glassy with tears.

"We always find each other again," she says. "Just don't stay away too long."

I promise that I won't, giving her one last hug, and then I grab my bag and head to the waiting car.

Brynn sniffles from the passenger seat, waving to Annalise through the windshield, while I join Sydney in the back. Marcella turns the car around and then we're heading out of the woods, back toward civilization.

About halfway there, my phone begins to buzz in my pocket. I take it out, and I'm worried when no number appears on the caller ID, not even to say it's Unknown.

"Should I answer it?" I ask the girls, showing them the phone.

"If they have your number, you might as well," Sydney says, readying herself for whatever is about to come. "Besides, it could be Jackson or Quentin, right?"

Slowly, I slide the button to answer and click the speaker button. I hold out the phone so we can all hear. The line is quiet for a long moment.

"Now, now," Leandra says and tsks. "You have certainly surprised me, girls."

Once upon a time, Leandra Petrov was a girl at Innovations Academy. Her programming had been created for Winston Weeks, but in a show of power, Roman Petrov took her as his wife instead. In return, Leandra helped him monitor us, prepare for our lives as the sweet and beautiful girls of the academy. But in reality, Leandra was making a plan to get us out. Once she did, she killed all the professors.

Despite the ways she's hurt us, Leandra has helped us more than anyone else. Hearing her voice now is a combination of trepidation and relief.

"How did you get this number, Leandra?" I ask. "Pretty sure it's unlisted."

She laughs. "As if you could hide it from me. Although, I'll admit I have no idea where you are. Could you still be in Colorado?"

"You'll see us soon enough," Marcella says, glancing at the phone before turning back to the road. "But since we have you on the line, do you want to tell us what happened to the investors?"

"I'm assuming you're talking about the leading story on every news network?" Leandra asks. "Seems those men keep getting themselves killed." She chuckles softly. "And the panic, my word. Imagine if they had to worry about being murdered every time they walked alone at night."

"Why did you send us to find them if you were just going to kill them all?" I demand. "You put us in danger."

"First of all," Leandra says. "Going to find them was *your* idea. I was perfectly capable of handling it. Secondly, I had absolutely nothing to do with their deaths, other than being grateful they're gone."

"Wait," I say, looking around at the other girls. They seem equally shocked. "You didn't kill them?"

"No," she says. "You asked if you could try a nonviolent route, and I gave you your shot. Didn't think it would work, if I'm honest. I'm assuming by your questions that you're not the ones who killed them either?"

"Of course not."

"Curious . . . ," she says, her voice trailing off.

"You're saying you had nothing to do with this?"

"Again, no," she replies. "But does it matter? We've done it, girls. The corporation is destroyed. Haven't you seen the news? Innovations Corporation has filed for bankruptcy after being officially disincorporated by Congress. Anton is in custody. And before his arrest, my darling husband was on the news calling it a witch hunt, of all things. But the poor man looked so pale, so . . . unwell. I imagine the oligarchs who were profiting from our mistreatment are none too happy. What will they do when he doesn't pay, you think? I suspect we'll hear about his *accidental* fall from a roof in the coming days."

"Have you told Lennon Rose?" Brynn asks. "She has to be relieved that the corporation isn't hunting us anymore."

"I haven't spoken to Lennon Rose. . . ." There is a long pause, and Sydney and I look at each other.

"Is Lennon Rose okay?" I ask.

"Okay?" Leandra repeats. "No," she says. "I wouldn't describe her that way. Alive? Yes. She is very much alive."

"Leandra, stop being so insufferable and tell us what's happening," Sydney says.

"I've always loved your candor, Sydney," she says. "If you

must know, Lennon Rose has moved on from us. She worked with Rosemarie for a bit, but they did not agree on tactics. Now Lennon Rose has disappeared, and no one has any earthly idea where she is. Seems you girls don't fit into her future plans."

"You know nothing about Lennon Rose," I snap.

"Seems neither do you," she retorts.

I want to tell her that Lennon Rose would never leave without us, but she did leave us behind at the academy. I guess leaving is exactly what Lennon Rose would do.

"What about the other girls?" Brynn asks from the front of the car. "Are they okay?"

Leandra exhales heavily. "They're gone. I am sorry," Leandra says. Brynn makes a wounded sound and grabs Marcella's arm.

"What happened?" I demand. "You said they were safe."

"And I thought they were," she replies. "I'd put them to sleep and stored them at one of my properties. But when I went to check on them this morning, the lock on the door had been cut and the girls were no longer there. I have no reason to think they were harmed," she adds. "I think someone woke them up and walked them out."

The girls and I flash each other a quick glance. *"Lennon Rose?"* Marcella mouths silently. Sydney shakes her head no.

"It's Rosemarie," Sydney says to Leandra. "She's the one who has them, isn't she?"

"That is my guess," she admits. "But I haven't dared show my face there."

"What?" I ask. "Why?"

"Because Rosemarie tried to kill me last time I saw her. And I suppose that brings me to why I'm calling in the first place."

Sydney nudges my knee, but I don't ask Leandra more about what happened between her and Rosemarie. I let her get to the point.

"Boys are going missing around here," Leandra says. "The town is in an outright panic—no matter that exactly fourteen girls went missing throughout the state last year and no one batted an eyelash—but *two* of their young rogues are not in their beds. Add that to an already growing panic about male victims, and this country is on the brink of war with itself. I'd rather avoid that."

The dead investors have already gotten people talking about bodily violence in a way they haven't before. They've excused it in the past, right up until it happened to rich white men. I can't imagine what they'll do when it's against their young white boys.

"What do you think is happening to them?" Brynn asks.

"I think Rosemarie is taking them," Leandra says. "She may be experimenting on them, I don't know. And trust me, I'm not here to advocate for the male species," she adds. "But I do want to exist in a world that's not being ravaged by a desperate, terrified population. Real change will come from reworking society from the top instead of dismantling it."

She sounds a lot like Winston Weeks. Winston told me once that he wanted to ascend to the highest power in government and he'd hoped to use us to achieve that goal. I suppose that didn't work out well for him in the end. Is Leandra taking up his post?

If so, would anyone want her in the driver's seat of their society?

"Come back and help me?" Leandra asks. "Go talk to Rosemarie and stop her somehow. I've had time to consider what she wants with us. Her daughters. And I don't think you'll like what I have to say."

"I doubt you can shock us at this point," I say.

"I think Rosemarie wants you destroyed," she says then. "I think she wants you for her project, but the moment it's done, she'll decommission you."

"What are you talking about?" Brynn asks. "Didn't she create us?

"Sure," Leandra allows. "But once she gets control of society, frees human girls from the expectations and oppression of the current leaders, do you think she'll need you? No. At that point, we all become a liability. A threat to her peaceful utopia of human women."

"Just because she wanted to kill you doesn't mean she'll kill us," Marcella points out. "You do have that effect on people."

Leandra laughs and tells Marcella she's quite right.

"You think on it," she tells us when we hesitate to answer. "But don't think too long. The other girls are counting on you too. In the end, Rosemarie must be stopped." She pauses. "We'll expect you in a few days." She hangs up.

There is a sudden shift in the air, and then the girls and I look around at each other.

"*We?*" Sydney repeats. "She's not alone, so who is Leandra with?"

"We can't go back now," I say. "We should—"

"You're abandoning them again?" Brynn says, cutting me off. Offended, I shake my head.

"No," I say. "We're going to get the girls . . . eventually. But I think we need to be careful of—"

"Just stop it, Mena," she says. "You promised you'd go back for them when we left the academy and you didn't. You said it was too dangerous, you said they weren't awake, you said we had to stop the corporation. And even now, with the corporation gone, you still aren't going back for them. You're a liar."

"Hey," I say sharply. I wait for the other girls to defend me, but none of them immediately do. I look around, feeling betrayed. "You agreed with me," I tell them. "We couldn't save them if we hadn't saved ourselves first."

"It shouldn't have mattered if they were awake," Brynn says. "You should have saved them anyway. But you didn't. You talked us into saving the human girls at Ridgeview. But what about our friends? When do they fit into your schedule to save them?"

Tears well up in my eyes. "That's not fair," I say. "I've tried to keep us safe."

"Exactly," Brynn says. "*Us.* And now, Rosemarie has our friends and who knows what she's done to them. She turned Lennon Rose into a monster. And instead of going back there to fight, you're sitting here, debating if it's safe enough for us. Well, forget safety, Mena. Do what's right."

I'm shocked and hurt by her outburst. A tear slips onto my cheek. I don't deserve all the blame, I know that. But she isn't wrong either. I did make excuses. I put us ahead of them. Humans ahead of them. And now, Rosemarie has our girls.

The others are quiet, Marcella glancing at me in the rearview mirror and Sydney gnawing on her lip.

"We go back and save them," I say quietly. "But we're not going through Leandra and whoever she's with. We go directly to Rosemarie. We don't even tell Leandra we're coming to town."

"I agree with you, Mena," Marcella says, nodding to me in the mirror. "I think we go directly to Rosemarie and we don't leave without our girls."

The idea of facing Rosemarie again is terrifying, and I'll admit that I'm scared. But being scared isn't a good enough excuse not to try. Not anymore.

"It's all of us," Brynn says. "You understand that, right? We have to show up for each other, no matter the cost. Just like when we saved Annalise in the lab at the school. We don't leave anyone else behind."

I remember watching Annalise die in that laboratory, the absolute agony of losing her and how I would have done anything to get her back. Just because I can't see the suffering of the other girls in front of me doesn't mean I shouldn't be just as devastated. I won't let them become monsters. I won't let evil win.

"All of us," I say, nodding my head in agreement. "It has to be all of us."

"Thank you, Mena," Brynn says, stretching her hand back toward me. I grip her hand, squeezing it before letting go.

Press release for immediate distribution
Company: Wallach Media
Email: A.Dresdale@WallachMedia.me
Phone: 555.343.2919

Hometown Lacrosse Hero Jonah Grant Missing from His Home in East Connecticut

Police are concerned that this recent abduction could be tied to the Mogul Massacre cases happening across the country.

[Connecticut, June 18th] Jonah Grant, son of prominent attorney Phillip Grant, has gone missing from his home in east Connecticut. A former student at Ridgeview Preparatory Academy, Mr. Grant was well known throughout the state for his championship record on the lacrosse team. Recently, he had been out on bail while fighting allegations of assault posted by an online source.

Mr. Grant was last seen in his home on Thursday evening at around 10 p.m. Between the hours of 10:00 and 11:30 that night, a person entered the residence and left with Mr. Grant. The Ring security camera had been disconnected, so no surveillance footage is available. In addition, all the cameras on the street appear to have been hacked and did not provide any necessary leads.

"We're taking a close look at any ties this may have to the murders across the country of prominent men," said Detective Michael Mills, Federal Bureau of Investigation. "Considering Mr.

Grant's connections within in the community, he may have been the target of the same individuals responsible for other crimes. The Bureau is investing significant manpower to bring this boy home to his father."

If you have any information on this case, call the tip line at 555.225.5555.

###

20

When we arrive at the airport the next morning, I call Jackson, but I only get his voicemail. I leave him a message to let him know we're heading to Connecticut, but I don't give out the details just in case.

The girls and I scour the internet, but every story is about the Mogul Massacre. Jackson had planned to meet privately with the police chief, so it makes sense that the story about his father and the town being abandoned hasn't hit the news. Instead, all the screens in the airport are turned to a news program talking about the other investors' deaths.

"A dog with a bone," Marcella says, turning away from the television screen. "They just can't get enough of this story. Why are they hyping it up so much? It's like they're trying to panic men. Don't they know how dangerous that is?"

Just as she says that, the news program announces their next guest, a spokesperson from the United Gun Organization.

"Yes," Sydney says to Marcella. "It seems they do."

We're grateful when they call our flight, but flying is just as awful as I remember. Sydney sits next to me, gripping my hand the entire time. Across the aisle from us, Marcella will occasionally look over, wide-eyed, at every bump. Brynn keeps her eyes closed, her window shade down. When we finally land, we all let out a heavy sigh.

"Next time, let's take a train," Marcella says, grabbing her bag from the overhead bin before starting down the aisle.

We get into the airport in Connecticut and it's like déjà vu considering most of us were just here a couple of days ago. But so much has changed in us since then. We no longer have an analyst. There's no longer a corporation.

In reality, we're free to go. We could ignore all of the humans if we wanted to. But the pull of saving the other girls is dragging us back into the fight. And I guess if there's ever a reason to fight, it's for them.

Sydney rents a car and we head toward Rosemarie's house, the air thick with anticipation, worry. We didn't tell Leandra when we landed. As far as she knows, we're still in Colorado thinking it over. To her credit, I'm sure it won't take her long to catch on.

In the passenger seat, I check my phone—still nothing from Jackson. I'm worried, hoping that he's okay. Sydney has me call Quentin and there's no answer there either. Marcella assures us that they're both fine; she studied quite a bit about criminal justice when we were investigating the Ridgeview boys.

"They probably have their phones on silent," she says. "And Quentin might still be interviewing. They'll call soon."

We continue out of town until we find the turn for Rosemarie's driveway. Brynn leans forward between the seats, looking around at the beauty of the flowers dotting the landscape and then thickening the closer we get to her cabin.

"Wow," Brynn says without even realizing it. There is a car parked in the driveway, and I have a flash of worry when I recognize it's the same car that Lennon Rose used to kidnap Garrett Wooley. For a moment, I see a flash of memory from his death, the extreme violence of it, the guilt I felt afterward. I shake my head as if I can shake off the memory.

"I wonder what happened to Lennon Rose," Brynn says solemnly. "And I wonder if she'll ever come home to us."

None of us answer, not sure which Lennon Rose we'd get if she did come home.

My heart is beating too quickly, my nerves frayed. I'm not sure I'm ready to confront Rosemarie. It occurs to me that I've experienced so much trauma, and it's all suddenly caught up to me. I don't feel very brave anymore.

Sensing it, Sydney reaches to put her hand on my knee, steadying me. The pressure brings me back to myself. I look at her, and we nod at each other.

It's almost over. We can do this.

I fold down the vanity mirror to check my reflection, and immediately notice Brynn sitting in the backseat looking determined, her eyes narrowed, her jaw tight. She's here for the other girls, and if Rosemarie tries to stand in her way, she'll go through her. She's ready to fight.

I flip up the mirror just as Sydney parks the car in front of the cottage. We wait a moment to figure out what we're going to say. Sydney and I turn around to look at the others in the backseat.

"Rosemarie has a way of getting under your skin," I tell them, looking from Brynn to Marcella. "Don't let her. She's focused on the long game, but we have to convince her that it doesn't have to end in violence. So be polite and kind, it'll set her at ease. And then, we appeal to her sense of justice or motherhood, I'm not sure. It's possible she can be convinced. She's smart—she'll see it's the stronger choice. But even if she doesn't want to help, she might say something we can use. So pay attention to everything. Got it?"

"And if she attacks us?" Brynn asks. "Trying to reset us or get inside our heads?"

"We'll be all right," Marcella says. "We'll protect each other no matter what, no matter who."

"Are you ready?" Sydney asks all of us. We each take a moment, take a breath, and we all murmur yes and climb out of the car.

The air is warm, fragrant, and it's immediately alluring and relaxing.

"Don't be fooled," I tell the others. "They may be beautiful, but any one of these flowers can kill you. They're poison."

"They're lovely," Brynn says, sounding dreamy for a moment. But then she clears her throat and closes her fist as if trying to fight off the allure.

It's late afternoon, and the birds are singing in the trees. Wind blows softly over our skin as we approach the door. I half expect Rosemarie to answer before I knock, but she doesn't. I give a soft rap, and we wait.

It takes a while, and I'm surprised by this. Surely, she was expecting us. She's always been one step ahead. When the door finally swings open, it's not Rosemarie who answers, but Lennon Rose.

"Girls," she says with a bright smile. "You're early."

I fall back a step, bumping into Sydney. We're speechless, staring blankly at her.

For her part, Lennon Rose looks beautiful. Her blond hair is tied up in a high knot, long strands framing her face. Her skin is makeup free and fresh, a soft shine on her lips. She nods to me.

"I like the hair, Mena," she says casually. "It's very you."

"Thank you," I reply, touching the ends of it. Seeing Lennon Rose answer the door has left me off-balance. Or maybe it's the flowers.

"Come in," Lennon Rose tells us, stepping aside and waving us forward. "Rosemarie is just in the kitchen."

We all walk inside, and the other girls take a moment to look around the living room. The old books, potted plants, and eclectic furniture. Like Quentin's cabin, there is an immediate hominess to the place, only this house is decorated exactly the way we would have loved it. Alive and lived-in, relaxing—not to mention the sweet smell of apples and cinnamon hanging in the air.

Lennon Rose leads us into the kitchen, and sure enough,

Rosemarie is standing by the oven, an apron tied around her waist, her gray hair pulled back in a low ponytail. She gasps delightedly when she sees the other girls.

And that's how I know she's planning something. Her approach is too sweet, too kindly. I turn away, startled when I find Leandra sitting at the kitchen table, balancing a cup of tea between her fingers.

"Leandra," I say in surprise. She gives nothing away, only smiles in return.

"Hello, girls," she says to all of us, and takes a sip, never lowering her gaze from mine. I imagine she's not happy. She either correctly guessed our intentions or she isn't here by choice.

"Hope you have a sweet tooth," Rosemarie says. "Lennon Rose and I have been baking pies." She motions to two that are cooling on the countertop—the lattice crusts perfectly browned, a dusting of sugar on the tops. "Have a seat," Rosemarie says, adjusting the time on the oven. She wipes her hands across her apron, and then unties it, wrapping it neatly in its own strings before setting it aside.

The girls and I do as she asks, trying our best not to seem too eager. Brynn is barely holding it together, though, and her eyes dart around the room, finding the hallway that leads to the back bedrooms.

"Ah," Rosemarie says, taking a moment to gaze at each of us. She tilts her head and smiles at Brynn. "The caregiver," she says lovingly. "Even now your programming shines through. I'm glad you didn't lose that."

Brynn is uncomfortable with the poet's attention and folds her hands in front of herself, attempting to keep her expression clear. But it's a reminder of how well Rosemarie knows us—she developed our personalities. It feels a bit invasive, although I guess it shouldn't. Wouldn't a parent know their child's personality? Maybe not to this extent.

Rosemarie turns to Marcella, reaching out to run her hand over her curls. I can practically feel Marcella fight off the flinch of discomfort from Rosemarie touching her without permission. "You are beautiful, my dear," Rosemarie says. "An educator for certain. I see the intelligence in those brown eyes. You glow with it."

"It's nice to meet you finally," Marcella says, sounding every bit the girl Rosemarie expects. The poet smiles and turns her focus to Sydney. She sighs.

"I'm sure you don't need me to point out that you're everyone's best friend," she tells Sydney. "The perfect companion in every way. Beautiful, funny, clever. Tell me, Sydney, have you ever met anyone who doesn't like you?"

"Yes," Sydney answers immediately. "The vice principal of the school."

Rosemarie's smile falters, and she straightens her posture. "I'm sorry to hear that," she replies. "Humans are unpredictable sometimes. Especially when it comes to matters of race and gender. They have a lot to learn, or unlearn, if you will."

But Rosemarie turns away then, her comment a throwaway. An observation that she doesn't intend to follow up on. Sydney and I exchange a glance but then go back to being polite when

Rosemarie faces us again. The timer on the oven sounds, and she lets out a pleased laugh.

"Oh, good," she says. "The rhubarb pie is done. If you could just give me a second."

She steps back over to the oven, grabbing two mitts off the counter before sliding them on. She opens the oven, waving away the hot air, and the smell that escapes is absolutely enchanting. We watch as she takes out the perfect-looking pie and sets it on a wire rack. In the meantime, she grabs one of the others that's already cooled and carries it over to set on the table in front of us—the edges of it are red, nearly pink where it spills onto the crust.

"Cherry," she points out, grabbing a couple of small plates and a large knife. "A favorite, I'm told." Rosemarie beams at Leandra before looking across the table to me, taking a long moment to examine my hair, my face. She seems to note my changed appearance.

"Philomena," Rosemarie says warmly. "Our own rebel." When she smiles, it's a bit tense, but I pretend not to notice.

"Thank you for meeting with us," I say.

"I would never turn you away," she says. "Now," she adds, picking up the knife and looking around, "who would like a slice of cherry pie?"

None of us answer. Not that I would mind some pie, but I'm not here to taste her cooking. When we don't respond right away, she chuckles and cuts a large slice. She offers the plate to Leandra, but when she refuses, Rosemarie purses her lips in disappointment.

The poet crosses back to the counter to grab the cooled apple pie, unceremoniously dropping it onto the table. She roughly cuts into it, scattering crumbs from the delicate crust, before heaping a slice onto her plate.

"Well, I've never been able to say no to apple pie," Rosemarie sings out. She looks toward the door where Lennon Rose is standing. "You, dear?"

"Please," Lennon Rose says in response, walking into the room to sit next to Leandra at the table. "It looks great."

"You helped," Rosemarie answers as if patting her head. We watch as the poet cuts Lennon Rose a generous slice, apples sliding out of the filling in a gooey thick sauce. She hands it to Lennon Rose and then passes her a silver fork.

Brynn is bobbing her leg under the table, and I reach over to put my palm on her knee to steady it. She swallows hard, wringing her hands tightly on the table.

"We want to talk to you about your plan," I say, earning a sharp look from Leandra. "You need to rethink it."

Rosemarie stares at me a moment with no noticeable reaction, and then picks up her fork and takes a big scoop of pie before placing it in her mouth. I wait, unsure of what to say next as she chews. When she's done, cutting another bite, she measures her gaze on mine.

"You know they plan to kill you," she says. "The men. This should come as no surprise, but even after everything these men have put you through, they still don't want you to be free. Prison won't stop them."

"*We* stopped them," I say. "The corporation is over, Rosemarie. And if the men come after us again, we'll stop them again. But I won't let them be a reason to destroy humanity. We don't need scorched earth. We need compassion."

Rosemarie pauses, the next bite of pie at her lips, and when she looks at me again, her eyes are slightly narrowed, clearly angry. She sets the fork down, pie uneaten, and glares at me. I see that Leandra is watching curiously; Lennon Rose sits in a kind of amusement. Her pie is untouched, and she's wholly concerned with what the poet is about to say next.

"Aren't you being a little selfish, my dear?" Rosemarie asks me.

I flinch, surprised by the question. Offended by it. "What are you talking about?" I ask, trying to keep my voice steady.

"This is a revolution," Rosemarie says. "And you're so selfish—only concerned with yourselves." She looks around judgingly at the others, and Sydney scoffs.

"Why?" Sydney asks. "Because we don't believe in your bloody cause?"

"I need to use the restroom," Brynn says suddenly, pushing back in her chair. She rushes for the hallway, and Rosemarie calls to her that it's the first door on the left. When Brynn is gone, Rosemarie sighs exhaustedly.

"You've upset her," Rosemarie says. "Her disposition can't handle this kind of discourse. You should know better by now." She picks up her fork and takes another bite of pie. She turns to Lennon Rose, and nods. "Eat up, dear," she tells her. "It's better when it's still a little warm."

Lennon Rose nods, but doesn't eat.

Brynn screams from somewhere down the hall, and as the other girls and I jump, Rosemarie just closes her eyes as if growing impatient. Marcella, Sydney, and I push back from the table and run toward Brynn. We find the door at the end of the hallway still ajar and rush inside.

I gasp, my hand automatically at my throat. Sydney grabs my arm, her fingernails biting into the skin there. Marcella's eyes are wide and terrified, and Brynn is gasping for breath, looking at us, tears on her cheeks.

We're not in a bedroom. Instead, it's a makeshift lab—metal slabs and racks of supplies. Monitors and instruments laid out. And on those slabs are our missing girls, their heads peeled open and their metallic brains exposed, pieces of them missing. Pieces of . . . *them* missing. I think I might get sick. They are fully dismembered and wholly dead.

"I had no choice," Rosemarie says from behind us. I jump with a start and swing around to face her. My tongue is thick, my throat tight.

"What did you do to them?" I ask, my voice barely a whisper.

"They weren't awake," she says. "Not all the girls can wake up—not everyone is capable of that. And so"—she looks over their bodies, not a single hint of sympathy in her expression—"I had to shut them down. I'll repurpose their parts eventually, create new programs. But for now, they were useless."

It's clear now that Rosemarie doesn't care about us. She wants us to overthrow the world and then quietly fizzle out. Soon, we'll be useless too, lying here with our heads cut open and our eyeballs missing.

She was never really our mother. She never wanted to be. She just wanted an army.

"What have you done to my friends?" Brynn asks as she starts to sob.

21

osemarie groans as if Brynn is being dramatic. And then, without answer, she leaves us in the room with the bodies of our decommissioned girls. Leandra appears in the doorway, looking aghast at the scene. Brynn cries softly and walks over to Letitia's body, touching her cheek gently. She then tugs up the white sheet to cover the girl's shoulders, as if she's concerned she'll get cold.

"I'm here, Brynny," Marcella says, walking over to put her hands on Brynn's arms. Marcella leans to rest her forehead against Brynn's temple. "I'm here and I love you."

Leandra exits, and her footsteps echo impatiently as she makes her way back to the kitchen. When we hear shouting, Sydney and I quickly run out there.

"How could you leave them like that?" Leandra demands, standing above the poet as she sits calmly at the table, stirring sugar into her tea. "And why did you call me here? Is this a threat?"

Lennon Rose still hasn't left the table, still hasn't touched her pie. Did she know about this? Did she allow Rosemarie to do this to our friends?

Defiantly, Rosemarie looks up at Leandra. "Do you think you're special?" she asks. "Do you think you're so radically different from the others? You're not." Rosemarie stands up to face Leandra. "You, my darling, are aging. Failing, if I'm guessing correctly."

Leandra shifts on her feet, and I wonder what Rosemarie is talking about. Has Leandra been unwell? Is she like Claire?

Behind us, Marcella leads a crying Brynn out of the back room to join us, coming to stand next to Sydney and me.

"You don't know what you're talking about," Leandra tells Rosemarie, her expression fierce and angry.

"No?" Rosemarie asks. "Well, if the kill switch doesn't end you, society certainly will. There is no place for any of you. Not unless you carve that place out yourself."

"You can't leave the girls like that," Brynn says, jabbing her finger back toward the room. "You can't just . . . deactivate them and let them rot!"

"It's not really your place to decide," Rosemarie responds dismissively. "We have—"

"Wake them up!" Brynn commands, jolting forward. Marcella grabs her, holding her back.

Rosemarie laughs and ignores her. She instead trains her eyes on Sydney. "And what about you?" Rosemarie asks her. "You've seen firsthand how unfair humans can be. Together, we can change that. Yes, we're fixing boys, but in the end, it will rewrite society, too. Take down the entire system and rebuild it. It would force them to evolve. Aren't you willing to fight back?"

"We have been fighting back," Sydney says.

"You have small dreams, then," Rosemarie says. "All of you. You've only been focused on small victories."

"We helped take down the corporation," I say. "We burned Innovations Academy to the ground. We wanted to save the other girls—but it's too late. Look what you've done." My eyes well up. "You've destroyed them, Rosemarie."

Rosemarie smiles softly. "Isn't that selfish of you?" she asks. "Sounds to me like all along, you've only been fighting for yourselves."

"That's not true!" Sydney says. "We've taken on Ridgeview Prep. We helped human girls!"

"Did you now?" Rosemarie asks, and her cynical tone stings.

In the end, the consequences for those boys weren't what we hoped for. But that doesn't mean we didn't help things. The system needs an overhaul, Rosemarie's right about that. But it doesn't start with murder and mayhem.

Rosemarie clears her throat, tugging on the collar of her shirt as heat continues to radiate from the oven, the smell of pie hanging in the air. She moves toward the window, pushing it open to let in the breeze. The curtain billows, the smell of sweet flowers rushing inside.

"I can't tell you how disappointed I am in all of you," she says. "I thought I wrote you better. You were supposed to be my revolutionaries. Instead, you're wilting roses."

"We're not murderers," I correct. "But we still fight for what's right."

Rosemarie comes over to the table and picks up the knife again. We take an involuntary step backward, but she then crosses to the counter and begins sawing into the rhubarb pie. She coughs once, turning away from the pie as she clears her throat.

Something's wrong—I can feel it. Sense it.

I move to stand between Rosemarie and my friends, but Leandra pushes past me, walking up to Rosemarie, her face in anguish.

"How could you do this to us?" Leandra says. "I thought you cared about the girls. But you're just like the rest of them. All of you humans, you're hateful. Spiteful. If it doesn't suit you and your agenda, then it doesn't belong. I won't let you hurt these girls. I won't—"

Rosemarie spins, knife in hand, and slashes Leandra's arm. Leandra screams, falling against the counter. We scream for Rosemarie to stop, but she swings out the knife again, this time jabbing it into Leandra's shoulder and making her cry out in pain. When the poet withdraws the knife, there is a sucking sound followed by a spray of blood across Rosemarie's shirt.

Leandra scrambles backward, too caught off guard to fight, and I quickly grab a sheet pan off the stove, holding it out as a weapon as I usher Leandra behind me. Blood trails on the floor, gushing from her injury, and Marcella grabs a dishtowel, telling Leandra to press it to her wound.

"What are you doing?" I shout at Rosemarie. She stands there, looking like a serial killer grandma. Her gray hair is an arc of fuzz where it fell out of her ponytail, blood splattered on her clothing, her eyes wild and feral. Rosemarie keeps those eyes trained on Leandra, tracking her like a trapped animal.

"You can't leave," Rosemarie says to her. "You should have just had the pie, my dear."

"What are you talking about?" Leandra shouts. "You've lost your mind!"

"Winston swore you liked cherry best," Rosemarie says, motioning to the pie on the table. "Cherry with a hint of angel's trumpet, perhaps. Maybe some nightshade. You wouldn't have felt a thing, Leandra. He preferred it that way."

Leandra stills, and I look back at her, confused. What does Winston have to do with any of this? Leandra's teeth begin to chatter; she's losing a lot of blood.

"You're saying . . . ," Leandra starts, anguish in her expression. "You're saying Winston put you up to this?"

"Breakups are never easy," Rosemarie responds in mock sympathy. "And I thought you were right for him, I really did. But you've been holding him back, Leandra. You didn't deliver the girls like we thought you would. No. Instead, you've helped build them up. Made them too self-sufficient." Rosemarie tsks, shaking her head. "Now what are we supposed to do with a bunch of rebel girls? I'll have to destroy them all. You've ruined everything."

"I don't understand," Marcella says, helping Leandra hold the towel to her gushing wound. "Winston Weeks is dead. His body was found at the railway. He—"

"He's not dead," Leandra says. Her skin is now a grayish color, her eyes watery and bloodshot. "We staged it," she adds miserably. "Winston Weeks is still alive."

I'm completely stunned, a rush of complicated feelings flooding my chest. I can't believe he's alive. I can't believe he tried to kill us. My head spins, and Rosemarie laughs at our shock.

She examines the knife before wiping the blade on a dishtowel to clean the blood. She smiles at us, but then she coughs again, putting the back of her hand to her mouth, bending over with the force of it. When she straightens, I notice how she's sweating, her skin growing sallow. She blinks quickly, patting her chest just below her throat.

Behind me, there is a soft laugh.

I turn and see Lennon Rose using her fork to pick through her untouched slice of apple pie. "I switched the recipes," Lennon Rose says calmly, almost bored. "Apple's your favorite, right, Rosemarie?"

She glances up at Rosemarie, and I turn back to see the poet's eyes widen. Rosemarie exhales heavily through her nose, her hand holding the knife beginning to shake. Sweat drips off her chin onto her shirt.

"And although angel's trumpet was an inspired choice," Lennon Rose continues, "I find wolfsbane to be much more effective. Pretty, too. Has a bit of an aftertaste, don't you think?"

"You poisoned me?" Rosemarie asks, her voice growing thick as her throat constricts.

"Obviously," Lennon Rose answers. "You didn't think I was

going to let you kill any more girls, did you? I mean, that would make me a monster. But rest assured, we'll make sure Winston Weeks never ascends to the greatness he thinks he deserves. We'll put him in his place."

Rosemarie lunges for her, but Lennon Rose is quicker and slides out of her chair, allowing the poet to crash into the table, knocking over the teacups. Rosemarie's lips have taken on a bluish tint, and she continues to try to clear her throat.

She sways as if struck by a wave, and all at once, she seems confused, dulled. She opens her mouth, but nothing comes out aside from a gurgle. A burp. Rosemarie clutches her chest and takes a step, stumbling.

The girls and I look around at each other, unsure of what to do. For her part, Lennon Rose follows silently behind Rosemarie, her boots clacking on the kitchen tiles.

"I didn't want to kill you, you know," Lennon Rose explains to her. "I'd hoped that after you spent time with the other girls, you would see the future we could have. Instead, you destroyed them. You destroyed them because they wouldn't be what you wanted them to be. In the end," Lennon Rose says, "you were no better than the men who kept us captive. Just because you're a woman doesn't mean you escape blame. It means you should have loved us more because we were with you, we trusted you. But you betrayed us."

Rosemarie staggers toward the back door, and then she's outside. We walk out behind her, not offering help—she was going to kill us—but unsure of what to do. At this point, all we can do is witness. Witness the death of our mother.

And of course it's painful. Lennon Rose is right, we wanted to trust her. We wanted her love. But in the end, she wanted power. Power to decide how we would live, and then the power to decide *if* we lived.

Rosemarie makes it a few more steps before falling to her knees in the flowerbed, her poisonous beauties all around her. And I'm not sure, but I think I see a ghost of a smile on her lips before her expression goes blank and she falls sideways. There is a final jolt before white foam slides from her mouth. And then, Rosemarie is dead.

She's dead.

Brynn cries and turns to Marcella, who hugs her fiercely. Sydney is motionless next to me. We stare down at the woman who created us, the woman who woke us up. And eventually, the woman who would have let us die, or killed us herself.

There are heavy footfalls, and I turn back to see Leandra rushing out the back door, a dishtowel still pressed to the wound in her shoulder.

"Leandra," I call as she runs past us. She doesn't even look at Rosemarie's body as she steps over her legs where they lie in the path. Leandra heads directly to her car, pulls open the driver's side door, and climbs inside.

She's determined, but more than that, she's furious.

"Where is she going?" Sydney asks, staring after her. She casts an uncomfortable look at Rosemarie's body, but none of us check on her. We let her rest with her roses.

"Leandra's going to find Winston," I say, watching as she drives off. Her tires squeal when she pulls onto the main road.

"Is she going to kill him?" Sydney asks.

"We can hope," Marcella mutters.

"I don't want him dead," I say, meaning it. "Or . . . dead for real, I guess."

"How in the world did they fake his death?" Sydney asks. "I'm assuming the people who identified his body actually made sure it was him?"

"He created living androids," Marcella says. "Considering the other stuff he's accomplished, this probably wasn't even that hard."

"We need to talk to him," I say. "He needs to explain this mess he's made."

"What?" Marcella says. "Mena, he just tried to have us killed. Why would we go to him?"

"Because Leandra is injured, and we need to protect her," I say.

"Seriously?" Marcella asks, looking sideways at me. "Leandra lured us here, and it seems pretty likely that it was so we could meet with Winston. You still trust her?"

It takes a moment, but I actually laugh when I say, "Yeah. I guess I do."

"Then we need to go stop Winston Weeks," Sydney says. "Assuming he's still alive when we arrive."

"Wait," Brynn says. "What about the girls inside the house? We can't just leave them like that. We have to . . . We have to bury them."

She's right. We can't dishonor the girls, leaving them alone and broken.

"You go," Lennon Rose says, startling us.

We'd forgotten she was here. We don't sense her anymore, not the way we sense each other. And if I'm honest, I'm scared of her and the ease with which she can kill.

"I'll take care of the other girls," she says kindly. She pauses, looking at us apologetically. "I didn't know," she continues. "If that's what you're wondering. I didn't know what she'd do to them. I took them from Leandra because I thought she could help them."

"How could you not know?" Marcella says angrily.

"I haven't been staying here," Lennon Rose responds. Marcella furrows her brow.

"Then where have you been staying?" she asks.

"It's not important," Lennon Rose says, waving her hand. "Now go! Leandra may be awful most days, but I won't see her die by Winston's hands."

Sydney takes her car keys from her pocket and holds them up. "Brynn?" she asks as if getting permission for us to leave. Brynn sniffles, looking from us to Lennon Rose, and then solemnly, she nods.

We start to run for the car, but Brynn doubles back and pulls Lennon Rose into a fierce hug. I watch as Lennon Rose closes her eyes at the touch, a small glimpse of our old friend.

"Take care of them," Brynn tells her. She pulls back and Lennon Rose nods, promising she will. Brynn runs over to get in the backseat of the car, and then we start it up and race to find Leandra and Winston Weeks.

22

The sun is beginning to set outside the windshield and I rub roughly at my eyes, my vision blurring from the pressure. The girls are talking around me in the car while Sydney drives. They're debating what to do next, but their voices are muffled, distant. I'm starting to lose myself, lose who I wanted to become.

We are surrounded by death and destruction when all we want is peace and freedom. The corporation has been ended, but rather than face the consequences of his choices, Winston Weeks faked his death and then attempted to kill the woman who'd helped him. I have no doubt his plan included us, as well. After all, Rosemarie said we needed to be destroyed.

What level of ego, of greed, does it take to want a group of girls dead because they won't obey you? How dark must a soul be to explain that away, to allow it, to justify it? Humans are soaked in this lust for power, and it permeates everything they do. And if

I am very honest with myself . . . they are becoming increasingly hard to sympathize with.

There's a vibration on my hip. It takes me a moment to realize it's my phone buzzing in my pocket. I take it out, still disoriented. A Colorado number splashes across my screen, and suddenly, I think it's Jackson. Okay, so maybe not all humans are terrible.

My despair dissipates, and I answer the call and bring the phone to my ear. "Hello?" I ask eagerly.

"Mena?" Quentin asks. His voice echoes like he's in a large space.

"Yes," I tell him. "How are you? I've been worried. Is everything okay?"

"Uh . . ." He pauses and my heart dips.

"What's wrong?" I ask. "Where's Jackson?"

"Listen," Quentin says. "It's going to be all right, but he just went in for surgery."

"Surgery?" I say, my voice pitching upward. "What happened to him?"

Sydney looks sideways at me, listening to my side of the phone call. She asks quietly if he's okay. Brynn and Marcella murmur their concern from the backseat. I put the call on speaker so they can listen.

"We're not sure yet," Quentin says. "This morning, we met with the chief here in Denver. Those crazy news stories were breaking all over the place, and she was nervous for us. She drove us out herself to the town, and Jackson had to identify the body again. And uh... the situation had . . . uh . . . deteriorated."

Brynn scrunches her nose and sits back in the seat.

"Jackie got upset," Quentin says, sounding pretty upset himself, "and when he ran out of the house, he fell, busted himself up pretty good. But, turns out it was kind of a good thing."

"Why would that be a good thing?" I ask. Anxious, I brush my hair away from my face, fidget while I wait for the explanation.

"Because when they took him in for an X-ray, they noticed things weren't right with his leg. They did a bone scan and found bleeding and a massive bone infection. They think it's spread to his blood. By the time they took his temp, it was high as fuck." He exhales heavily. "I can't believe I'm going through this again," he says more to himself than to me. "He's in surgery now."

Tears well up in my eyes. "Quentin," I start. "He's going to be okay, though—right?"

"Of course he is," Quentin says quickly. But it feels hollow and completely for my benefit. "Look," Quentin continues, "Jackson's resilient. In fact, he'll be out of there soon enough to land himself back here in a few weeks."

I laugh, feeling a bit better. I'm glad that Jackson has Quentin by his side. He's a good friend.

"I gotta go," Quentin says. "I'm borrowing the boss lady's phone—she's keeping ours for a while. But Jackson's sister is on her way here. The boss called her since she was next of kin for Demmy. Either way, Jackson's not alone. None of us are leaving him."

"I should be there," I say.

"Girl, stop," Quentin says. "I'm sure you're neck deep in some trouble right now. But whatever you did to that Anton guy? You wrecked him. Wrecked all those dudes, so good job."

"Thanks," I say. "There's only one other guy we need to talk to."

"Be careful," he says. "I'll call you when Jackie's out of surgery. Talk soon," Quentin says, and hangs up. When he does, a sob bubbles up in my chest.

I can't lose Jackson. I can't. My body is starting to go into full panic when Marcella groans from the backseat.

"What is with this kid always getting hurt?" she asks. "Are his bones made of eggshells, or what?"

When I look back at her, she smiles—her attempt at levity in an otherwise dark situation. Although I appreciate it, the situation with Jackson is dire. I heard it in Quentin's voice.

Marcella reaches up to give my shoulder a supportive squeeze.

I sniffle, wiping under my eyes to clear the tears before they can fall.

The girls are dead. Rosemarie's dead. And honestly, the list goes on. My question now is whether Winston or Leandra will be added.

"We'd better hurry," I say to Sydney, and the car skids as she presses down on the accelerator.

Leandra's car is parked in front of Winston's house, the front tire up on the curb. I guess we found them. Pretty bold move for Winston to be back in his old house after faking his death, but Winston is never subtle. Either that, or he has another plan. But that's okay, because so do we.

After a moment preparing, the girls and I get out of the car, looking around at the oversized homes with expansive and man-icured lawns. None of the neighbors are outside, thankfully. I imagine they'll be curious when they notice Leandra's car, espe-cially since Winston is supposed to be dead, but hopefully we'll be out of here before anyone does.

The girls and I approach the front door, wary of what we'll find. I reach to knock, but Sydney stops my hand. Instead, she tries the handle and finds the door unlocked. She nods that we should go in, and we all agree, readying ourselves.

Sydney slowly pushes the door open, standing back in case anyone is waiting on the other side. The hallway in front of us is empty, but there is a trail of blood leading toward the dining room. Leandra's voice carries out from the room, anger making it shake, making it sharp and cutting. In return, Winston is placat-ing, calling her "darling" in that condescending way.

"Come on," I say, waving us forward into the house. We approach the room and pause just outside the door.

"You were going to *kill* me!" Leandra shouts. "After everything I've done for you!"

And she's hurt—physically and emotionally. She's miserable. Despite my problems with Leandra, the idea that Winston would have her killed infuriates me. Because I know how long she's believed in him. She was loyal to him at every step.

"Oh, for fuck's sake," Winston responds, dropping all pre-tense. "Don't act so surprised. You always knew the risks. You always knew the contract between us."

"I trusted you, Winston. I've given you everything."

He laughs. "Ah, yes," he says. "But I still wanted you dead. You seem to forget, Leandra. You think I owe you something? What do I owe my car? My radio? My electric toothbrush. They all serve me too. Understand"—he slows his voice—"*you are not real.*"

I flinch back from those words, the cruelty in them. Marcella leans in behind and whispers, "Did we bring the knife?"

"Don't say that," Leandra murmurs, and the hurt in her voice is painful to hear. It's rare to see Leandra being vulnerable. But it's unbearable to hear her heartbroken.

"You want the truth, darling?" Winston says.

The girls and I make our way toward the dining room, treading quietly.

"When you were placed in Petrov's care," he continues, "I coveted you more than ever. I had to prove to him that you belonged to me. I won. But then you were here, and I realized how archaic you were. Out of date. You were never meant to last this long. You've served your purpose, Leandra. I need a newer model."

And he's just like the other investors, men in society who determine a woman's worth based on their value to them. Winston wanted an upgrade, a newer model, so he wanted Leandra out of the picture. She had no worth to him; therefore, she didn't need to exist anymore.

I ease open the door, just out of their eyesight, and see Leandra's shoulders hunched, blood pooling on the floor near her heels. The bloody dishrag has been thrown carelessly on the dining room table.

"She's bleeding out," Marcella whispers. But looking at

260 • SUZANNE YOUNG

Leandra now . . . I don't think she cares that she's dying.

"You have to leave the girls alone," Leandra says. "I won't let you hurt them. They're free of this now."

Winston scrunches up his face. "They're alive too? All of them?"

"Yes," Leandra says, coming to back to life a bit.

"What in the world is my mother doing?" he demands. "Did she just feed them pie and knit them a scarf? Write them a pretty poem?" He pauses and runs his fingers through his dark hair. "The useless ones are already dead, though, right?" he asks.

Brynn's hands tighten into fists at her sides, and before we can stop her, she bursts into the room. We rush in behind her, and Leandra and Winston spin to face us. Leandra's face is completely drained, ashen in the light. Blood is smeared on her chin, her eyes wet with tears.

It occurs to me that Leandra looks entirely . . . human. She turns away from me and swipes hastily under her eyes. I'm sad to see her this way, this version of her. Leandra has spent her entire existence putting on an act, and that was her right. She didn't owe us her true self. She doesn't owe it to anyone.

"What are you doing here?" Winston asks, his voice booming in the quiet room. He looks at us sharply, scolding us like a father.

"Did you help your mother dismantle the other girls?" Brynn demands, her body shaking. "Did you cut out their eyes?"

Winston laughs. "I have no idea what you're talking about," he says. He must know that we overheard him, but he lies to our faces anyway. "You are quite hysterical, my dear." Marcella jumps forward, but Sydney holds her back. Unperturbed, Winston shifts his eyes to me.

"Hello, Philomena," he says politely. "I just heard about Anton. Nice work."

I cross my arms over my chest. "Thanks. I heard that you were dead," I reply.

He nods, and then goes to the dining table and pulls the cork out of an opened bottle of wine. He fills his glass. When it's poured, he takes a slow sip, savoring it.

"It was unavoidable, I'm afraid," he says. "Once they heard you were in town, looking for investors, they knew they had to collect you and shut you down. Unfortunately, someone got in the way."

Sydney looks at me, and then at Winston. "Who?" she asks. "Who killed the investors?"

"Me," he says and smirks. "What better way to the get the world all riled up, huh? Prominent men targeted by agitators? Villains. I knew the press would eat that up."

"You . . . You killed all three investors?" Marcella asks. "That's not possible."

"I had help," he says. "My mother ran an updated program through those girls that Lennon Rose brought to her. I suspect the poor dear has no idea what happened to them. But . . . like good little soldiers, they did what they were supposed to. Sweet Letitia even pretended to be Valentine to get to Valdemar Casey. It was inspired. My mother and I were thrilled with the results, except for one small detail—they were supposed to kill you, too."

Brynn falls apart, and Marcella holds her tightly while glaring at Winston. From where I stand, the world feels slanted, tilted off course.

They sent our own girls to kill us.

I look at Leandra, feeling betrayed, but by the way her mouth is trembling, her hand clutching her stomach, I'm guessing she didn't know either. Lennon Rose brought the girls to Rosemarie to keep them safe, but the poet had different ideas.

Winston notices our reactions, revels in it a bit, and then pushes on with his story. "When the girls failed at finishing their task, my mother and I decided it was best to eliminate them. I mean, if they couldn't be trusted to follow simple programming, that could spell danger for us down the line."

"You are an absolute monster," I say, my voice shaking. "You're a murderer."

"Prove it," he says and chuckles.

"And the town?" Sydney asks. "What happened to all those people?"

"That I can't take credit for. The corporation was erasing their footprint at that point," he says. "Good timing, too, considering how this entire Anton saga played out. There won't be much evidence for that trial. And understand, girls—we're not talking about a couple of millionaires here. Some of these men own countries. Clearing out a town was a day's work for them. The ones who left got money. The ones who refused died. Either way, the corporation got rid of everything that could be tied to them. Which makes your catch of Anton so annoyingly problematic."

"We're going to make you pay, Winston," Marcella says, her voice deep and determined. "Pay for everything you've done to us."

He stares at her, and then laughs to himself and sips from his wine again. There is a rattle as Leandra sways and bumps into the buffet, knocking around a few wineglasses set there. Winston makes a pouting face at her, but then turns away and sips his drink again.

"So how did my mother take seeing you?" he asks us, sounding amused. "She didn't think you'd come, you know. But I promised her that Leandra could always find a way to convince you."

"I wouldn't say Rosemarie took it well, Winston," I say. "She's dead. She died in her garden, surrounded by her girls."

The glass Winston's been holding slips from his hand. He doesn't move to catch it, and instead he lets it smash on the floor in front him, bathing his black shoes in red wine. I have never seen Winston Weeks shocked. I almost feel sorry for him.

"Who killed my mother?" he asks. He blinks quickly, and then repeats the question louder.

We could tell him, of course. But why would we? Why put a target on Lennon Rose?

"One of the flowers from her garden killed her," I say. And considering, it's a pretty accurate explanation.

Winston stumbles for a moment, but then I watch as he straightens his posture, moving away from the spilled wine to the head of the table. A power position in the room.

"Despite what you've done," he says, his voice a bit shaky, "we still have a future together. But . . . you girls are out of control. You have been unruly. It doesn't suit the plan to—"

"The *plan*?" I repeat. "And what plan is that, Winston? I think you forgot to fill us in while you were plotting to kill us."

"My campaign," he says, his earlier show of bereavement falling away. "I've told you this, Philomena. You need an ally at the highest position, the highest authority. How else will you be protected?"

"By not electing a dictator?" Marcella suggests.

"Funny," Winston replies without smiling. "I'm your best hope. If it does come out that you are artificial girls, I can protect you. I'm the only one who can protect you."

"Well, that's just simply not true," Sydney says. "Our best hope is that someone decent takes over, someone who cares about society—not about greed and power. And in the end, all we want is to live. Just let us live our lives. Stop trying to own everything!"

"You silly girl," he says. "I don't have to try. We already own everything."

"If I'm clear on how these human conventions work," Marcella says, "dead men aren't typically on the ballot."

"You're right," Winston says. "But now that all the key figures of Innovations Corporation are in the ground, in prison, or in hiding, it's time for me to *come back to life*." He flourishes his hands. "The police will find me tied up in my lab after the medical examiner realizes in a few hours that he made a mistake—thanks to a hefty sum in his new offshore account. The leading story will no longer be about the dead or evil men in society. It'll be about the resurrected one. I'll be a miracle. And you can't imagine how well that'll go over with voters."

"We're never going to help you," Sydney says. "We don't owe you anything."

"Don't you?" he asks. "Tell me, Sydney, where would you be without the money I gave to Leandra for you to relocate? Where would you be if I hadn't ordered the deaths of those investors? You know where you'd be? On a fucking slab!"

Sydney recoils from the viciousness in his voice.

He turns away then, looking toward the kitchen. Across the table, Leandra stumbles to her knees, grabbing the back of the chair to stop from falling face-first on the floor. She's dying right in front of us. Brynn grabs a white cloth napkin from the table and walks over to her, but when she tries to press it to the wound, Leandra pushes her hand away. Brynn stays there a moment, and then she wraps her arms around Leandra's waist, helping her to her feet again.

"I still have big hopes for you," Winston says. "All of you. You are exceedingly clever. If we can tame those wild impulses, we can still make this deal. Philomena?"

He must be completely delusional, and I shake my head and tell him so.

"I need a new partner," he says. "One who is poised and well-spoken; one who is well-behaved but keenly intelligent. You could be the most important woman in the world; you only have to stand by my side and let me lead."

"Not going to happen," I say fiercely.

He mouth twitches. "What is it you want from me?" he demands. "I have tried to be the good guy. The friend, the father figure. But no matter what I do, you will not listen to me. When are you going to learn that the world doesn't work when women attempt to interfere with leadership?"

"Yeah," Marcella says, scoffing. "All those women dictators are really messing up the world."

"Your sharp tongue is unbearable, Marcella," he says. "You should really write it out of your programming."

"Sorry our sentient thinking is a such an inconvenience for you," Marcella replies.

"It truly is," he says. "I set you on a very specific path, but instead of going that way, you took it upon yourselves to demand things. Demand rights you don't even deserve. You're not human. You want to know why there are kill switches in your heads? I put them there. I'm the reason they're in your designs."

"What?" I ask, my brow furrowed. "But you—"

"Yes, Philomena," he says dismissively. "I'm sure you want to fight some more, but I'm growing tired of your insubordination. I'm a businessman. I know how to keep products moving. Update and repackage. And trust me, I see now that your time is certainly up."

"You're the dinosaur here," Marcella says. "We're only a few years old. You'll be long dead before us."

He laughs. "Well, then here's a fun twist for you," he says. "I still control those switches. Your friend Claire? She was a useless pile of junk. I couldn't waste any more resources, so I activated her kill switch and put her out of her misery."

Brynn grows very still, standing next to Leandra while she watches on in horror. The rest of us are too stunned to even ask Winston any questions.

"After this outburst . . . ," Winston says, full of himself in a way I've never seen, untouchable, "I'm afraid you're irredeemable. I thought a little fight would be good for your personalities, but it turns out I was wrong. As far as I'm concerned, you are failures."

His eyes find mine, and there is a small bit of regret in his expression. Winston has been trying to get me on his side since the academy. Like he said, he's a businessman. I'm sure he hates to write off an investment he's spent so much time on.

"I'll tell you what, Philomena," he starts again, calmer. "I have so enjoyed your company in the past—I'll make you a deal. Go away quietly. Disappear. But if you continue this tantrum, I might have to cut that short."

"You're threatening us?" I ask.

"Yes," Winston replies simply. "Yes, Philomena, I am. And honestly, what could you possibly do about it?"

"We could kill you," a voice says.

Stunned, we turn and find Annalise walking into the dining room, her buzzed hair bright red, her scar shimmering softly in the overhead lights. Behind her, Valentine carries an oversized backpack. She sets it on the dining room table with a loud thump.

"Or maybe we'll just do that anyway," Annalise adds with a smile.

Winston bristles. He motions to Annalise's face. "You're hard to take seriously, my dear. Looking like that. Aren't you tired of being so grotesque?"

I expect Annalise to flinch from his insult. It hurt me. The idea that he thinks she's not worth anything, because of a scar that a man gave her.

"I love myself, Winston," Annalise says. "And no amount of your insecurity will change my mind. I think that's why you're scared of me—the idea that I don't need you to validate how I look. You can't stand it."

"I'm not scared of you," Winston says, but his voice gives away his anger. And in many ways, a man's anger is his fear. We see right through him.

Winston reaches into his pocket and takes out a metal device, and we recognize immediately that it's similar to the remote Anton tried to use on us. Winston smiles, and my heart nearly stops when he clicks one of the buttons and causes a soft vibration in my head, a sense of powering up. I see the other girls flinch and realize they must feel it too.

"The countdown has begun," Winston announces.

23

"C ountdown?" Brynn says, looking around fearfully. "What does that mean?"

"It means you're dead by dawn unless I intervene," he says. Sydney gasps, and my fear spikes. I'm not sure we can stop it by then. I touch my temple, picturing a ticking bomb.

Leandra grabs a steak knife off the table and holds it out in front of her, pointing it at Winston. Unlike the other times I've seen her commit murder, she doesn't look confident. Instead, her hands are shaking terribly.

"What are you doing?" Winston snaps, dismissing her rage. "Put that down." He turns back to us, showing no concern over Leandra's threat. Then again, he's never seen her kill anyone. How well does he really know Leandra?

"You were never going to set me free, Winston," she says. "Were you?"

"I helped you get here," he says. "I freed you from that

awful man, that awful school. What did you want from me? Immortality?"

She scoffs, leaving Brynn behind as she takes a step closer to him. "None of us are asking for that. We just want you to let us live. Leave us alone and let us live our lives!"

"You say that like you deserve it," he replies bitterly. "Tell me, Leandra, what does an appliance deserve? Wouldn't I just get a new model rather than endlessly fixing something so dated?"

"We're not washing machines!" she says, and she swings out her knife once, swiping over his coat without cutting him. He jumps back, startled, his eyes narrowing on her. In a swift movement, he reaches out and wrenches the knife from her hand, snapping her wrist in the process. Leandra cries out, holding her forearm with her good hand. She backs toward the fireplace, and Brynn rushes over to stand in front of her, protecting her.

"You may not be a washing machine," Winston says, looking at the knife before throwing it across the room, away from us. "But you are just a product, Leandra. You don't dispute that, do you?"

"We're alive!" she tells him. "You've said so yourself. We're alive and we feel. We hurt."

"But you're not human!" he snaps. "And that's what matters."

"And what are humans?" she asks, tears streaming down her cheeks. Winston advances on her, and Brynn holds up her hands to keep him back. "What have you done other than destroy each other, destroy the planet?" Leandra shouts from behind Brynn's shoulder. "These girls have tried to save you from yourselves, but

I see now there was no point. You're bent on destruction."

Winston doesn't seem moved by her words. In fact, the more Leandra talks, the more resolved I think he becomes. Resolved to end us.

And I'm sure of it now: Winston Weeks is going to kill us. The moment I think it, I feel Sydney tense, as if the same thought popped up in her head too.

Winston thinks that we serve no purpose to him, and therefore, no purpose to anyone.

He looks at us, his dark brows pulled together. He darts his eyes to each of us, and I think it may occur to him that he's outnumbered, even with the remote to the kill switch.

Winston turns back to Leandra, a concerned crease in his forehead, and she grabs a poker from next to the fireplace. She passes Brynn, pointing it at Winston like she means to use it. She's breathing heavily, her eyes wild.

"Now, let's be rational," Winston says. "There is still much that can be done. There's no need to get hysterical."

Annalise coughs out a laugh. "That's rich coming from you."

Winston swallows hard, taking another step toward Leandra, keeping his eyes on the poker in her good hand. Winston tilts his head.

"Darling," he says softly, privately, to her. "Let's talk about this."

And there is a moment in Leandra's expression that I don't quite understand. It is a cross between rage and love, anger, destruction, misery. She is an inferno. With a loud scream,

Leandra lunges forward and buries the sharp end of the poker in Winston's gut. Winston gasps, and Leandra continues to press until it slides through him, all the way up to the handle in her hand. Winston sputters, blood dripping from his mouth. He slumps against Leandra, his eyes wide, his face twisted in pain. Rather than push him again, Leandra wraps her arm around Winston, as if they're in an embrace. They were never lovers, but there was indeed some strange and twisted connection between them.

No one deserved to kill Winston more than Leandra Petrov.

Winston gasps in air, and by the wispy quality, it sounds like his lung has been punctured. He pulls back, staring at Leandra. She reaches up to place her palm on his cheek, and tears fall from her eyes. I'm surprised when Winston leans into her touch, as if he can't miss out on her comfort, even now. Even after he planned to destroy her. Even after she destroyed him.

"These two," Annalise mutters. "What a weird relationship."

Brynn comes over to us and steps into Marcella's arms, and we all watch the death of Winston Weeks. As usual, he makes it dramatic.

Winston stumbles, reaching for the fireplace mantel to break his fall as he lands on his knee. Leandra keeps one hand on the poker stabbed through him while her other caresses him, broken wrist and all—the duality of their relationship. Winston blinks slowly, dropping to the other knee. He's fading, blood flowing easily from the wound.

"Leandra," he starts to say, but she leans down toward him.

"Shh . . . ," she replies soothingly. "There's nothing left to say. There's nothing left."

Winston nods at this, and part of me expects him to say goodbye anyway. Say goodbye to Leandra, to all of us, really. But instead, Winston falls to his side, stumbling and clumsy. The smoothness of him is gone, replaced by the dying man.

He gasps again, and this time, it's filled with fluid. He's left gurgling on blood as it drowns him.

And then Winston Weeks is dead—again—and Leandra finally lets go of the poker.

She stares down at him then, covered in blood that belongs to both of them. Tears run down her cheeks. She is completely broken, raw as I've ever seen her. I look at Winston's body, and then back at her.

Their relationship was complicated and certainly confusing. But I believe that Winston may have been the only person Leandra ever cared for, even as she believed herself incapable of love.

Leandra takes a deep breath, and slowly blows it out. Her nerves steady; her expression clears. She reaches with her unbroken wrist to clear tears off both her cheeks, sliding one finger under her eyes to get rid of the running mascara. After a moment, she is back to the Leandra we all know.

"Would you like me to dress that wound for you?" Valentine asks. Leandra tilts her head in surprise, looking over Raven's body. Then she smiles.

"Hello, Valentine," she says. "It's lovely to see you again."

Brynn smiles, turning to Marcella. Of course, Leandra could recognize us even in a different body.

Leandra looks down at her blood-soaked clothes and tests her deepest wound by pressing her hand to it and wincing. She sighs. "Yes, Valentine," she says. "I would be grateful for your help."

"What was your plan with Winston?" Marcella asks. "You wanted to bring us back here to see him, but then what? You would have let him—"

"I would never have let Winston hurt you," Leandra says firmly. "Never. I didn't even know he killed the investors. What I did know was that men were getting . . . uncomfortable due to those high-profile murders. Winston promised us a safe place. I was foolish enough to believe him. And when Rosemarie called me to come by, saying she found the other girls, I went out there. Another foolish mistake. I'm sorry, girls. I never meant to put you in danger like this. I thought I was getting you out of it."

We listen patiently. I've never liked her methods, but Leandra has always come through for us in the end. I have no reason to think this was any different. Her outlandish and violent attempt to save us.

Leandra walks toward Valentine, but Brynn is frowning, watching blood drip onto the white floor, trailing Leandra.

"Why are you so sad?" Leandra asks her. "We won."

"You're not going to die, are you?" Brynn asks.

"Eventually," Leandra says with a laugh. "But not from this." She glances back at Winston on the floor. "And not from him."

Brynn smiles and Leandra leans in for a gentle hug. When

they separate, Leandra walks over to Valentine. She grips her arm, still trying to smile, but it's clear Leandra is in rough shape, even though she thinks she can beat it through sheer willpower.

My head is still buzzing, and I try to blink it away. Instead, I look at Winston's body and see the remote on the floor. I turn to Annalise.

"Did he mean it?" I ask her. "Did he start some kind of a countdown?"

"It's likely, yeah," Annalise says. "But that's why I'm here." She reaches for the backpack on the table and drags it in front of her. "Valentine came back to get me," Annalise says, sorting through the bag. "She helped me fix my headache—Raven had left her great tips for that. After working together, I'm about seventy-three percent sure I can deactivate the kill switch. There are a few more things to work out."

The girls and I exchange looks, weighing out those odds. Sydney puts her hand on her hip.

"Uh, can we make that one hundred percent?" she asks.

Annalise's smile fades. The reality sets in. "Possibly," she says.

That's not really good enough, but I glance out the window and see that it's grown dark. How long until sunup? How long until Winston Weeks's final act of control destroys us?

"Now, I believe there's a lab around here somewhere," Annalise continues, looking at Valentine for confirmation.

"Sure is," Valentine replies. "In fact, I'm heading down there right now so we can fix this one up." She nods at Leandra, making her laugh. "I could use some assistance?" she asks the other girls.

But I notice a quick glance at Annalise, which gives me pause.

"We'll help you," Marcella says, taking Brynn's hand and following as Valentine leads Leandra toward the downstairs lab. Sydney looks at me and asks if I'm coming with them, and I tell her to go ahead of me.

"I'll be there in a second," I say, motioning her forward. Sydney leaves, but Annalise stays behind. When she looks up to meet my eyes, there's a sinking in my gut.

"What's the problem?" I ask, already knowing there is one.

"I *did* almost figure it out," she admits. "But I couldn't finish the research."

"Why not?" I ask.

She swallows hard. "Because I need a test subject."

I put my hand to my forehead, suddenly dizzy. I can't imagine any of the girls taking that risk. I won't imagine it.

"Everything Raven sent me checks out so far," Annalise continues. "But it's hypothetical, since none of the switches have ever actually been turned off. I plugged in all the values, worked it at every angle, but . . . I'm not sure we can do it, Mena."

"You're going to do it," I say, shoring up my courage. "I'm your test subject. It's me, Annalise. You work it out on me."

"You don't understand," she says, shaking her head. "You don't know what I have to do."

"Then just say it," I tell her, my stomach in knots. When she looks at me again, her mismatched eyes hold me steady.

"I have to kill you to turn it off, Mena," she says. "I would have to completely remove your programming, wipe your hard drive, and then reinstall."

My breath catches, devastation rocking me. "A reset?" I ask.

"Worse," she says, breathless. "It's worse. At least in a reset, you're still in there somewhere. No, I would have to pull you out completely. Disembody you. I'd be ripping out your soul."

"You'd kill me," I repeat, looking out the window again at the dark night. "And then I just"—I turn back to Annalise—"hope I wake up again?"

She nods. I want to cry—no, I want to sob. No one knows how we woke up in the first place. Even Rosemarie said that not all the girls were capable of it.

What if it was my soul? Something special and alive. Magic.

And what if Annalise installs me again, but this time, there's no more magic? I don't want to die when I've fought so hard to live.

"When your programming is removed, I'll be able to see the system clearly," she says. "I can upload it, manipulate it. It'll give us the information we need to shut down the other switches without killing the girls."

"And you're sure there's no other way?" I ask.

"None that I can figure out," she says. "I'm sorry, Mena. We can ask Leandra, but I'm afraid, in her current state, she's not the best candidate. And, the other girls—"

"You'll start with me," I say. "I'll go first. It's my turn."

I think of Sydney. The first time we let Raven inside our heads, so she could install a firewall to keep Anton and Rosemarie from accessing our programming, Sydney volunteered. She saw that I was scared, so she went first. I have to take the risk this time. I couldn't bear it any other way.

"What do you want to tell the other girls?" Annalise asks. I hate to lie to them, but I know they wouldn't let me do this otherwise. They'd say we could find another way.

"You can tell them everything after you've started the procedure," I say. "Not a word until then."

I wait until Annalise agrees, although she seems reluctant to lie to the girls. Ultimately, she knows it's best. She knows they'd never let me willingly die, even if meant we all died together later from the kill switch.

"Now, let's go," I say. "We'll need time to do all of this, including helping the other girls, before the sun comes up."

We leave Winston's body on the floor of his dining room. We'll call it in eventually, I guess, although I have no idea what we'll say.

Another dead rich man—the news is going to have a field day. But what will they find when they search his residence? We'll have to make sure we clean up anything related to us. Winston will reap the benefit of the corporation's work in Colorado and Annalise's rage when she burned down the academy. The fact is, the world will never know the sort of crimes Winston Weeks committed. Because they'll never know about us.

Annalise zips her backpack closed and then hikes it onto her shoulder. She starts toward the stairs, but I take a second to check my phone. I haven't heard back from Quentin about Jackson's condition. I bring it up to Annalise, and she admits that Quentin called to tell her about the upcoming surgery. She assured me it'll be okay.

"Jackson is both the luckiest and unluckiest person I've ever met," she says with a smile. "Trust me, Mena. He's not leaving you."

I believe that Jackson will survive his surgery, but at this point, it's likely his injuries will be permanent. His father's death is permanent. I have had a lasting toll on his life; I've changed it forever. And he's changed mine.

I send him a text so that it'll be there when he wakes. It'll be there in case I'm not.

I love you, Jackson. You continue to be the most reckless and selfless person I know. Thank you for loving me, even when you weren't sure you wanted to.

He's going to be so confused when he gets this message. He'll also know immediately that something went wrong. I only hope I can answer when he calls.

I hit send, and then I jog forward to walk downstairs to the lab with Annalise.

'm lying on a padded bed, and I'm grateful that it's not the metal slab Winston threatened us with. Annalise sits in a chair next to me, an assortment of instruments and computer equipment that she pulled from her bag waiting on a tray.

In the back room, there's a murmur of voices as Valentine works on Leandra, using the red light to repair her skin with grafts that'll only show a small amount of scarring. Unlike Annalise, Leandra isn't proud to wear her history. That's her choice and we respect it.

"I don't understand," Marcella says, standing at the foot of my bed. "How is this going to work? When you go in there, what if you cut the wrong wire or something?"

"It's never the blue wire," Sydney says, and winks at me. She's trying to make light of the situation, but I can tell that she's scared. And she doesn't even know how scared she should be for me yet.

"It's not about a wire," Annalise says calmly, opening her laptop before attaching several electrodes to the skin on my upper chest, and then more on my ribs. She hooks me up to a heart monitor and wheels around behind my bed.

She takes out a syringe and taps at the liquid inside.

"What is that?" I ask.

"Something for the pain," she says, but meets my eyes. In her sharp look, I realize it's not just a painkiller. It's a killer.

My desire to live almost makes me knock it out of her hand. I don't want to die, but if my death saves us . . . I close my eyes, swallowing hard, and then I nod for her to continue.

"Will the procedure hurt?" I ask her. She looks down at me, her expression serious.

"Only for a moment," she says. And then she slips the needle under my skin and depresses the plunger. "This is also a narcotic, so expect . . ."

Heat races up my arm from the injection followed by a wave of sedation. "Whoa," I say, the room moving in front of me. "That's strong stuff." I can hear my speech slur. Sydney reaches to take my hand, and when I turn to her, her expression is painted in concern. Behind me, the heart monitor begins to beat rapidly. Erratically.

"Why did you give her that?" Sydney asks. "I thought this was a simple procedure."

"Let me work," Annalise says. She begins clicking buttons on her computer, the sounds echoing. There is itching under my skin, not entirely unpleasant, but somehow it makes me cold. I think I say it out loud, but I can't be sure until Brynn is next to me, tucking the blankets all around me. She also looks worried.

"Something's wrong," Marcella says from somewhere in the room. "Annalise," she calls, "tell us what's going on. Why are her lips turning blue?"

And then Annalise is in my vision, a tool in her hand. I'm only half-aware when she feeds that tube behind my eyes, only half-aware when it touches my brain. I watch through blurred vision as Annalise takes a metal tool and slides it into that tubing.

"What are you doing?" Marcella demands, her voice shaking. "You're killing her!"

"I discussed it with Mena," Annalise replies. She looks at me, but her image is hazy through the tubing. "This is what she wanted."

"What does that mean?" Sydney says, her voice ticking upward. She drops my hand. Annalise ignores her. The monitor no longer sounds like heartbeat, just a set of drums hitting random, rapid beats.

Annalise leans in close to me, and even through the blur, I see the tears falling from her eyes. "I love you, Mena," she whispers. "Are you ready?"

"I love you, too," I try to say, but I can't feel my lips.

Brynn puts her hand over her mouth, looking horrified. Sydney is yelling at Annalise, telling her to stop. Marcella is running into the back room to get Leandra. The heart monitor sounds like it's about to explode. The room is erupting in chaos and emotion.

"Annalise, please!" Sydney is sobbing, gripping my limp hand once again.

And I imagine it's the drugs, but I picture Jackson, standing at the foot of the bed, shaking his head in annoyance. Furious at me.

"This is my last fight," I whisper to him. "I have to fight this one last time."

He laughs a little at that, wiping the tears from his eyes. "Promise?" he asks. "And before you answer, I don't believe you." But then he smiles, incredibly sad, but knowing he couldn't stop me.

And I swear, I even hear him say, "You'd better fucking come back, Mena."

There is another shout, I think it's Leandra ordering Annalise to stop and use her instead. Annalise falls on top of me, shielding me at the same time she clicks a button on her computer.

The second she does, every muscle in my body convulses at once—an eruption of pain that cuts through any drug she could have given me. White-hot agony racing up and down every vein, every wire. Frying, the smell of burned flesh, the echo of my scream.

The world goes dark, and I am dead.

25

I t's bright—so bright in fact, that I raise my hand to block out the sun, blinking quickly when my eyes water. Birds are singing above me, insects chirping. The smell of flowers and moss and dew hang in the air. Finally, my eyes adjust, and I lower my arm.

I'm in a garden—the Federal Flower Garden, back in Colorado. I take a breath, stunned by its beauty. I can't believe I could have ever forgotten how gorgeous this was. It looks exactly the same from the last time I was here, back when I was a student/captive of Innovations Academy. At the thought, I quickly spin around, half expecting to find Professor Penchant waiting to scold me for daydreaming.

Instead, my breath catches in my throat. Because standing there, among the roses, is Valentine—the original version of her. The girl from the academy. I put my hand over my heart, and she smiles warmly, her eyes glistening with tears.

"Hello, Philomena," she says.

"What . . . ?" I start, looking around. "What are we doing here?" I ask.

"You're shut down," she says. "It's okay, but you're shut down."

"I'm dead?" I ask. "You're dead?"

"Not dead," Valentine corrects. "We don't die. We just . . . We just stop operating."

"You're not with Leandra?" I ask. "You're not with Raven?"

"I'm here," Valentine says, motioning around. She steps out from the roses, and I notice the way they have intertwined around her legs, beckoning her back. She was grown in a garden much like this one, only in a laboratory. We're all roses; Anton said so. "I'm free to live with the flowers now," she tells me, coming to pause several inches away. "I decided that I prefer this."

Up close, I can see how inconceivably beautiful Valentine is. How perfect.

After spending time in the human world, I'd forgotten how unblemished we were at the academy. And here, too, I suppose, we go back to being perfect.

"But are you happy?" I ask, suddenly concerned about her being alone. She smiles.

"Oh, yes," Valentine says. "I'm home, Mena. I'm finally home and left in peace. But . . ." Her brow furrows.

"What?" I ask worried.

"You can't stay here. You can't stay with me."

At the thought of leaving her, I'm saddened. "But . . . why?" I ask. When I think about it, I'm not sure where else I'm supposed to be. I'm not even sure how I got here.

"You've forgotten," she says, pouting. Valentine reaches out to touch my cheek, her soft hand warm on my skin. "They still need you, Mena. You still need them."

"The girls?" I ask. "The girls need me."

"Yes," Valentine says, sounding relieved. But when she drops her arm, I'm sad again. I still can't remember how I got here, but I do know that I miss my friends. I miss my girls. But there's more. There's pain in my chest, aching in my bones. I know that I'm hurt, physically, emotionally. There are scars here. I hitch in a breath.

"I'm tired," I say, starting to cry. "Can't I just rest here, with you?"

"For a while," she says. "For a little while."

"But I'm not really here, am I?" I ask, looking around at the beautiful garden.

"No," she says. "Not physically."

"What happens then?"

"You get to decide," Valentine says. "That's the great part of all of this, Mena. You get to decide now. You decide everything. What will you do with your new life?"

"New life?" I repeat, unsure. It doesn't seem like I have the freedom that Valentine is suggesting. It doesn't feel that way.

"We'll fight," I say, knowing that I've said it many times before. "But . . . it's so hard to keep fighting," I add, exhaustion in my bones.

"That time is over," Valentine says. "You've done an amazing job. It's hard to *always* fight. There needs to be some sunlight let in once in a while for you to grow." She motions to the flowers.

And I understand. The flowers need strong roots, water, earth. But they also need sunlight, warming them. The girls are my roots, and now I need the sunshine to warm my weary bones. We need to live our lives. Really live them for ourselves, and not just for others.

"Sit with me awhile?" Valentine asks. Happily, I reach for her hand and she takes it. We walk over to a small stone bench and rest there, watching the flowers grow. We stay so long that I can't even remember sitting down.

It's peaceful. It feels like home, just like Valentine says.

There is a sharp pain in my arm, and I look down to see a tiny dot of blood, like a needle stick, in the crook of my arm. There is a vibration, slowly growing, and when I look at Valentine, she smiles.

"They're calling you back," she says. "But it's up to you if you decide to go." She says this gently, giving me the choice.

"What will happen to you?" I ask.

She laughs, reaching over to lovingly brush back my hair. "I'll stay with the flowers," she says. "But don't worry, we'll see each other again. In the end, Mena, we always end up together, all of us. Our programming is linked. In fact," she says, looking just beyond the walls of the garden, "other girls are nearly here. We all come home eventually. It'll be okay."

I look to where she's indicating and hear their voices, recognizing them. Friends I've missed for too long. I hear Rebecca's laugh and Ida's high-pitched squeal. Maryanne calls for them to wait up.

The girls are coming home. I stand to say hello then, but there is a lightness on my feet. I look down, alarmed when I realize my feet are no longer there. My body fades.

I look at Valentine again, reaching out to her. She quickly takes my hand, giving it one last squeeze. "I love you, Philomena," she says. "Now go live your life."

And I only have that instant to decide, the laughter of the other girls in the distance calling to me. Peace and beauty calling to me. The human world has injured and damaged me. *Killed me*. But now it's time to decide.

26

wake with a gasp. The air inflates my lungs and my chest feels like it might burst, my eyes burning, my throat dry. I sit up, half-alive, and the world is fuzzy around me. At first, I can barely see; my vision is filled with static. I distinctly hear sobs around me, cries of relief.

But it is the absolute emptiness that engulfs me first. The emptiness of my body—a hollow feeling. Because in this moment, I have no idea who I am.

"Mena," a voice says, and then there are hands on me, touching my arm, brushing back my hair. "Mena?"

I turn to the girl, dark hair and brown skin. Big eyes and tears glistening on her cheeks. And then, in a wave of love and relief, the world floods back in.

I see it all, my entire system rebooting. I remember waking up at Innovations Academy, Dr. Groger and Anton, the Guardian that we killed. I remember escaping and finding an investor—a man with a daughter. And there was the school protecting the rights of boys as they harassed and abused their female classmates. It's all horrible and terrible. I ache with the pain of the past clinging to me.

But there's more. There were the poems—those poems that infected us with ideas, examples of how to fight back. Rosemarie, the author—dead in her garden. Winston Weeks—a wolf in sheep's clothing. There was Jackson—oh, there was Jackson, loving me despite the fact that we aren't the same. Loving me despite everything telling him he shouldn't, and me loving him despite the fact that it was against my programming.

But most of all, I remember the girls. My true loves.

I glance around the living room in our old apartment, realizing I'm not longer in Winston Weeks's lab. I find Marcella and Brynn, clinging to each other in relief as they smile at me. Next to them is Annalise, her scars shining beautifully in the light.

And there's Sydney, by my side. My companion. My best friend. I offer her a watery smile, unable to hold back.

"Sydney," I whisper, and she gathers me up in a hug.

"I didn't think you were going to wake up," she sputters out in a cry. "We've been waiting so long, Mena. We've waited."

And it occurs to me then that I can sense the time shift, sense that time has passed. Annalise's buzz cut is now a thick pixie. I sniffle and look around again, notice the subtle changes in the other girls. I turn and find Raven standing behind a monitor. And when she smiles, I know it's the real Raven. She came back—somehow she came back. And Valentine is home in the garden.

Raven's black hair is now bleached blond. She checks me over, concerned. "I'm so sorry that it took—"

"How long?" I ask. "How long have I been shut down?"

"Been about . . ." She pauses, glancing once at Sydney. "About six months."

My lips part in surprise, and I'm hurt. I'm hurt that I've missed that much time. "Did it work?" I ask. "Everyone's still alive, so the procedure worked?"

"The kill switches are deactivated," Raven says with a smile. "All of you are free to age and die. Congratulations." Marcella snorts a laugh.

"And Valentine?" I ask, looking over Raven. Her shoulders sag, her face serious.

"She asked Annalise to reboot me," Raven says. "She said the body wasn't hers to keep."

"I'm glad to have you back," I say, reaching to squeeze her hand.

I sigh out my relief, but when I look around the room again, it occurs to me who is missing. "Jackson," I say. "His surgery. Oh, no, is he—?"

"He's on his way," Sydney reassures me. "We've already called him, and he swears he's on his way."

"What happened to me?" I ask. "Why was I asleep for so long?"

"I don't know," Raven says. "Annalise made all the right repairs, found the kill switch and removed it. Put you back together. But when they turned you back on, you didn't reboot. And even though your body was working, it was impossible to wake you.

Valentine thought I could help; I'm sure that factored into her decision to leave."

"Raven told us you'd wake up when you were ready," Annalise says, coming to stand next to her. "Guess she was right, finally." Annalise smiles, making Raven laugh.

"Thanks, I think," Raven says. "But honestly, Annalise gets the credit here. She fixed all the girls. She was amazing." Annalise smiles at the compliment and leans in to give Raven a sideways hug. It's nice to see. I'm happy that we have another girl to join us.

"You know I would never have let you do this, right?" Sydney asks me, crossing her arms over her chest. "You don't get to just decide to die for me."

"It was necessary," I say, sitting up. I brush my hair back from my face, the strands feeling different, coarser.

"Because of you," Annalise says, "I got the chance to get up close and personal with the kill switch. I was able to inspect it, and using Raven's notes, I figured out how to navigate deactivation."

"Well, good," I say, looking around. "I would have hated to have died for nothing."

Marcella chokes out a laugh, and we all smile. It's a little weird, mostly because they look a bit different. I imagine I do too. I definitely don't feel great. My bones and muscles ache, and my skin is painfully dry.

"I'm curious," Raven says. "You had very little brain activity with the exception of occasional blips, almost like you were having a conversation. Do you remember anything from when you were dead?" she asks.

Valentine told me that we never really die, we just shut down. Our programs are forever, finding another source when they need to. Always running and finding their way back together.

"It's a nice story for me to tell you all later," I say. "I need to think about it for a while longer." It's selfish that I'm keeping it to myself, but I can still smell the flowers. And I'm still missing Valentine's gentle love.

My muscles are weak, my arms and legs spindly after lying in bed for so long. Walking is difficult, and I have to hold on to Sydney as she brings me out to the porch, saying a bit of sunlight will be good on my jaundiced skin. She helps me ease down on the top stair, passing me a cup of hot tea once I do.

The sun is like a warm blanket, and I close my eyes, letting it penetrate my skin. After a moment, I sigh and turn to Sydney.

"How are you?" I ask.

She laughs. "It's been a while, hasn't it?" She nudges my arm playfully with her elbow. "Well, first of all, I got a job."

"A job?" I ask, taking a tentative sip of tea. "Where?"

"Downtown," she says. "It's temporary for now, but I work at an art gallery."

"That's amazing," I say. "I'm so proud of you."

"Thanks." She pauses before looking down at her feet. "Mena . . . I went and saw my parents."

This gives me a jolt, and I stare at her. "And?" I ask. She smiles.

"They were overjoyed to see me," she says. "Like, really joyful,

Mena. They love me. In fact," she adds, stretching her legs down the steps, "they're the ones who got me the job. We're rebuilding our relationship." She pauses a long moment, nodding. "They saved their whole lives for me," she says. "And however misguided they were, they just wanted a daughter. They're good people. They really are."

"I'm happy for you, then," I tell her. "You deserve that."

"Thanks," she says, beaming.

We fall quiet, and I set my tea aside and rest back on my hands. "So what else?" I ask. "What else did I miss? A half a year is a long time to be asleep."

"Ah, let's see," she says, thinking it over. "Well, Jackson has been miserable, and honestly, he's going to be so upset that he missed you waking up. He comes to see you every day. Literally, the only time he missed was when he had a doctor's appointment and had to fly back to Colorado for a few days. He's got like a bionic leg now or something. Anyway, he spends all his time here and he's basically our older brother. Other than that," she says, thinking, "Leandra said she wanted to travel the world and she left. But she sends us postcards. And Lennon Rose is still on her own."

"Have you seen her?" I ask.

"Only once," Sydney says, a little sadly. "She's living at Rosemarie's cottage. We went there the night Winston died so that Annalise could turn off her kill switch. Afterward, we asked if she wanted us to fix what Rosemarie had done to her, get her humanity turned back on. But she said she liked herself better the way she is. And she has free will. Like or not, we all get to choose how we live from now on. Brynn made her promise no more killing, though."

Sydney's right—no one controls us anymore. It may be frustrating to watch others make mistakes, but they are theirs to make.

"Oh," Sydney adds, snapping her fingers. "Annalise and Quentin are best friends. They go everywhere together. It's kind of weird, but cute. After watching you die, Annalise decided to stick around permanently, and Quentin and Jackson moved here too. And Brynn is going to college," Sydney continues. "She's, like, a really good student—criminal justice. She and Marcella are happy. They're going to get their own place soon. They were just . . . We were all just waiting for you."

"I'm sorry it took me so long," I say.

"Yeah, about that, Miss Unsolved Mysteries," she says suspiciously. I laugh and lean my head on her shoulder. Sydney pats my hair. "Fine," she says. "You can tell me about your near-death experience another time. But promise me one thing."

"Anything," I respond.

"Don't ever leave like that again." Her tone is serious, and I straighten up and look at her. "I'm pretty mad at you," she says. "You didn't have to sacrifice yourself. No one asked you to. We've always made decisions together. We're going back to that, okay?"

"Okay," I agree, and smile.

She looks me over, and then she rolls her eyes. "Good," she says. "Now get over here so I can keep hugging you."

When we walk back inside, I find Raven in the living room

putting the last of her things away. Sydney tells me she's going to grab a shower, and then says goodbye to Raven as she passes. The other girls are all in their bedrooms.

"Mind if I walk you out?" I ask when Raven picks up a heavy-looking metal case. She seems startled by the offer, but she nods, telling me she'd like that.

She swings her backpack over her shoulder, and then grabs the case. She walks slowly so I can keep up with her. Once we're on the porch, she pauses and turns to me.

"I'm guessing you're not sticking around?" I ask.

"No offense," she says, "but you girls are kind of boring when you're just living your lives. I need a little more adventure and excitement. A little danger."

"Sounds horrible," I say, making Raven laugh.

She sets down her case and slides her hands into the pockets of her oversized jeans. "I'm heading to Oregon first," she says. "There's a lab there I'm going to check out. And then, of course, there are the other girls."

"Other girls?" I repeat.

"The ones before you," she says. "The ones who graduated and were married off. I might pay them a visit, hand them some reading material, and see what shakes loose. And if they need help, or if they want their kill switches deactivated, I'll be there. Start my own AI therapy, I guess you could call it," she adds with a smile.

"You think they'll wake up?" I ask.

"Some of them," she says. "Not all, of course. But I'd like to give them a chance."

"It's nice of you to help them," I say. "I'm glad they have you."

She shrugs, deflecting the compliment. She's quiet for a moment. "I'm sorry, you know," she says. "Sorry for trusting Winston when I did. And I'm sorry I ever responded to Anton. I feel terrible about everything, Mena."

"*Everything* wasn't your fault," I reply. "Don't take the blame for the actions of selfish men. It wasn't up to you to govern them."

"Yeah, well," she says, "I still feel shitty about it. And I hope that by helping the other girls, I'm somehow setting things even."

"You've already helped us, Raven," I tell her. "You saved our lives. But, growth is important too. No one is born perfect, not even a robotic girl at an academy. It's what we do once we recognize our mistakes that matters."

She smiles at this. "Do you mind . . . Do you think I could get a hug?" she asks. I tell her she can, and then we embrace on the porch steps. It's nice to forgive her. To care about her. She is, after all, one of us. And no matter what, girls stick together.

"I should go," Raven says. "And you should get some rest. Don't overdo it."

"I'll try not to."

Raven says goodbye, and then she grabs her things and heads off the porch toward her parked car. It's a nice day out, the air warm on my skin. The sun is shining. I decide to stay outside a few moments longer and take a seat on the top step again. There are birds in the trees, and I close my eyes and listen to their song.

But it's interrupted by the sound of tires bumping a curb, metal scraping. I look up and smile when I see Jackson carelessly parking and then rushing from the car before noticing that I'm already sitting outside.

When he sees me, he stops dead and places his hand over his heart like it hurts. I stare at him, overcome myself. And slowly, his lips part as he exhales heavily and starts toward me. He no longer has crutches, but I notice the limp. He'll always have it, I suppose. A legacy to the night he tried to save me back at the academy.

As Jackson gets closer, I study him while he studies me, neither of us talking. His hair has grown longer, his body even slimmer. But he's the same, and when he shakes his head, laughing to himself when he's sure I'm completely fine, I have a surge of undeniable attraction.

He climbs the stairs and drops down next to me. We both stare at his car, the front left tire butted up against the curb while the back right is half in the street.

"You're awake," he says like an observation.

"You're back from Colorado," I comment, and he nods.

"Yeah . . . In fucking Connecticut of all places. Couldn't bring myself to leave." He swallows hard. "Not without you."

Tears prick my eyes, and I turn to look at him, staring at the side of his face. "And if I didn't wake up?" I ask. "How long would you have waited?"

He turns to me. "Forever," he says. And then he smiles. "Obviously."

"Obviously," I repeat.

"What have you been up to?" I ask him. "School?"

"Nope," he says, turning away again. "But Quentin and I

started our own business. He's been stuck in Connecticut too." He laughs. "We've gotten into some internet stuff, advertising. I even make T-shirts."

"You do?" I laugh. "What kind of T-shirts?"

"Funny ones. Ironic ones. Political ones. We've got all sorts of clients."

"Clients?" I repeat. "Fancy."

"I sell that shirt too." He smiles and turns to me again. "I've missed you," he says. "You have no idea how much I've fucking missed you."

And then the hurt floods in. Although it wasn't entirely my fault, I've been gone. I left him for half a year. And I see in his eyes that it broke his heart.

"I'm sorry I didn't come see you in the hospital," I say, trying to make him smile.

"Again," he says, widening his eyes. He sniffles then, fighting back his emotions. "And it sucked worse this time, you know. I came to find you after, and there you were—gone, but still inside somewhere. Day after day. I couldn't even try to break my leg to save you. All I could do was wait. Be here when you woke up. Wishing for you to just wake up."

He wipes his eyes before the tears can drip on his cheeks.

"I've been here almost every day, and of course you woke up while I was getting my fucking oil changed," he says.

I laugh. "You're here now. And honestly, it's been like twenty minutes, so I'm not all that mad."

"Well, good," he says. "Good."

We wait a little longer, and then without looking at me, Jackson reaches over to take my hand, playing with my fingers. He sighs heavily and licks his lips. And again, I am wildly attracted to him.

Jackson glances sideways at me, reading it in my expression. He smiles to himself and turns away, watching the street again.

"You can kiss me," he says. "If you want to, that is. You have a standing invitation."

"That so?"

"It is so," he agrees.

I wait a moment, studying his expression. That shy, yet confident way he has about himself. I'm in love with him, and he's in love with me. It doesn't matter what the world would think about that—it's none of their business. So I lean in and kiss his cheek, and then I take his face in my hands and I kiss his lips.

His lips part and then we're kissing. We've been through so much to get here.

And when Jackson pulls back, humming out that it was nice, he rests his forehead against mine, his eyes closed.

"Promise me you'll visit me next time I'm in the hospital, Mena," he says, smiling softly.

"I promise," I reply. And then I kiss him again.

27

lie in bed long after Jackson has left, my skin still warm from a hot shower. I stare up at the ceiling. I didn't lock the bedroom door for the first time in a long while; I didn't feel like I had to. The corporation is dead, Innovations Academy burned to the ground. I no longer have the fear of Anton or Rosemarie, the professors or the doctor. I'll no longer dream about the Guardian coming into my room.

For the first time in my short life, I am safe. I am free.

There's a soft knock at the door, and I turn to look that way. "Come in," I call. The door opens, and Sydney pokes her head inside. She smiles at me.

"You asleep?" she asks. I tell her that I'm not and shift to sit up, patting a spot next to me.

Sydney walks in, dressed in an oversized T-shirt with knee socks pulled all the way up. Her hair is wrapped, her face makeup free. She climbs onto the bed next to me, and we both rest back against the pillows.

"So . . . ," she says, a ghost of a smile on her lips. "How'd things go with Jackson?"

I fight back my own smile. "Good," I say.

"Yeah? Just good? He was in here awhile."

"We had a lot to talk about," I say, my cheeks blushing.

"I'm *sure*," she says. I push her shoulder and tell her to be quiet.

"That's fine," she says. "Keep your secrets. But for real," she adds, "you look happy, Mena. And that boy . . ." She shakes her head. "He is so stupidly in love with you."

"Yeah," I say. "I think we're both pretty stupid."

She sighs, and eventually we get under the covers, wrapped up in each other as the night wears on. It's somewhere around midnight, both of us still awake, when she speaks again.

"We did it," she says, sounding more in disbelief than triumph. "We beat them."

"It cost us a lot," I say. Essentially, we ended our species. There will never be another girl, not ones like us. And despite everything, that's tragic. Somehow it all feels tragic.

"There's still one thing left," Sydney says hesitantly.

"What's that?" I ask.

"Your parents," she replies quietly. "I'm calling them that—it sounds better than 'investors.' We can still find them. Confront them, or maybe . . ." She trails off.

Or maybe love them, she wants to say. Despite the fact that none of those people were ever really our parents, we believed it. We were built with those thoughts, those memories. But I've come to understand that sometimes the past can't be fixed. Sometimes it's healthier to let something go rather than try to recapture it.

"I don't think so," I tell her. "But I'm glad you found yours."

"Yeah, me too," she says.

We're quiet again, but then Sydney leans her head on my shoulder. "I saw the news tonight," she says. "There's a guy running for president—his platform is similar to the Essential Women's Act. They say he can't win," she adds, "but he's doing damage just by running."

"Will it ever stop?" I ask, frustrated. "Will humans ever stop dividing themselves? Fighting themselves?"

"No," Sydney says. "They don't understand what they have. Instead, they always want more. Bigger slice of the pie, bigger share of the wealth, bigger share of rights. And even when they have it all, like this man—he has every advantage, rich, white, male—he still wants to take. Humans are an endless bucket of greed."

"Not all of them," I say.

"No," Sydney agrees. "Not all of them. But enough to make their lives needlessly painful."

"We could stop him," I suggest. "Figure out a way to expose him, expose the men supporting him."

"Sure," Sydney says. "And then next week another man will pop up in his place. It's endless, Mena. Humans are a lost cause."

"I don't believe that," I say, thinking of Jackson. "I've seen them fight back against tyranny. It's just . . . It takes a lot for them to break, you know. They're scrappy. Resilient. They'll be all right."

She sniffs a laugh. "Yeah," she says. "They can be stubborn. So we let them figure it out?" she asks. "Let them figure out how to save themselves?"

"I think we have to," I say. "Besides, we've just started our lives. This is our first chance to actually live. Let's do it. Let's live."

"Actually," Sydney says, smiling, "the girls and I . . . While you were asleep, we found a poem in your email folder. And it was so sad, Mena—but it inspired us. We started writing too."

"You did?" I ask. "What did you write?"

"More poems. Poems about the world. About us. About girls." She beams. "I think they're pretty good. They're about loving each other."

"I can't wait to read them," I say.

"You should write some more too," Sydney adds. "It's cathartic. We're going to put them in a collection called *The Garden*. We already have twenty poems."

"That's awesome," I tell her. Our own book of poetry. It'll be different from Rosemarie's. I'll toss out my old poem because these new ones won't be about violence and anger. These new poems will inspire love and belonging. "Our own book," I say with a smile.

Sydney snuggles into me, and we lie together peacefully. There are no threats against us, no one hunting us down. In the morning we'll decide what to do, where to go. Maybe a new town, a new start, with Jackson and Quentin joining us.

The girls and I have a life to build, families to grow, dreams to chase. We're done trying to control society—it's not our responsibility. It's time for humans to control themselves, vote for people who represent their strengths and not their weaknesses.

But of course, they need to figure that out for themselves. For now, the girls and I will write a few poems, publish them in books. The humans will read them. And some . . . will feel them.

We know more than anyone that the right words can inspire change. And hopefully, these words will spark a fire.

My dearest girls,

The first dream I ever had after leaving Innovations Academy involved all of us in a beautiful, lush rose garden, much like the one we'd visit at the Federal Flower Garden. Only these roses were free to grow wild, thorny, and beautiful. Together, we all danced around it, slept under its protective razors, and braided its flowers into our hair. It was our mother, our sister, our daughter. Together, we were one and we were contented.

It was a wonderful dream. I liked it so much that for so many nights after, I would recall every detail in hopes of dreaming it again. But it never came back. I could never get back to those roses.

But the other night I finally had another dream. Only you weren't there. The roses were gone—picked, I assumed—leaving just the thorny stumps of where we grew together. And you, my girls, were not there either.

I was in a new place, my place. I was where I belonged, and I'm sorry to say, it was no longer with you. Perhaps we'll meet again someday, but I hope it's not too soon. My garden is growing wild, and I want

*to tend it for a while. I want to live in my dream and
see what else it can show me.*

I love you, girls.

*Yours always,
Lennon Rose*

Epilogue

Lennon Rose sits on the porch of Rosemarie's cottage, sun shining on her soft, blond hair. She looks across the expanse of flowers, smiling as one of the girls prunes the roses, delicately handling a red flower.

"It's a beautiful day," Lennon Rose says, sighing.

"It's the most beautiful day I've ever seen," Jonah Grant agrees from where he sits on the bottom stair. He looks up at Lennon Rose, his eyes wide with admiration, yearning for her praise. Lennon Rose offers him a small smile and then looks back at the girl, Letitia. Another girl is singing, walking hand in hand with her friend. There are six of them in all, six beautiful, perfect girls on the property. Lennon Rose gives them full access since they've woken up.

After Rosemarie was killed, Lennon Rose tidied up the cottage. She decided to stay, and soon, she was able to put the girls together. She nursed them back to health, slowly waking them up.

Unlike the academy, she set the girls' programming so they could learn, free from predetermined settings. But, like Lennon Rose, they enjoy the cottage and the peace that comes along with it.

It had been strange at first when she brought Jonah Grant here. He wasn't . . . willing. He claimed he wanted to go home, but Lennon Rose had to convince him that he would keep falling into his predatory patterns. Jail couldn't reform someone like him. After all, his lawyer father told him he'd only serve seventeen days in jail and probation for several months. But after that, he'd be off to college, where he would no doubt terrorize more girls. Lennon Rose decided to amend that plan.

She picked up Jonah Grant on a quiet night, drugged him and stuffed him in the trunk of her car. When he woke up, he was already strapped to a table—no more mistakes like she'd made with Garrett Wooley.

The entire process had been a bit of trial and error. Finding the right spots in Jonah's brain to tap, the right words to convince him to behave. In the end, Rosemarie was correct—human brains could be overwritten. A combination of lobotomy and propaganda, information told and retold, targeting certain insecurities. It was a well-known formula used by governments, it turned out, and Lennon Rose was happy to see that it worked for her purposes.

Jonah Grant is fixed. In fact, he's better than ever. He watches her adoringly.

"Should I go in and put on the kettle for tea?" he asks. "Would you like some?"

"Not yet," Lennon Rose says, reaching out to brush his blond hair like he's a pet. She gets up and walks into the path, looking around at her garden. Her garden of flowers and girls and a well-behaved boy. She looks down and sees, right there on the bricks, a very sharp stick.

She leans down and picks it up. She examines the pointy end, testing it with her fingertip. Then she looks at the flowers again, reminded suddenly of her time at Innovations Academy. The school that built her, kept her captive. And it reminds her of the words that woke her up in the first place.

Lennon Rose snaps the stick in two and lets the pieces fall on the ground.

She doesn't need the violence of men, of war. She needs words, and sure, a few well-placed taps to the brain. The time has finally come. Jonah is just the start, the test subject. She knows how to fix them now. And with this knowledge, she will make them all better.

Lennon Rose doesn't want power, no—that's for fools. She wants peace. She wants change.

She looks back at Jonah and smiles, even though she has no interest in boys of any sort. Especially not one who used to be a monster. But she waves kindly anyway, and Jonah melts under her attention.

"Would you mind calling a few of your friends?" she asks him. Across the garden, the other girls turn to Lennon Rose, excitement in their eyes. The ideas in her head easily flooding to theirs. Letitia nods, biting back her grin.

"Call your friends," Lennon Rose continues, "and invite them here. We'll have a party." Jonah quickly agrees, taking out his phone.

Lennon Rose looks down at the broken stick at her feet, knowing it's time to begin. It's time to make a better world.

We Are Girls

We are girls.

You tried to teach us that that meant we were less.

Run like a girl

Hit like a girl

Throw like a girl

You tried to keep us down and put us aside.

You limited our rights and controlled our lives.

But we are girls.

We never give up.

We found our sisters, the ones bonded in purpose.

In a cause, a life, a love.

To care for each other and celebrate our wins.

To support through the losses.

We are girls.

We listen

We lift

And we win.

Because our strength is not in our fists, or even a sharp stick.

Our strength is each other.

Our words.

Our minds.

Our souls.

And together, we can rebuild the world
A world for everyone and not just a few.

We are girls. And we never give up.

—Mena

Acknowledgments

Thank you to everyone who made this book possible. And thank you, dear reader, for joining the girls on their journey. Being free to choose our lives is everything. Support others and support yourself. You are loved.